CHRISTMAS DAY 2010

Mags unlocks the wardrobe. With cold fingers she parts the thick wall of hanging clothes, sliding a hand through to the darkened depths behind. She leans in as she feels around, fabrics brushing against her cheek, their movement releasing the dusty, perfumed scent of the past. Her breath catches in her throat when she finds it, its edges rigid lines under the flimsy folds of an old, threadbare shawl.

The shoebox.

Her eyes close as she lifts it out, only opening again when she perches on the edge of the bed and settles it on her lap. She doesn't need its contents to remind her: she carries the secrets in her head. Always.

But sometimes she gets scared.

Scared that the passing of time might dim the memories. That what happened might somehow fade to nothing without a regular shot of proof. As she carefully eases off the lid, she hears PJ downstairs in the kitchen, his tuneless whistling while he attempts all the jobs she'd thought she'd be doing herself. She's glad he's taken over: she wouldn't be able for it today. Mags has never been mad about all the trouble to do with Christmas anyway. The huge amount of preparation, the frantic running around like the end of the world is on the way. But . . . she's always looked forward to that time, late on Christmas Eve, when there's no more gallivanting to be done. When a gentle peace has settled all around and the three of them sit by the blazing fire, Mags looking at her husband and her daughter and trying to thank God for what she has, instead of berating Him for what she's lost. And seeing, in PJ's eyes, his hope that the coming year might be easier for her than the one almost passed.

But none of that has happened this time. Orla hasn't made it home.

There was Mags on Christmas Eve, hoping against hope. Making sure everything was right: the tree positioned exactly in the front window so that Orla would see the twinkling lights as she drove into the yard; the homemade mince pies laid out on the tray with the best china; the fire roaring in the grate. As the morning wore on, she knew in her heart it wasn't going to be possible. They'd heard on the news that parts of the Dublin road were impassable. There hasn't been snow like it in years. Not since before Orla was born. All over the country people are stranded, stuck in places they don't want to be. For the past week, PJ has spent the best part of an hour each morning clearing the yard. Only for the jeep, they'd have found it difficult even to get down to the village. When Orla had phoned at lunchtime, Mags had managed to hold it together. But later, as the night closed down around her, she'd

Praise for Susan Stairs

The Boy Between

'A vivid and emotionally powerful story of the past's long hold on our lives'
Joseph O'Connor

'Absorbing and assured . . . *The Boy Between* is a powerful, moving story that stays with the reader long after the last page has been read. Stairs has most assuredly confirmed her place within the voices of quality Irish fiction'
Irish Independent

'Superb read . . . (Stairs') flair for characterisation and her ability to keep the reader in suspense are among the more masterful elements of this novel . . . A very human and moving story' *Books Ireland*

'An un-put-down-able mystery with an unexpectedly emotional impact'
Stellar magazine

The Story Of Before

'A bewitching read . . . I can't recommend it highly enough'
Kathleen MacMahon, author of *The Long Hot Summer*

'Stairs revels in sharp physical description, tinged with implication . . . Familiar and unsettling . . . An assured debut'
The Sunday Times

'A tale of childhood secrets and lies with a wonderful sense of time and place'
The Bookseller

'*The Story of Before* is a mesmerising psychological coming-of-age novel'
Irish Examiner

'Nuanced . . . visceral . . . will consume the reader for more than 300 pages'
Sunday Business Post

The Boy Between is Susan Stairs' second novel. Her first, *The Story of Before,* was published in 2013. She lives in Dublin with her family.

www.susanstairs.com

@SusanStairs

The Boy Between

SUSAN STAIRS

HACHETTE
BOOKS
IRELAND

First published in 2015 by Hachette Books Ireland
First published in paperback in 2016

A CIP catalogue record for this title is available from the British Library

ISBN 978 14736 1808 4

Typeset in Cambria by redrattledesign.com

Printed and bound by Clays Ltd, Elcograf S.p.A.

Hachette Books Ireland policy is to use papers that are natural, renewable and recyclable products and made from wood grown in sustainable forests. The logging and manufacturing processes are expected to conform to the environmental regulations of the country of origin.

Hachette Books Ireland
8 Castlecourt Centre
Castleknock
Dublin 15, Ireland

A division of Hachette UK Ltd.
Carmelite House
50 Victoria Embankment
London EC4Y 0DZ

www.hachette.ie

Darkness settles on roofs and walls,
But the sea, the sea in the darkness calls;
The little waves, with their soft, white hands,
Efface the footprints in the sands,
And the tide rises, the tide falls.

'The Tide Rises, The Tide Falls'
Henry Wadsworth Longfellow

stared hard at the fire with tears in her eyes, trying to make sense of the fact that, for the first time ever, her daughter would not be at home for Christmas.

And here is Mags now on Christmas morning, sitting on her bed, looking into the box and thinking that, this time twenty-eight years ago, Orla was just about becoming a tiny speck inside her. That's what makes her absence now all the more unbearable. She'd been conceived on Christmas Eve. Mags is sure about that. When she'd discovered why it was she hadn't been feeling herself, she'd cried for hours, her tears as much of sadness as of joy. PJ had grinned widely when she'd told him. He said they'd given themselves the best Christmas present they could have wished for.

Today Mags can hardly stand the empty feeling she has inside. No amount of PJ trying to cheer her up has worked. He's upset too, she knows that, but he's better at coping. He was up well before her, brought her breakfast in bed, made sure she took one of her pills. It's helped a little, has sanded down the sharp edges of her thoughts. But it hasn't stopped her thinking altogether. She has too much time for thinking today, that's the problem, reminding herself of things she doesn't need reminding of. The events of that summer when Orla was growing inside her. And all that came before. She keeps everything safe in the box. Letters. Postcards. Photographs. Each memento plays a role in the secret story that's always in her thoughts. A story that can't remain hidden forever.

She lifts out an envelope. How many times has she read this letter over the years? Countless. She almost knows every one of her sister's neatly written words by heart.

Weds, 20 July 1983

Dear Margaret,

You're probably wondering why I'm writing again. No need to worry, nothing's changed. Tim's still catching the afternoon sailing from Holyhead on Monday, please God. We haven't told him yet. We're saving the excitement till Friday, when he gets his holidays from school.

I've been thinking a lot about all this and I just want to say, Margaret, that I trust you. If we dithered over letting him go on his own it wasn't because we didn't think he'd be safe. It hasn't been an easy decision, I'm not going to deny it, but Ed and I know you'll look after him.

Things have been a bit cool between us over the years. But I really feel that's about to change. Once the baby arrives, you're going to be so much happier. I can tell from your letters that you're already a lot brighter in yourself. It's been a rocky road for all of us. But things might have been so much worse. We did what was best. I still believe that.

Will be in touch. Look after yourself.

Much love,

Joan

PS Make sure Tim writes to let us know he arrived in one piece.

Tim. Lord almighty. Had she been mad to invite him to stay that summer and she seven months gone? She's asked herself that question a thousand times. What had she been trying to prove? That she'd be up to it? That she'd be able to cope?

And how would things have turned out if he hadn't come? Perhaps they'd all still be in her life now. Imagine that . . .

She reads the lines again and thinks back to the day Tim arrived, all those years ago. How she'd kissed PJ through the van window before he set off for Dún Laoghaire. How she'd sat anxiously waiting in the kitchen, the sun and shade playing chase across the floor and the baby twisting and turning, like a water creature, inside her. She remembers being a bit put out at what Joan had written. *I trust you* . . . What had she been trying to say? That Mags should be grateful her own sister trusted her? Sure didn't she send the lad over on his own – wasn't that evidence enough? She'd hardly needed to go writing it down. Making Mags feel like an eejit and she thirty years of age. Being the oldest, Joan was always the bossy so-and-so. Still and all, Mags had cried when she left for England. She missed having her sister around. Mammy and Daddy were always so busy with the farm, and the boys . . . well, they were boys. *We did what was best.* Mags often wonders if that's really true.

She remembers again how she'd pushed Joan's letter into her apron pocket after she'd read it that day and hauled herself upstairs. How she'd had the feeling she might be able to see the ferry from the window in the spare room. She'd stood gazing out at the shining silver strip of the sea beyond the golden-green stretch of fields, staring until her eyes had stung and she'd felt her legs might buckle beneath her.

She takes a mass card from the group of several stacked together in the box. *With deepest sympathy.* The small cutting of newsprint she keeps inside it floats down onto the bed. Her eyes crease as she reads the printed words, then cloud with tears as they always do. Such a tiny notice of a tragedy so huge.

The memories unfurl themselves, drifting out from the coral ridges of her brain.

The bright blue of the sky and the biting cold wind.

The shoving and rolling and heaving. The water deep and black and endless.

And the space around her closing in. Squeezing. Turning her inside out.

'What in the name of . . . ?' PJ pokes his head around the door. Mags's face is hidden, the pillow muffling her gulping sobs. 'Mags? Are you all right?' He sits on the bed beside her, places a huge warm hand on her back. 'Come on, love. 'Tis Christmas Day. You can't be stuck up here on your own.'

When his wife turns to him, he sees her cheeks are wet and blotched, her eyes red-rimmed. 'I'll be grand,' she croaks. 'Just leave me a while.'

His shoulders rise and fall as he sighs. 'I will not and well you know it.' He takes her arm, helps her to sit up. 'I know 'tis not easy. I do. And now all this upset with the weather. We could've done without that, so we could.'

'I just wish Orla was here,' she whispers. 'I know I wouldn't feel so bad if she was.'

PJ pulls her close, winding his heavy arms around her thin frame. 'All your fussing over her would've taken your mind off of the rest of it, isn't that so?' he says, over her head. 'Listen. I'm sure a thaw is on the way. She'll be down in a few days. Isn't that right?' Mags stays silent, and statue-still. His embrace tightens, then loosens. He pulls away and looks hard into her face. His voice is grim, stony. 'All this has got to stop. You know that, don't you?' She keeps her eyes down. 'I mean it, Mags. I don't want to walk in one day and find . . .' He runs his fingers over his bearded chin and swallows hard. He knows there's no point. Not today. Not when she's in this state. 'Look,' he says, softer now. 'We'll say no more about it for the moment. Let's just try and enjoy the day as best we can.' He stands up. 'Come on. You go and sort yourself out. Get dressed and all that.'

Mags sniffs, pulls a tissue from her sleeve and holds it to her nose. She drags herself to standing and shuffles out to the bathroom.

PJ looks at the shoebox sitting on the bed. For a moment, he's seized by the strongest urge to carry it downstairs and hurl it into the fire. It's not the first time he's felt like that. But he wonders if it could be the last. If there may be some way to put an end to all this pain. He's not going to get rid of it – he'd never do that to Mags – and what he's thinking about may not even work. But he's prepared to take the chance. He leans down, rifles through the box and finds the photograph he wants. He scans it for a second, flinching at the bittersweet memory, then jogs quickly around the bed to the wardrobe, slipping it into the pocket of a tweed jacket he never wears.

Tim fell asleep that July afternoon and woke up in another country. When he felt the ferry crunching into the dock he knew he'd arrived, but he had no memory of the journey. Before he opened his eyes, he lay there for a moment, still curled in his seat, and he knew things were not the same. That time or space – or something inside him – had shifted. A lot or just a little, he couldn't tell.

He listened to the shuffling passengers, to the trundle and squeak of suitcase wheels and tried to make sense of the way he felt. He'd fallen asleep on journeys before – in the back of the car for the annual two weeks in Cornwall, on the airless bus to and from school – but this was different. And then there was the dream. Back home, his dreams were shallow, almost transparent, fading as soon as he woke. This dream still swam around his body, fusing to his skin, like barnacles on a whale. Dreaming on water was different, it seemed. And the deeper the water, the deeper the dream.

He dreamed he was a ship.

Not just any ship, but the actual ferry he was on. He was

on it and he was it. He'd felt the huge, hard bulk of himself slicing through the greasy waves; the painted silver steel of his flesh; the pump-pump of an engine-heart deep inside his hull. Felt the sea propelling him forward, squeezing up against his sides in great swirling billows that came and went, push-pushing him on through the depths. And sometimes in the dream he was the sea. The sea and the ship together. He was the suck and the swell and the bow and the stern, rolling, sliding, surging through a cloud of deepest, blackest black. Now was all he knew. There was no memory behind him. And yet, as he dreamed, he sensed there was purpose in his journey, in the course his sailing self was charting. It was greater than the metal carcass, greater than the push and pull. Something certain had hold of him in that dream: he could feel it. And it wasn't letting go.

He stretched out his legs and sat upright in his seat. His stomach was raw and it stung, as if he'd swallowed then puked up a bellyful of salt water. The funny thing was, he hadn't felt seasick at all, despite Mum's worries. In fact, he'd found a peculiar sort of comfort as soon as he'd stepped onboard. But now he felt inside-out, slippery, almost skinless. Not like himself at all.

It wasn't surprising he'd slept: he'd lain awake for hours the night before. Around three in the morning he'd tiptoed down to the kitchen for some squash and on his way back to bed had quietly pushed open the door of his parents' room. He'd stood watching them for a moment: the dark cave of Mum's open mouth; the oily tentacles of Dad's hair, out of place and exposing the pink shell of his head. There was something fragile and dry about them that night, as though whatever made them real had been sucked out. It was the nearest thing to them being dead. Tim had felt his heart flutter, his breath shudder at the back of his throat as he looked at them. Six weeks away from home. A summer in Ireland with an aunt and uncle he'd never met. How was it possible to be so scared and so excited at the same time?

It should have been the two of them. Tim and Mum. That had been the plan. Tim's Auntie Margaret – Mum's sister – sent him a birthday card every year without fail. Always the same greeting in the same loopy handwriting. *Happy birthday, Tim, love from Mags.* (Mum didn't call her 'Mags'. It was always 'Auntie Margaret'.) And in the last few years, she'd added, *Would love to see you all. You're more than welcome to visit over the summer.* 'Can we go?' Tim would ask. 'Please?'

'Not this year,' Mum would reply. 'But we will. Some day.'

And then they'd end up going to Cornwall. Again. Not that Tim didn't enjoy Cornwall. But he would've liked a change. The journey took forever and he hated having no one his own age to talk to for such a long time. Last year, he'd wanted his best friend, Mark, to come along, too. 'He's already asked. He's allowed,' he'd pleaded.

Mum had wagged her finger. 'Not by me, he's not.'

'It's a family holiday, Tim,' Dad had said. 'It's not a free-for-all. We can't have just anybody tagging along.'

Tim had sulked. Mark wasn't 'anybody'. But they couldn't be persuaded.

Earlier in the year, Auntie Margaret had told Mum her 'news'. She was going to have a baby. Some time in September. That was that, then, Tim had thought. There'll be no invitation this time. So, when his birthday card arrived, he was amazed to see, along with the usual greeting, something that opened up a whole world of possibilities: *Now that you're fourteen, Tim, you'd be well able to come over on your own, if your mammy and daddy allow it.* When he'd shown it to Mum, she'd looked at Dad. A long, loaded gaze.

She frowned and shook her head. 'I'm not sure.'

I'm not sure? Tim had been expecting an out-and-out 'No.' Even 'Absolutely not.' 'I'm not sure' suggested there was hope. On his own? Surely he'd never be allowed.

Dad had stroked his nose and pursed his lips. Actions that usually showed he was thinking hard. He'd ummed and hmmed and paced about the kitchen, opening his mouth several times before shutting it again. Eventually he spat it out: 'Why don't the two of you go? You bring him over, Joan. I'm sure Margaret would appreciate some help, what with she ... you know ... the baby coming ...'

Mum's eyebrows slipped. 'I don't know, Ed. I ... What about Cornwall? What about—'

'Just do it. You haven't been over since the funerals. Show Tim your home country.'

Mum's parents had died within months of each other when Tim was about eight. He'd never met them. Had barely known they existed. Mum had gone over both times. Flying visits. Over and back in twenty-four hours.

'Go on,' Dad continued. 'Once and for all. It's about time.'

'All right, then,' Mum said, with a sigh. 'We'll go.'

Just like that? Tim was shocked. OK, so he wasn't going on his own, but it'd been settled so easily. Without any pleading on his behalf. Parents. They were hard to understand sometimes.

Arrangements were made. They'd leave just as soon as the school holidays began. Tim was really looking forward to it. He'd never been on a boat before. Never been in another country.

Then things went wrong. Two weeks before they were due to go. He'd known it was all too good to be true.

Tim took the blame. He'd meant to go back and pick up his Rubik's Cube after it had dropped on the stairs. He'd been on his way to bed and carrying too much, trying to avoid having to make two trips. A glass of cold milk in one hand, a quartered orange in the other, a pair of freshly ironed pyjamas draped over one arm, his schoolbag on his shoulder (last-minute revision for the summer exams), and his Rubik's Cube tucked into his armpit. He'd buried his face in his pillow when he heard Dad yell. The hospital doctor said Dad wasn't the first person to break an ankle falling *up* the stairs. And it wasn't the first injury he'd seen brought about by the careless placement of a Rubik's Cube either. A complicated fracture. Eight weeks in plaster. He'd be off work for the duration. It was hard to look Dad in the eye. Especially when he was hobbling around on his crutches.

'That's the end of our trip, then,' Mum said. 'Can't leave Dad on his own.'

Tim didn't know which feeling was worse. The guilt or the disappointment. He came home from school each day and there was Dad. Watching *Countdown*. Leg up on a footstool. Miserable. Dad was used to being out and about. He worked as a claims assessor for an insurance company. Tim wasn't exactly sure what that was. Something to do with people getting money when their houses flooded or went on fire. Boring. Tim wanted to be a photographer. He wanted to travel to out-of-the-way places and bring back pictures of things most people had never seen. That had been his plan for the trip to Ireland. Not that Ireland was an undiscovered country or anything like that, but he would've made good use of his camera there all the same. He'd imagined showing Dad his photos, telling him all about the trip. What they'd seen. What they'd done. Now all that had been thrown out of the window and he'd nothing to look forward to. It made him not care about his exams. He'd told Dad maths had been 'easy' but was pretty sure he'd failed. The summer stretched out before him like an empty road – long, grey and unexciting.

Until the morning of the last day of school. 'We've been thinking, Tim,' Mum had said, as she'd spread her thinly buttered toast with lemon marmalade. 'Haven't we, Dad?'

'Hmm? What?' Dad looked up from his porridge. Mum winked. 'Oh. Yes. Indeed. We've been thinking.'

'Go on. You tell him,' Mum said, biting into her toast.

And there it was. The adventure. Mum had already written to Auntie Margaret and had received her reply in that morning's post. (It wasn't as easy as just giving her a call. Auntie Margaret didn't have a telephone.) 'We're trusting you,' Mum said, after Dad had explained. 'Allowing you go on your own. It's a big thing, Tim. You understand that, don't you?'

Tim nodded. This was big. This was *huge*.

'It's not been an easy decision,' Dad said, 'but, well … you're growing up and …' he sprinkled more sugar onto his porridge '… take it from me. Do you good to get away for a while. Make you appreciate what you have at home.'

'Dad's right,' Mum said. 'Auntie Margaret says you're welcome to stay until you need to come back for school. She'll look after you well. And your uncle PJ will, too. I know I only met him the once. At Daddy's funeral. But he seems like a good sort.'

Tim could hardly take it in.

'I didn't want you thinking I'd ruined your chance of a holiday,' Dad said.

Tim protested: 'But it was me who—'

'It was an accident. Don't be blaming yourself.' Dad poured himself a cup of tea. 'Water under the bridge.'

'And you're ... you're happy to let me go? On my own?'

Mum stood up, smoothed her skirt and started clearing away the breakfast things. 'Hurry up now. You don't want to be late.'

Dad leaned in and whispered to Tim, 'Took a while to persuade her. You know how she is.'

'If she's not happy about it, maybe I shouldn't go.'

'You go and enjoy yourself, son.' He smiled and landed a pretend punch to Tim's cheek.

A few days later, Tim found himself on the way to Holyhead to catch a three o'clock ferry. Mum drove, with Dad stretched out on the back seat issuing instructions. He only made things worse. She was nervous enough as it was. She knew how to drive, all right, but usually just short journeys. To the shopping centre. To town. Places she knew well. By the time they arrived, her face was pretty much the same colour as the sea. Green.

In the waiting room, Dad shook Tim's hand. 'Good luck on the voyage, son,' he said, sounding all serious.

'It's the Irish Sea, Dad, not the Pacific Ocean.'

Dad fumbled in his trouser pocket for his wallet and produced a handful of Irish notes.

Tim counted them. 'Thirty quid? Thanks, Dad!' He stuffed the money into the pocket of his jeans.

'Fiver a week,' Dad said. 'If you're staying for the whole holidays, that is. Let's see how you get on, shall we? Play it by ear, as they say.'

Mum pulled a crumpled length of pink toilet paper from her handbag and held it over her nose. A weird noise escaped from her throat. She'd probably have attracted less attention if she'd just gone ahead and cried instead of trying not to. Dad tried to put his arm around her but he couldn't balance on just one crutch. He coughed. 'Now, now, Joan. Everything's going to be all right.'

Mum gave Tim a long, tight hug. 'Write as soon as you arrive,' she said, pulling away and taking his face in her hands. 'Let me know you got there safely. Don't forget.'

'I won't.' He pulled away. 'Promise.'

She held on to his fingers for as long as she could, only letting go when Dad said Tim really needed to board. 'Want to be sure he gets a seat, love. Big enough crowd all the same.' He patted Tim on the back. 'Enjoy yourself, son.' He grinned. 'Don't do anything I wouldn't do, eh?' Mum elbowed him and made a face. She was trying not to laugh now.

Tim turned away, a smile flickering about his lips as he walked towards the ferry. Just as he was about to board, right at the very last second, he glanced back and caught Mum's eye. He wasn't sure if it was the look she gave him, or if it was because he was hovering between earth and sea, but something wild and tingling had galloped up and down his body and he'd had to grab hold of the rail and lean into it, he was so dizzy. Once inside the ferry, he'd flopped down in the first empty seat he could find, drawn his knees to his chest and fallen asleep in minutes.

Now that he was awake, he wondered what had gone on

around him as he'd slept. Had his things been touched? Was anything missing? Hurriedly, he unbuckled his rucksack. The packed lunch Mum had given him was still there – a Tupperware box containing a pork pie, a hard-boiled egg and a slice of Battenburg. He wolfed down a bite each of the pie and the egg, then stuffed the slice of cake into his mouth. He pushed his hand down into the rucksack, past his clothes and the ordered way Mum had packed them: the jeans and T-shirts carefully rolled into tight sausage shapes; the rain jacket folded into its own pocket; the socks and underwear stuffed inside the shiny brown brogues she'd insisted on buying for him. He wouldn't have been upset if the shoes had been stolen. He couldn't ever see himself wearing them. He felt around some more. Phew. His camera was OK, wrapped in the woolly cushioning of his cricket jumper.

As he pulled his hand out, his fingers slid over the shiny cover of a hardback drawing pad. He groaned. His summer art project. He'd shoved it in at the last minute. Miss Thistle, his art teacher, expected it to be 'completed in full' by the time he went back in September. Tim liked art. But Miss Thistle made it a lot less enjoyable than it should've been. 'Complex Patterns in Our Natural Surroundings' was the title she'd chosen. She made it sound as boring as maths. At least she'd said she'd allow the use of photographs as well as drawings to illustrate it. He could use his Kodak, get the film developed once he got back home. He stood up, lifted the rucksack and slung it over one shoulder. It felt as though the ferry was still moving when he walked: his steps wavered, bouncing through what seemed like an altered gravity. Is this what happens when you go to another place? Is somewhere else just a different kind of real? Floating down the gangway, his heart quickened. He knew he hadn't, but he couldn't help thinking he'd left something behind.

Dún Laoghaire. (Pronounced 'Dun Leery', Dad had said.) That's where the ferry docked. In the atlases and maps he'd studied before his journey, Tim had seen it spelled several ways – Dún Laoghaire, Dun Laoire, Dunleary – which was all a little confusing. But, then, everything was confusing that day. Even the light. It was sharp, blinding, yet it was soapy and soft. And everything around – the dissipating crowd, the string of cars worming from the ferry, the jagged skyline of spires and roofs – it all made him feel as if he was looking out through other eyes, that he was in a different body, that he wasn't really fourteen-year-old Tim Swift, only child of Joan and Edward, who'd left Holyhead three and a half hours earlier. He was sure he stood out, too. Like a tropical fish in a flock of garden birds.

He sat down on a low wall and waited, as he'd been told, for Uncle PJ. 'Don't worry, he'll know you,' Mum had said. 'I sent Auntie Margaret a picture.' But what did PJ look like? What kind of person was he? It was strange, waiting for someone you didn't know. The only uncle he'd met before was Dad's younger brother, John. 'Gentle John', Mum called him. He and Dad were close – it'd been just the two of them growing up. No other brothers or sisters. Mum came from a larger family. She was the eldest, Auntie Margaret the youngest, with four or five brothers in between who'd all emigrated to Canada years ago. That was about all he knew. Mum didn't talk about her childhood much, where she came from, stuff like that.

Tim looked up. The sky was paper-white with cloud, the kind that could start spitting rain or might just as easily break apart to blue. The sounds and smells – the electric buzz of waves, the lonely cry of seagulls; bitter exhaust fumes, the briny tang of the sea: he felt, somehow, that they should be familiar, that he should know them. Maybe someone had described them to him once and their memories had become his own. And the way people were speaking, their accents. They all sounded like Mum.

'Tim, is it?' A beanpole of a man appeared. Tim had to lean back in order to look at his face. His hair was a sunburst of orange curls and his beard was much the same. 'I'm your uncle PJ.' He stretched out his hand and Tim took it, feeling reassured by the strength of the shake. The introduction over, PJ grabbed Tim's rucksack. 'This way,' he said, taking off at top speed. Tim slid from the wall and began to follow, his uncle's torso swerving around bodies, bending left and right as he zigzagged through the crowd. Tim almost had to run to keep up. They went along the seafront then crossed the road, PJ dodging cars and disappearing down a lane when he got to the other side. Tim hung back, waiting for a break in the traffic, catching up just in time to see PJ toss his rucksack into the back of a dusty, tobacco-coloured Hiace van.

As his uncle folded himself into the driver's seat, Tim climbed in on the passenger side and the van pulled away, sailing out onto the main road and straight through a red light, serenaded by a chorus of horns that only faded when they turned right at the next junction.

It was hard to get comfortable. The footwell was cluttered: black welly boots caked with what looked and smelt like fresh cow shit; a plastic tub of tile glue; the head of a pickaxe; a Maxwell House coffee jar filled with nails. Papers littered the dash: hand-written receipts; parking tickets; brown bags scribbled with sums. And a biscuit tin, its battered lid gouged with the word 'screws', was wedged between the front seats. Tim wriggled about, moving his feet until he found a space for them to rest. Once he was settled, he studied his uncle from the corner of his eye. PJ's head touched the roof of the car – at least, his hair did – and his knees got in the way of his arms. He stroked the fur-covered steering wheel with the palm of his right hand, whistling through his teeth, not very tunefully. With his over-long limbs and wild hair, Tim thought he looked like a cross between a lion and a giraffe. Some sort of mutant animal dressed in a mustard sports jacket and a pair of mud-splattered brown slacks.

With the town behind them, PJ broke the silence and asked how Tim had enjoyed the journey.

'It was . . . it was OK.'

'Choppy, was it?'

'Uh, a little. Maybe. I think so,' Tim said.

'Don't seem too sure.'

'I . . . I was asleep.'

PJ glanced at him, then let his eyes wander back to the road. Miles passed without either of them speaking. Tim felt awkward. It wasn't that his uncle was unfriendly, but he wasn't doing much to put Tim at his ease.

As they drove, Tim glimpsed patches of sparkling blue sea to his left every now and again. They passed through a small, bustling town with narrow streets barely able to contain the traffic. Rainbows of plastic buckets and spades and blow-up rings were strung across shop fronts, twirling and flapping in the breeze. Crowds of people filled the paths, spilling out onto the streets – the holidaymakers: T-shirted kids waving ice-creams, ambling adults displaying sunburned flesh. And the locals: agitated women hauling plastic bags of groceries, weather-beaten old men leaning on sticks, watching the world going by. PJ seemed annoyed at having to slow down to a crawl. He mumbled under his breath every time he had to brake.

The miles passed. The sky cracked apart in places, spattering the sheep-dotted fields with fleeting patches of shadow and sun. Then the road began to climb and, from his vantage point, Tim could see a bigger expanse of the Irish Sea. Far out on the misty horizon he spotted the white smudge of the ferry making its return journey to Wales. Watching it, his heart pounded as the breadth of the distance he'd travelled became clear. He hoped it wouldn't be long before they got to Lissenmore, the village where Auntie Margaret and PJ lived. Tim didn't expect there'd be much to it. When he hadn't been able to locate it on any map, Dad had said it was more than likely a blink-and-you'll-miss-it kind of place. It wasn't too far from where Mum had been born. About thirty miles or so. He'd been able to extract that much information from her at least.

'Not too long now,' PJ said, reading Tim's thoughts. 'Far side of that hill.' He took a right turn. The hill ahead rose up from the earth like the arched back of a waking beast and, as they drew closer, Tim saw its surface was a fur of purple-green heather while, in sloping lines near its summit, bands of pale rock showed through like bone. Skirting round the edge, they came to a crossroads where a flat-capped man in a dark suit and a headscarfed woman with a bicycle stood chatting beside a butter-coloured telephone box. The man saluted and PJ sounded his horn as he drove straight on without slowing. The road widened out for a stretch and, on the left, standing in a verge of recently cut lush grass was a white metal sign painted with black letters that read 'Lissenmore'. Tim noticed a playing field with a peculiar-looking set of goals on the right and, further along, what he guessed was a school – a long, low prefab building, its tarmac yard deserted and its gates chained shut for the summer. The village was a cheerless little place, one street lined with dusty, old-fashioned shop fronts that had all seen better days. One had its windows blacked out with yellowed sheets of newspaper, another featured a sparse display of faded cornflakes boxes and tins of beans. On the left, a terrace of tiny cottages with front doors opening onto the street faced a large, grey, double-fronted house, one half of which appeared to be a post office. A humpbacked old man sat in an armchair outside the open door of what looked like a bar – a maroon-painted place with a couple of beer bottles sitting in the window and fading letters spelling out 'Whiskey Bonder' etched across the glass. The sleeping dog at the man's feet raised its head as the van passed but the man remained frozen, like one of the waxworks Tim had seen in Madame Tussaud's the one and only time he'd visited London.

If the village appeared sleepy, it woke up a little at the end of the street. Sitting on the corner was a shop that sold anything and everything, judging by the number of items in the window, hanging from its front, or displayed on the path outside. From fruit and vegetables to wheelbarrows, ice-cream to tins of paint, Kavanagh's seemed to have it all. Tim watched as some teenagers emerged from inside. Two boys and a girl. He locked eyes with the tallest boy for the second or two it took the van to pass. His hair was a squirrelly auburn, cut short at the sides, with a spiky fringe that fell down over one eye. He nudged the chubby boy beside him, who shot a look in Tim's direction. Tim felt uncomfortable. It seemed his arrival in Lissenmore had been noticed. He slipped down in his seat as they left the village behind.

'You don't exactly live *in* the village, then?' Tim plucked up the courage to ask.

'Half-mile up ahead,' PJ answered. The road curved left, then right, then left again before it straightened out and narrowed so much Tim wondered what would happen if they met an oncoming car. All around was green – fields, hedgerows, trees – and not a house or any traces of life to be seen. Tim's heart sank a little. Surely they'd travelled half a mile by now? He looked over at his uncle but PJ showed no sign of slowing down. Tim was used to living on a street lined with houses, a bus stop right outside and shops on the corner. A library, a swimming pool and cinema all within walking distance. He gazed out of the window at the bare landscape. This is what nowhere looks like, he thought. And I'm in the middle of it.

'Nearly there,' PJ piped up, as they passed a solitary house on the right – a squat, pebble-dashed cottage half hidden behind scrawny trees. With its moss-covered roof and small windows hung with grubby lace curtains, it didn't look as though it could be habitable. Yet a washing line of flapping clothes was strung across the part-concreted yard and a hairy black and white dog tied to a gatepost went berserk when he saw the van. And belting each other with sticks at the front door was a group of small boys. One of them broke away and ran out to the road as the van passed, swinging his stick above his head and roaring something Tim couldn't understand.

Shortly after, PJ slowed down. 'Here we are,' he said,

swinging left through a wide gap between two fir trees.

There she was. Auntie Margaret. Waiting in the yard with a huge smile spread across her face. She held one hand on her rounded stomach and waved the other excitedly.

PJ parked the van, jumped out and slammed the door behind him. Auntie Margaret hurried over, opening Tim's side before he got a chance to do it himself. 'You're here in one piece!' she cried.

Tim climbed out, his legs wobbly after the drive. She looked younger than he'd expected. Very like Mum. Smaller, though, and a tiny bit chubby, with orange-brown freckles peppering her face and arms. Her thick, almost-black hair had been tamed into a short cut that showed off her neck, and her dark, deep-set eyes gleamed like pebbles under water. She wore a bright yellow dress with a white lacy collar and, over her shoulders, a short-sleeved navy cardigan. 'Hello, Auntie Margaret,' he said.

She pulled him close and hugged him tightly. 'It's Mags,' she said, breathing into his hair. 'It's Mags. All right?'

Tim was a little embarrassed. She smelt of flour and fresh air and earth and he could feel the hardness of her stomach pressing into his own. 'You're a fine lad,' she said, when she finally released him. 'The size of you! And the Lord save us but look at those gorgeous blond curls!' Her words quivered slightly in the back of her throat. 'We're so glad you've come to stay. Aren't we, PJ?'

PJ was unloading the van. He lugged a bag of cement out and thumped it into a wheelbarrow. 'What?'

Auntie Margaret – Mags – threw her eyes up and smiled at Tim again. 'Tim,' she said, louder this time. 'We're glad he's come to stay.'

'Oh. Aye.' He pulled Tim's rucksack out and tossed it over. Tim caught it and held it to his chest.

'In a world of his own,' Mags said quietly, circling her arm around Tim's shoulders. 'I suppose he had the ear bent off of you all the way from Dún Laoghaire?' Tim looked at her, puzzled. 'Ah don't be minding me,' she said. 'I'm only pulling your leg. PJ's never been one for the talking.'

As she guided him towards the open back door, Tim glanced around. The house was old, two storeys, with tiny windows and flaking whitewashed walls. The yard around it was bordered by scraggly hedges growing through a collapsing fence, and beyond that were open fields. A tidy pile of old furniture – a broken armchair, a chest missing its drawers, a cast-iron bed frame – lay in a corner of the yard.

Mags brought him through the door and straight into a big room that ran the full width of the house. To the left, in the far corner, was the kitchen; to the right was a living space. The windows allowed only a small amount of light to filter in and, probably to make up for that, Tim thought, the place was decked out in bright, lively colours. The uneven walls were painted cherry pink to waist height and lemon yellow above, and the floor was covered with a sea of blood-red lino, worn through in places and showing old flagstones underneath.

'Sit yourself down there,' Mags said, indicating a circular table covered with a patterned oilcloth. 'I've the dinner made. You must be starving. I'll show you to your room after. But . . . I'm sure you'll need the bathroom first?'

Tim smiled, relieved. He hadn't wanted to ask.

'Upstairs,' she said. 'Second door on the left.' He wrinkled his nose. He could smell food he knew he wouldn't like.

Back downstairs, Mags set a plate in front of him, along

with a glass of cold milk. He was right: thick-sliced pink bacon, mashed cabbage and boiled potatoes bursting out of their skins. Not one thing he'd enjoy. 'There you are now,' she said. 'Get that into you.' She settled herself down in a chair opposite.

'Is there any . . . gravy?' Tim asked, trying to sound cheerful. 'Or ketchup?' Either would do. He needed something to disguise the taste.

Mags reached over and ruffled his hair. 'Sure why would you want to go destroying the taste of good food like that? Now eat up. And when you've finished that, I've apple tart for after.' She watched intently as he began to saw through the meat, smiling widely whenever he looked up. There was no way out of it. As he chewed, he tried to distract himself by concentrating on the sounds that filtered through the open door: the low *murrr*s of distant cattle; the far-off drone of farm machinery; the delicate notes of breeze-blown birdsong. He focused on the details of his cutlery: the tarnished prongs of his fork; the blunt, serrated edge of his knife; the faceted, mother-of-pearl handles. Anything to take his mind off the food. The whole process was torture. The potatoes weren't too bad, once he'd removed the gritty skins. And the bacon wasn't the worst meat he'd ever eaten. But the slippery over-boiled cabbage was another matter. He picked through it, hoping Mags wouldn't notice that he wasn't actually eating it. He could feel his cheeks redden as she stared. He mashed a forkful of green into some potato, pushed it into his mouth and washed it down with a gulp of milk. Abruptly, Mags shoved her chair back, stood up and walked over to the kitchen. Tim felt terribly guilty. Her breathing grew heavy as she leaned into the sink. There was silence for a moment and then she spoke.

'How was the ferry?'

Tim winced. 'Fine, thank you.'

'You managed it all right? You didn't find it strange at all?'

He swallowed a piece of bacon whole. 'Maybe. A little.'

She spun round. 'You did? How so? In what way?'

'I . . . I'm not sure.' Tim was taken aback by the force of her questions. 'I can't really describe it. Maybe . . . maybe it's just that I've never been on a ship before.'

Her eyes on him were like those of a bird. She opened her mouth and drew in a breath as if ready to speak, then closed it and walked past him, out to the yard. He stared at his dinner and wondered how long she'd be gone, if he'd have enough time to scrape it into the bin and get away with it. But then she was back, her eyes wide and glistening, her cheeks high with colour. 'It's all right,' she said, taking his plate. 'Suppose you're more used to . . . what? Fish and chips? Bangers and mash? You did your best. That's all that matters.' She sniffed and kept her head down, as though she didn't want Tim to see her face.

Was she *crying*? Was that why she'd walked out of the house?

Tim felt awful. Could she have been *that* offended he didn't like the meal she'd made? He dug his nails into his palms as he spoke. 'I'm sorry.'

'What in God's name have you got to be sorry for?' Mags said, clearly trying to make her voice sound cheery.

'I . . . I don't know. The dinner . . . I mean . . .'

'Ah, don't be ridiculous,' she said, smiling. 'No need for apologising, do you hear me?' She slid a slice of apple tart into a bowl and drizzled it with cream. 'There you are now. You'll enjoy that, no doubt.'

This was good. More than good. Warm and sweet and delicious. As Tim ate, he watched her wiping a cloth around the sink, over and over again. She seemed lost in her own thoughts, silent and focused, and Tim wondered if she'd forgotten he was there. Then she turned just as he swallowed his last mouthful. 'Come on,' she said. 'I'll show you your room.' She ushered him up the narrow staircase and down to the end of the landing. 'I hope it's all right. I got PJ to clear it out and do it up for you.' A good-sized room, it had two windows – one that looked out the front of the house, the other that faced the back. 'I'll leave you to get settled, then,' she said, half closing the door as she left.

Tim looked around. It had been a hurried job. The wallpaper bubbled badly in parts and none of the strips had been lined up properly, making the dated pattern of yellow climbing roses crazily mismatched. A carpet of orange and emerald-green splashes covered the floor, though it hadn't been cut properly and its edges were short of the skirting. The wooden panelled ceiling had been painted lilac and the thin, unlined white curtains looked like they might once have been bed sheets. Against one wall stood a small, rather rickety mahogany wardrobe with mirrored doors and, under the front window, a white-painted chest of drawers. Tim opened his rucksack. He put his things away carefully, placing his camera in the top drawer of the chest. Then he lay down on the bed. He liked the smell of fresh paint and new carpet and felt happy that they'd gone to the trouble, even if the effect made him a little dizzy. He heard Mags coming back upstairs, tapping lightly on the door before she entered. 'Everything all right?'

'Fine, thank you,' Tim answered.

'Exhausted after coming all that way, isn't that it?' she said, when she saw him curled on the bed. 'A long journey to be making all on your own.' She hovered over him for a second, as though she was thinking about sitting down on the bed, but then she stepped away and stood looking out of the back window. Her face glowed in the last of the evening light and she smoothed a hand over the curving outline of her stomach.

Tim wondered when exactly the baby was due but he didn't want to ask. It scared him, the idea there was another life inside her, a little being squirming about, waiting for its time to emerge. 'You know,' Mags said, her voice soft and whispery, 'you can see the sea from here. If you keep walking out over the fields, you come to the cliffs at Faranboy. I came up here today and well . . . I got this notion I might be able to see the ferry and . . . I think I did. 'Twas only a speck, mind, but I'm sure I saw it. And I thought about you being on it, away out in the middle of the sea. And now you're here, in the room, and . . .' She turned around and eased herself onto the bed. 'What was it about the journey that was strange?'

Tim shoved over to make more room. He cringed. Why did she want to know? It would sound ridiculous if he tried to put it into words. 'It . . . it was nothing. It—'

'No, go on. Tell me,' she said, fixing her eyes on his.

He felt silly as he tried to explain the dream and the way he'd felt when he woke up. But she didn't laugh or even smile. She listened, nodding, as though she understood exactly what he was trying to explain.

'I know,' she said, when he finished.

'You've been on the boat, then?' he asked, sitting himself up on the bed.

'I have. I went over once.'

'And you didn't like the journey either?'

'Not one bit.'

'Did you come over to see us?'

'I did.'

'I don't remember.'

'Ah, you were only a baby, so you were.' She stroked his arm. 'Well, never mind the strange dreams. You got here safely and that's all that matters. Now, are you going to come down and sit with myself and PJ or will you be wanting to go to sleep?'

PJ wasn't exactly talkative. It might be awkward. 'I ... I think I'll go to sleep,' Tim said. 'I'm a bit tired.'

Mags smiled. 'Don't want to be stuck with the pair of us for the night, isn't that it? Don't blame you, so I don't. You'll feel better when you meet some of the young lads living around.' She reached out to him. 'Now, come here and give me a kiss goodnight.' Before Tim could move, she had him enveloped, his face squashed up against her own, her lips pressed hard to his forehead. He could hardly breathe. When she pulled away, he could feel his cheeks burning. 'Night night. Sleep well,' she said. 'And don't forget to write to your mammy in the morning. I promised I'd remind you.'

Tim listened to the stairs creaking under her feet. He could still feel the strength of her embrace as he got undressed and put on his pyjamas. And as he brushed his teeth in the bathroom, he looked away from the mirror when he saw how red his face was. In bed, he pulled the blankets right up to his chin.

It was so quiet. He was used to the rattle of late-night buses, squealing ambulances, barking dogs. The lack of sound – it was almost as though he couldn't understand it. He lay in the dark thinking about the events of the day. About the drive to Holyhead and saying goodbye to Mum and Dad. About the ship and his dream and waiting for PJ. And about Mags. Was she a bit strange or was it just his imagination? Not *crazy*-strange but maybe a little ... odd? He wasn't sure. But, then, everything had been strange today. Everything. He'd never had a day like it before. He closed his eyes and felt himself sinking deep into the soft, empty silence. It didn't take him long to fall asleep.

Deep in the night, he part woke. And though he was half in and half out of slumber, he was aware the space around him was unfamiliar. With a racing heart he tried to figure it out, his eyes flickering, opening and closing, just a split second but enough to remind himself of where he was. Reassured, he felt his body sinking again, teetering on the edge of unconsciousness. And, as he fell, his brain told him that he'd seen her. Mags. Standing over him like a ghost. Staring. He wrestled with the image, tried to keep it clear and real, but a thick sleep took over, and by morning, he'd forgotten all about it.

I've always known something was missing. For as long as I can remember, Mam's never been fully there. Even as a small girl I noticed. Things would usually start to slip once August came around. I used to think it was because she'd miss me too much when I went back to school, after all the fun we'd had over the summer holidays. Just the two of us. Making memories. Walking across the fields to the beach at Faranboy, clambering over hedgerows, scaling fences, until that magic moment when we'd spy the glittering strip of blue. We'd bring salty ham sandwiches, wedges of porter cake, a flask of tea, and sit for hours on a rug laid out on the warm sand. Mam would stare at the sea, holding up her hand to shield her eyes from the sun. I could tell she was in some other place when she did that. As though she was searching for something she wasn't even sure she had lost. If ever I asked what she was looking at she'd smile a little and answer, 'It's nothing, don't mind me,' but wouldn't pull her gaze away for ages.

Wandering home on those summer evenings, we'd see Dad waiting for us in the yard, standing stock still, peering out over the fields. When he'd spot us, he'd wave both arms over his head, like a mad thing, before turning back to the house. He always looked relieved. I often wondered if he worried we might never return. Other days, Mam and I would stroll to Crowe's farm to pick strawberries to make jam. But I'd eat so many on the way home we rarely had enough. She never minded. Those were the good times, when I could do no wrong, and Mam seemed to drift along on a soft cloud just shy of the ground. But then summer would end and she'd fall to earth. I'd go back to school, another year older but no wiser to her moods. On the bus home in the afternoons, I'd dread what awaited me. I might find her curled in bed, covers over her head. Or in the spare room, shivering at the open back window, staring at 'nothing' again. Those were the bad times. When not much I did was right. If I offered tea she wouldn't want any; if I didn't, she'd complain.

Dark winter nights it was often just me and Dad for dinner in the kitchen. Mam wouldn't make it out of bed. I taught myself to cook. Dad used to joke about being a guinea pig. He just got on with things. He'd learned to deal with it, I suppose. He'd circle around her, mindful but not fussing, knowing when to advance, when to retreat. Another man might not have had the patience. I found it more difficult, convinced that at the back of it all it was somehow my fault.

In recent years it's been a little better. The new pills help. She said the other ones gave her headaches, made her dizzy. Dad used to try to make sure she took them. In as much as he could. 'Mags,' he'd say gently, cocking his head to one side and giving her a half-smile. 'You're being good, aren't you?'

She'd know what he meant. 'What do you take me for, PJ? Of course I am.' But he could never truly be sure. This latest descent is the deepest in a long time. By the time my birthday came round in late August, she was already in freefall. Refusing to venture out, making minor issues into major ordeals. She'd sent a text: *Happy birthday x*. At least she remembered, I told myself. And it's not as if turning twenty-seven is special. It doesn't bother me now. Not like it did when I was younger. I used to long to have a party. 'Please, Mam. Everyone's asking me to.' She relented once, on my tenth. When the day came and no preparations had been made, I was left to lie to my friends that she'd had to go and look after a non-existent sick relative, when in reality she was foetal under the bedcovers, curtains drawn against the late-summer sun. I used to wish I'd been born in an earlier month. April. Or March or May. Just not the one that heralded the onset of darkness.

Christmas. The coldest winter for twenty-five years puts paid to me driving home as I usually do. They take it badly. I'm sure I hear a tremble in Dad's voice when I call on Christmas Eve to let them know. I don't think I've ever felt so guilty. I've left it as long as I can, hoping conditions might improve. But the entire country is under several feet of snow. Everything has ground to a halt. Roads treacherous, many impassable. Buses and trains cancelled. People snowed in all over the place. No sign of a thaw for at least a week. It simply isn't possible. 'I'm so sorry, Dad. You know I would if I could.'

'It's all right,' he says. 'Don't worry about it.'

But it isn't 'all right'. How can it be? The two of them, on their own, without their only child at Christmas. If they could hire a helicopter to fly me down, I've no doubt they would. When I call again on Christmas morning, Mam isn't even up. 'Not a great night,' Dad says. 'Awake for ages, so she was. She'll phone you after.'

I'm forced to spend Christmas with Luke's family. I say 'forced', though, in truth, I know it'll be no hardship. Quite the opposite. I get on well with them. Luke and I have been going out over a year and it's not the first time I've had dinner at his. His family welcome me as one of their own and I like the way I feel part of it, just one among the crowd of brothers and sisters, not the focus of all attention. Throughout the day, though, I'm jumpy, waiting for Mam's call and not knowing what to expect.

In the end, it's Dad who phones. Mam's asleep. Been out for the count on the couch for over an hour. 'Didn't want to leave calling any longer,' he says. 'I'll be hitting the bed myself soon.' He tells me he managed to stuff and cook the turkey but it remains largely uneaten. He's taken the tree down. Mam's orders. Christ. Talk about a guilt trip. 'Sure what use is it now?' he says, trying to justify her wishes. 'Shedding needles all over the place anyway it was.'

That pretty much proves what I've long suspected: if it wasn't for me, they wouldn't bother with Christmas at all. Mam did her best every year. And Dad. When I was a child, Santa delivered. Whatever I asked for and more. But, it being only the three of us, I've always felt under pressure to carry the day. I pretended to believe long after I figured out the truth about where the presents under the tree came from. It was never the same once I finally let slip that I knew. That pressure, I still sense it. And now, because I'm not able to be with them, it's even stronger. I know it's not my fault, but why do I feel like I've ruined their Christmas? 'Is Mam OK?' I ask Dad, and screw up my face as I wait for his reply. I'm relieved I don't have to talk to her. I'd probably feel like chartering that helicopter myself if I had to hear the sadness in her voice.

'She'll be grand,' Dad says. 'But she'll be counting the days till you're here.'

'Everything all right down in the sticks?' Luke asks me, when I've finished the call.

I nod. 'As well as can be expected, I suppose.'

After New Year's, another week goes by before a thaw sets in and I finally manage to make it home. Though conditions aren't treacherous any more, they're bad enough. I take it easy. The journey is bleak. A grey tunnel. Sky lead-heavy and spitting rain. Roads edged with half-frozen blackened slush. Windscreen wipers working overtime the whole way down. To top it all, it's Sunday. Back to work tomorrow.

I'm late. I said I'd be down at two but it's that time now and I've another fifteen miles to go. My mobile rings in my bag. I know it's them, wondering if I'm all right.

Dad's waiting at the gate when I pull up. Face tense. Body rigid. And not just because he's worried about me. I'm sure of that. I roll down the window. 'How's Mam?' He presses his lips together, raises his eyes. I drive on into the yard. When I get out of the car and head for the door, it's as if the sky has lowered itself to within inches of my head.

I hand Mam the bunch of white lilies I bought in my local florist's yesterday. Her face lifts. 'Lovely. Lovely,' she says, laying them on the dresser. We hug. Her cheek is cold and dry against my own. 'Wasn't the same. You not being here. Not like Christmas at all.'

'I know,' I say, pulling away and noticing the film of tears in her eyes. 'But I'm here now.'

She does her best to smile. 'I have the dinner ready.'

I can smell it. The works. 'Turkey?'

Dad puts his arms around me. 'I said there was no need. But there's no telling your mother.'

'Well, I'm glad you insisted, Mam,' I say into Dad's shoulder. 'I'm starving.'

She pads into the kitchen. I take the crystal vase from the top of the dresser and follow her. 'I'll put these in water, will I?'

She bends to open the oven. 'Put what in water, love?'

I turn on the tap. I don't want to answer. She'll get flustered, afraid I'll think the lilies have made no impression. It isn't that she doesn't appreciate the thought. And there's no worry on my part about early-onset Alzheimer's or anything like that. Sometimes things happening around her aren't as clear as whatever's going on in her head. She doesn't seem to notice that I haven't replied. 'Pass me another tea-towel there, Orla,' she says.

'Here, let me do that,' I offer. The turkey is huge. 'You'll never lift it.'

'That's a man's job, so 'tis.' Dad swoops in and takes over. 'Fine bird,' he says, setting the roasting tray on the counter. 'Done a great job, so you have, Mags.' He looks at me. 'Hasn't she, Orla?'

'Looks amazing, Mam. So good of you to go to all this trouble.'

''Tis no trouble at all. Wouldn't have it any other way. Now, settle yourselves in at the table. I'm ready to serve.'

'So, Orla,' Dad says, when we start to eat, 'how's work going?'

I chew and swallow a mouthful. 'It's OK. Not too bad.'

'You're managing?'

'Keeping my head above water. I'm sure it'll get better. It's just . . .' I hesitate. I'd hoped we'd at least get the dinner over with before I'd tell them. But now or in an hour's time, what does it matter?

Dad reaches out and places his hand over mine. 'You know we'll support you as best we can.'

I give him a smile. 'I know, Dad. But . . .' I sigh. 'You've done enough already. Luke and I, well, we've been doing a lot of thinking and . . .' Mam's eyes. Already worried. Oh, God. I can't make this any easier. Here goes . . . '. . . we're heading over to the States. We're going to do the New York Bar exam. We—'

'You're going away?' Mam lays her knife and fork on her plate. She sounds breathless. 'You can't. You can't just . . . go.'

'We know a few who've already done it. But, look, we're not making any plans beyond doing the exam. We'll just see how it goes.' I try to make myself sound casual, as if it's something I've given barely any thought to. I knew Mam wouldn't like the sound of it. 'We mightn't even pass!'

'But you might,' she says. 'You probably will. I don't know how I . . . I mean we . . .' Her chest heaves with the effort of breathing.

Dad takes his hand from mine. I catch his eye. He's a little annoyed. Not because I'm thinking of doing the exam but because Mam's upset. I should've run it by him first. I realise that now. 'Look. It might not even happen,' I say. 'We could change our minds. Forget about it for the moment, OK?'

Dad continues eating. Mam stares at her plate, dark eyes

unblinking. 'Eat up, Mags,' he says. 'We'll talk about it later.' She waits until her food grows cold, then scrapes it into the bin.

Later in the afternoon Dad lights a fire. He shoves the couch close to the hearth as soon as Mam dozes off in her armchair and I sit in beside him while he reads the paper. I stare at the flames and think about Luke. About the two of us. Partners in a top law firm. At home in a Manhattan loft. Hailing yellow taxis. Strolling in Central Park. Crazy dreams. Maybe not so crazy. Others have done it. But will guilt hold me back? Fifty miles is all that separates me from Mam and Dad at the moment. How will I feel about three thousand? Dad would probably be happy for me. Not thrilled at the thought of me leaving, but able to see the broader picture. Mam won't want me to go. But should I allow that to colour any decision I might make? I have before. School trips. I'd really wanted to do the German exchange. Dad had paid the deposit. The excitement. Then the jealousy when they all arrived home. The stories. The fun. And college. Erasmus. Mam sank into a deeper trough than ever when I told her I'd applied. She tried her best. Said she was proud of me, hoped I'd get it and all of that. I could see through her. I hated myself for giving in. But I'd have hated myself more if I'd gone and she'd ended up getting worse.

'Mam won't want me to go, will she, Dad?' I whisper. I pick up the poker and stick it in among the red-hot coals. 'To New York, I mean.'

He throws a glance over his shoulder to check she's still asleep. He keeps his voice low. 'Don't hold yourself back.' He closes his paper, folds it, lays it on his knee. 'If you want to go, then do. She can't keep you here forever. It's just . . .'

'Just what, Dad? What is it?'

'Ah, I don't know.' He runs a palm over the naked pink skin of his head. 'She just hates the thought of . . . of leaving. Always afraid of . . . well, people going and never coming back. They all went. You know that. Left her on the farm to look after your grandparents.'

'I'm sure it wasn't easy.' I split a lump of coal in two, sending a flurry of orange sparks up the chimney. 'Is that why she'd be against me going to the States?' I give him a gentle elbow. 'Afraid there'll be no one to look after you both in your old age?'

He laughs. 'Have we not hit it yet? I'm feeling a lot like an old man at the minute.'

'Ah, Dad. You're still in your fifties, for God's sake!'

'Not for long!'

Dad is fifty-nine, Mam fifty-seven. They'd both reached their thirties when they had me. Not unusual by today's standards, but back in the eighties, it would've been considered they'd started a family quite late. Started, then stopped.

I trace S shapes in the sooty hearth with the tip of the poker. 'Did you ever wish you'd had a bigger family?'

Dad leans in towards the fire. He holds his huge hands up to the heat. 'Aren't you headache enough?' he says. I smile. That's as far as I'll get with that question. I often wonder what it'd be like to have a sister, a brother, lots of siblings. Not to be the only one.

'It might be about control,' Dad says, into the fire. 'If you're looking for reasons why she won't want you to go.'

'Control?'

'Aye. If she doesn't keep a tight grip on things, she feels everything'll fall to pieces.'

'I wish she wasn't like that.'

He blows out a mouthful of air, making his cheeks balloon and the flames quiver. 'I know, love. But, well, every time your bundle of sticks comes undone you tie the knot stronger.' He pats my knee. 'Gets to the stage when you can't undo them at all, they're so tightly bound.' Dad's not a philosophical man. He doesn't go in for explanations. Deeper understandings. Reasons. It's almost comical to hear him speaking like this. 'No one likes letting go,' he continues. ''Tis frightening, so 'tis.' He turns to face me. 'She likes to think you'll always be around.'

'Is that fair, though? On me?'

He pulls at his ear. 'That's for you to figure out. You make your own decisions.' Mam shifts. Mumbles something. 'You're back in the land of the living, then?' he asks her.

I stand up. 'I'll make some tea.'

Mam has already tidied the kitchen. Wouldn't hear of me lending a hand. It's spotless. Her pride and joy. Dad put his heart and soul into it for her. Did a fabulous job. Solid oak cupboards. Marble worktops. Porcelain tiles. He spent years trying to get her to agree to the refurb. When he finally persuaded her, he went all out and gave it a top-quality finish. He even cleaned and restored the flags hidden under two layers of lino. He had help, of course. That was boom time. When he employed four men and still had to turn down work. He was doing so well, he was able to pay the considerable fee for my year in the King's Inns and hardly even notice it. He wouldn't hear of me repaying him. He's back out on his own now, spending most of his time pricing jobs rather than actually doing them. 'People want the work done,' he says. 'Just don't have the money to pay for it.'

We drink our tea by the fire. Dad relates a few newsworthy stories he's digested from the local paper. Then we chat about how we're over the worst of the weather, and Mam produces a plate of scones she made earlier. There's no more mention of my plans – from me or from them – though it's clear from Mam's silence that she's thinking about nothing but. Soon after six, I say I have to get going. The nights are still freezing. I want to get back early enough in case the roads ice over. Dad tries to get me to stay.

'I can't. I'm in court in the morning,' I tell him, as I zip up my coat. 'Otherwise I would.' Though, in truth, the thought of sleeping in the spare room doesn't really appeal. If my old bedroom wasn't cluttered now with Dad's work things – his huge, untidy desk, boxes of files all over the floor (I still haven't been able to convince him to buy a computer) – I might have more inclination. I've never been keen on the spare bedroom. It's looked the same for as long as I can remember. Horrible wallpaper with creepy yellow roses. Orange and green patterned carpet. Purple ceiling. Awful.

Mam pulls her cardigan tighter round her chest. 'If you change your mind, I mean if the roads are bad, just turn back. Don't take any risks.'

'I won't, Mam. I promise.' We hug at the back door. I make a parting pledge to be down again in a few weeks. 'Or maybe you'll come up,' I suggest. 'You haven't been in the city for ages.'

Dad answers, rubbing his hands together: 'I'll be up the end of the week, so I will. Not right into the big smoke, but near enough anyway. Pricing a job there in Dún Laoghaire.'

'That'd be a fair distance to travel every day. If you get the job, I mean.'

'Ah, sure, lookit, don't I know. But I have to take the work wherever I can.'

'Well, give me a call. Maybe we'll go for lunch. You might come with him, Mam?'

She nods. 'We'll see.'

I usher them both back indoors. 'Go on in. It's freezing. Wave out the window.'

I use my Laser card to scrape the thin layer of ice off the windscreen, then climb in and start the engine. Waiting for the hot air to clear the mist from inside the glass, I look towards the house. I just about make out Mam watching me from the kitchen. A shadowy form like a stiff, unmoving ghost. I can sense it. The nothingness that hovers around her. Is it a yearning for something? A mourning? Or a searching? It's as if it's not me she's watching out for at all.

I switch on the headlights, roll the car gently across the gravel.

Jesus!

A figure looms out of the darkness to my right. I push my foot down on the brake.

A tapping on the side window.

Dad.

I scrabble for the button, end up opening the door instead. He bends his rangy frame down and thrusts an envelope into my lap.

I try to push it back into his hands. 'Ah, Dad. I'm grand! You already gave me plenty!' He'd posted me a cheque for Christmas. Four hundred euro.

'Go on with you,' he says, holding his hands up. 'I'm not

taking it back.' Then he leans in and hugs me tight, his smoke-scented beard scratching my face. 'It's just . . . just a little extra.'

'Thanks, Dad.' I shove it into my bag.

'You be careful now.' His breath plumes white in the freezing air. 'Take it slow, do you hear me?'

'I will.'

I do. The night is deepest black. In the lighted arc of the headlights, hoar-frosted trees zoom scarily in and out of the darkness. Bleach-boned bodies stripped of flesh. As I leave Lissenmore, the journey seems more about the miles behind me than those that lie ahead. Half an hour in, the red light on the petrol gauge begins to blink. I pull into the service station at Kilmacanogue, shivering in the bitingly cold air as I fill the tank. Inside, I pick up a couple of overripe bananas and a litre carton of milk, catching sight of myself in the mirrored side panels of the fridge. In the unforgiving strip lighting, I look like I've been awake for days. Skin washed out and white as the frost outside. Eyes ringed with smudged flecks of mascara. And my hair. I spent ages straightening it this morning, taming the wild waves I inherited from Dad. Now the night air has undone all my work and it curls in ringlets round my face.

Back in the car, I check my mobile – a text from Luke: *Hi, you ok drive careful icy out see you tomorrow x.* I smile at his unpunctuated stream and tap out a reply: *On way. Road not too bad. Text you when I get home. X.*

I pick up the envelope Dad gave me. Jesus. Another hundred and fifty. He's too good to me. But there's something else. It's not just cash inside.

There's a photograph. Rounded corners. Postcard-sized.

I sit on the forecourt, still parked at pump No. 2, and look closely at the image. There's Dad in his younger days. Thin – skinny, even. Dressed in shades of brown. An awful mustard jacket and similar-coloured trousers. With a beard bushier than his present one and a roaring red Afro to match. Gas. And Mam. Hair in a pixie cut. Wearing a shapeless tartan dress. Hideous. But then, she had an excuse. She's pregnant. She's holding one hand on her stomach, on the bump that will turn out to be me. How strange that I'm in this picture with my parents. But that I am, essentially, invisible.

But stranger still . . . the boy who stands between them.

Mam has her arm around him, pulling him tight to her side. His face is scrunched up against the sun, his hair a mop of thick, white-blond curls. He's about fourteen, maybe fifteen. Hard to tell. Awkward. Serious. But a stranger to me. I've never laid eyes on this photo before. Mam and Dad have so few pictures from the past, I'd definitely remember if I had.

Dad usually just pushes a rolled-up wad into my hand. He's never used an envelope before.

He wanted me to see this picture. But why?

Dear Mum,

I'm here now. At Auntie Margaret's house. She told me to call her Mags. I wasn't seasick on the ferry, just so you know. It was quite late when I arrived so I haven't much to tell. I'll buy a stamp today and send this. There's a post office in the village. How is Dad? I hope you were able to drive home OK.

Love from Tim

The inviting smell that had wafted up from the kitchen when Tim woke made his stomach rumble. He was starving. He dressed quickly and scribbled the note to his mum, as he'd promised, then picked his way downstairs to see PJ at the kitchen table, chewing his way through a plate of bacon, sausage and egg. After his night's sleep, his hair was even wilder, reaching up out from his head in matted, springy curls, his cheeks and chin pinpricked with spiky golden stubble. He nodded when Tim sat down. 'All right?' he asked, through a mouthful of meat.

'Yes, thank you,' Tim replied, as Mags set his breakfast in

front of him. After the dinner he'd had to endure the evening before, the fry-up looked delicious.

'You wrote to your mammy?' she asked.

'I did. I have the letter here in my pocket.'

'Good boy. I suppose you could give her a ring from the phone box one of the days. Cost you a fortune, mind. Anyhow, PJ'll drop you down to the post office after your breakfast. He's going that way this morning. Aren't you, PJ?'

'Suppose I'll have to whether I like it or not,' PJ said to his food.

Mags gave him a playful punch on the arm. 'Go 'way out of that and don't be teasing the lad.'

PJ grunted a laugh and looked at Tim. 'Once you're settled in I'll have you off with me for a day or two. Bit of work'll do you no harm. What would you think?'

Tim nodded. 'I'd like that.'

'Keep you out of trouble, isn't that right?' Mags said, taking the slice of toast from Tim's plate and plastering it with a thick layer of soft butter. 'There you are now,' she said, when she'd finished. 'Would you like me to cut up your rashers?'

'No, thanks,' Tim replied. 'I'm fine. I can manage.' Mags hovered over him while he ate, offering more toast, another egg, some beans.

'Leave the lad be,' PJ said, irritated. 'Stop your fussing over him.'

Mags looked wounded. She took PJ's empty plate and went over to the sink. PJ got up from the table. 'Will you be taking the whole morning to eat that?' he asked Tim. 'Going to be leaving in a minute, so I am.' He strode out to the yard.

Tim chewed and swallowed as fast as he could. When he was done, he brought his empty plate over to Mags. She slid it into the sink full of suds. PJ yelled from outside. 'I . . . I think we're going now,' Tim said. 'Thanks for the breakfast.'

'Be careful walking back, you hear me?' she called after him.

Tim felt sorry for her. PJ had been a little hard. And now he hadn't even said goodbye. Still, it was a bit much offering to cut up Tim's food. He wasn't a baby.

It had rained overnight and the road showed slick under the bright morning sun. The hedgerows glistened, beads of moisture clinging to leaves and stems, like strings of sparkling diamonds. PJ drove far too quickly, swerving wildly to avoid a pothole and almost ending up in the ditch – the one on the wrong side of the road. Tim thumped his head hard against the window but PJ didn't seem to notice and continued to bump along at the same speed. As they passed the pebble-dashed cottage, the crazy dog strained at his tether, yapping furiously. There was no sign of human life in the yard, but when Tim glanced in at the house, he saw someone at a window, holding back a curtain and peering out. A girl. Heat rushed to his face and he was glad, then, that PJ was driving so fast.

As he slid down, he was thrown forward without warning, then slammed back violently against his seat. They'd come to a sudden stop in the middle of the road. An oncoming green Fiat, all shiny paintwork and glinting windows, pulled up alongside the van. PJ rolled his window down, as did the Fiat's driver, and the two men started chatting away, laughing and joking loudly over the engines' rumble. Tim leaned forward a little and saw that the other man wore a black shirt and a stiff white collar. A priest. With rosy-apple cheeks and eyes like shiny blue glass marbles. He chuckled like a cartoon character, his shoulders shaking, his breath wheezy and short. He nodded at Tim. 'And this is the little visitor from across the water, I take it?'

'Aye. 'Tis,' PJ said. 'Stuck with him for the summer, we are. Isn't that right, Tim? This here eejit is Denis Coffey. Father Denis Coffey. Though I'm a holier man myself. You needn't be believing a word he says to you.'

Father Coffey guffawed. He dabbed at his watering eyes with a handkerchief. 'Dear God! You're a man and a half, PJ Hyland. Do you know that? A man and a half.' Then he leaned further out of the window, fixing his glassy gaze on Tim. 'And how do you find it here, Tim? PJ looking after you, is he?'

'I ... he ... I only arrived yesterday. I ...' Tim couldn't think what to say.

Father Coffey roared with laughter. 'Seems you haven't made much of an impression yet, PJ! Lad's not sure about you at all at all!'

'Ah go 'way out of that, Dinny,' PJ said, edging the van forward. 'None of your blackguarding.'

'I'd best be away myself anyway. Holy man or no, I've a quare few visits to make all the same.'

'Right you are, Dinny. Dropping this fella down to Katty's, so I am. Good luck now.'

As PJ pulled off without even a glance in the rear-view mirror, Tim looked behind. There was the girl. Standing out on the road now, her slight, shadowy shape receding into the grey dust as they gathered speed. He watched her signal to Father Coffey when he passed. Tim recognised her now as the girl he'd seen coming out of Kavanagh's shop the evening before. When he turned back in his seat, the beats of his heart were running ragged. Some faster. Some slower. Some not there at all.

Despite the fine morning, the post office was gloomy and cold. The flagged stone floor and brown-painted walls gave the place a dead-end, hopeless air. Tim imagined it was like a prison cell. Or a funeral parlour. Although he'd never been in either. The postmistress, who went by the abrasive-sounding name of Miss Katty Hackett, looked up from her newspaper when he entered. Seeing him, she became flustered, trying to make it appear she was busy. She started flicking through a stack of forms and fiddling with the few items of stationery on the well-worn wooden counter. She knew who Tim was. It was her business to know everything, it seemed.

'The little English boy, isn't it?' she said, when he asked for a stamp. 'That's not an accent we hear in Lissenmore too often.' Her suspicious eyes, magnified several times behind large, pink-framed spectacles, gave him a good long gawk. 'You've a look of Mags, right enough. Not a lot, mind, but 'twouldn't be hard to believe someone belonging to her spat you out. And how are you liking us?' She didn't wait for an answer: she'd spied the address on Tim's letter. 'Writing home already! And you only after arriving? Aren't you marvellous altogether?' Tim couldn't be sure if she was genuinely impressed or just making fun of him. He smiled at her all the same, licked the stamp and stuck it down. 'Wait!' she called, as he made for the door. 'Give this to your uncle PJ. Furzy Madden over by Backwellstown was on to me, wanting some class of a hay barn taken down. Not much of a job but 'twill keep him going a couple of days. I wrote it all down.' She thrust a folded brown envelope in Tim's direction. 'And don't go losing it on him, do you hear? He needs every bit he can get. What with the baby coming and all that.' Tim shoved it into his pocket. 'Hold on!' she said, as he pushed open the door. She'd obviously been starved of human contact for some time. 'Tell himself and Mags I just heard from the P-and-T. Waiting list is still more than a year. They won't be getting the phone in for a good while yet.' She lowered her voice and pointed her finger, glancing left and right. 'Between yourself and meself, we could do with the likes of your Maggie Thatcher over here, so we could.' She leaned her bony frame out over the counter as Tim backed into the street. 'She'd show our lot how it's done. I'm telling you now.'

Tim was glad to escape. He slipped his letter into the emerald-green postbox and started the walk back. He felt good. Mum would be glad he'd kept his promise. The village was quiet. No one on the street. Except a couple of kids standing in a dark doorway, eyeing him as he passed. The bigger one – a shaven-headed boy with strawberry-red cheeks – munched a jam-smeared hunk of bread. He stuck his tongue out, showing the contents of his mouth. Tim put his head down, afraid to make eye contact, and—

SLAM!

'What the fu—' It was the boy with the squirrelly hair he'd seen the day before. He'd just shot out of Kavanagh's carrying a cardboard box piled high with shopping. 'Watch where you're bloody well going!' A cauliflower toppled from the box and rolled onto the road. Tim watched, helpless, as it bounced between a car's front wheels, like a football, then hit the kerb, ricocheted against the back wheels and smashed into pieces. The driver of the car – a wizened woman who must have been close to ninety – didn't seem to notice and drove on as if nothing had happened. Tim tried not to, but he couldn't help giggling. Squirrel-hair stared with narrowed, flinty eyes. He set his box down on the path. 'Think that's fucken funny, do you? All right for you, what? Some of us have work to do.'

Tim blushed. 'I . . . I'm sorry. Really I am. It was an accident. I—'

'Sorry, are you?' he said, mimicking Tim's accent. 'Sorry enough to pay for another one?'

'What? I . . . Of course.' Tim pulled a pound note from his pocket. 'I'll go in and buy one.'

Squirrel-hair snatched the note from Tim's fingers. 'My turn to be sorry now. 'Twas the last one. Shame. But don't worry . . .' he pushed the money into his back pocket '. . . I'll pick one up another day.'

How much could a cauliflower be? Surely a lot less than a pound. Probably only a few pence. Tim looked up. The boy was about sixteen. Tall. With icy-blue eyes, tanned, sinewy arms and red-skinned hands that looked like they belonged to someone much older. Above his top lip grew the spidery sketchings of a hoped-for moustache. 'But what about . . . I mean . . . shouldn't I get some change?'

Squirrel-hair laughed. 'Change? *Change*, is it?' He leaned in closer to Tim. 'I'll give you a bit of fucken change, if you like. How about I change your face for you? Would that be the kind of change you'd be thinking of?'

Tim's heart hadn't long settled back into its regular rhythm after seeing the girl. Now it was off again, thumping a drumbeat he could feel in his head. 'But—'

'But what?' the boy interrupted. 'But that's not fair? But that's all the money I have? I'll tell you something for nothing and look at my face when I say it.' He was even closer now and he spoke through clenched, crooked teeth. 'But I couldn't give a fuck. Now. There's a but for you.' He bent to pick up his box. 'You see that up there?' he said, jerking his head to the left. 'Read what it says, why don't you?' Then, crossing the road, he kicked a lump of cauliflower, sending it skidding up onto the path. Mumbling under his breath, and with the box balanced on his knee, he struggled to open the door of a rusty orange car. Dumping the box in the back, he climbed into the driver's seat and rolled down the window. 'Don't forget to have a good look now,' he said, pointing backwards with his thumb. A stinking black smoke cloud spluttered from the exhaust as he drove away.

Tim watched, astonished. Surely he wasn't old enough to drive a car? Not legally. Maybe there were different rules about that sort of thing in Ireland.

'You one of them?' Tim felt a tug on his sleeve. The boy with the bread and jam.

'One of . . .' Tim shook his head, puzzled.

'What it says up there on the mountain.'

Then he looked up to where Squirrel-hair had pointed and saw the other side of the 'hill' PJ had referred to on the drive to Lissenmore the day before. Daubed in what must have been enormous white letters on a sheer piece of rock about three-quarters of the way to the summit, two words: 'BRITS OUT'.

Tim had come across bullies before. Who hadn't? At school, it was the older boys. The ones who sat at the back of the bus. It was what you learned to expect. An unwritten rule. On the street, it was the bigger ones. Ones who went to different schools. Or those who thought they were tough. They all had their reasons

– however ridiculous – for picking on him. He bit at a rough fingernail, wishing Mark was there. He'd have known what to say, how to deal with Squirrel-hair. Mark was lucky. He had a big brother. If Tim had a big brother, he'd feel different. Safer. Mark was never as afraid as Tim was, didn't mind shouting back. 'I'll get my big brother!' he'd yell. 'He'll beat the shit out of you!' Sometimes it was hard being an only child.

The road back seemed a lot longer on foot than it had in the van. The walk was slightly uphill and the sun was hot. By the time Tim reached the pebble-dashed cottage, he was sweating. Great. He was sure his face was like a beetroot. And there she was. The girl. He arrived just in time to see her waving as the orange car drove away. The box of shopping the cauliflower had escaped from sat on the ground beside the gatepost. Two small boys appeared and took a side each, carrying it across the yard and in through the open front door of the cottage.

'Hiya.' The girl pushed her long brown hair from her eyes. 'You're Tim, aren't you? Mags told my mam you were coming over for a while. I'm Maeve Mooney.' Flustered, his heart speeding up again, Tim held out his hand. She took his fingers for a moment, her grip soft but sending a sizzle along his arm. 'Pleased to meet you, Tim,' she said, trying not to giggle. Oh, God. She found his greeting funny. What was he thinking? A handshake? He swallowed. They looked at each other for an awkward moment. 'Barry Kilbride that was,' she said, after a silence. 'Dropping off some messages for us. Does the deliveries for Kavanagh's. Supposed to be fifty pence but he never charges us. Very good is Barry.' She mistook Tim's raised eyebrows for curiosity. 'On account of my dad,' she explained. 'Feckin' off, like. Took the car and all, so he did.'

'Oh,' he said, as if he understood. 'Did he ... did he say anything about the cauliflower?'

She frowned. 'Cauliflower? My dad?'

'No ... not your dad. I mean, uh ...' he was already sorry he'd mentioned it '... that boy, Barry. I just thought he ... It's just that ... uh ...'

'Don't think he said anything about a cauliflower,' she said, puzzled. 'Should he have?'

'It's ... it's OK. It's nothing. Forget it.'

She tried not to stare. Tim tried not to keep looking at her. The skin on her face, her neck, her arms – every bit of it that he could see – was an even sandy cream. No glow on her cheeks, no stray freckles or moles, no sunburn. Her eyes were sea-coloured. It was hard to tell if they were green or blue or grey. Her lips were pink and pearly. She wore a lilac vest with thin, fraying straps that stretched loosely over the bones of her shoulders, and a pair of yellow jeans with the legs rolled up above her ankles. The big toes of both her feet poked through holes in her black canvas slip-ons.

One of the wiry boys who'd carried the box away reappeared, brandishing a bamboo cane. His shorts and T-shirt were several sizes too small, showing limbs that were little more than skin-covered bones flecked with scabs and bruises. He climbed easily to the top rung of the open gate, slicing the cane through the air and wincing at the swishing sound it made. 'D'ye hear that?' he shrieked. 'Jaysus! Cut the legs off of ye, so it would.'

'Get down, Declan,' Maeve said firmly. 'You'll have someone's eye out.' Declan, who couldn't have been more than ten, told her to 'Fuck off, ye bitch, ye,' and continued swiping the cane, leaning closer to Tim clearly in the hope that he might make contact.

'Declan! I said get down! You're making a holy show of yourself.' Maeve tried to grab the cane. 'And who do you think you are with that sort of talk?' Declan smirked as he almost allowed her to grab his weapon but pulled it away before she could get her fingers around it. It was her turn to blush as he teased her. 'Stop! Do you want me to tell Mammy on you? I will. I mean it.'

'I'm tellin' *Ma*-mmy, I'm tellin' *Ma*-mmy,' Declan sang. 'Go on then. D'ye think I care, d'ye? I'll tell her ye hit me.'

'Well, it's a mighty clatter on the backside you need, Declan Mooney! Give me that stick!' She made to grab it once and for all but he was too quick and whipped it out of her reach again. Tim stepped closer to the gate. Declan eyed him up and down and stabbed at him with the cane. Then, surprising even himself, Tim made a lunge, snatched it right out of the boy's hand and flung it to the ground. Declan shrugged and ran back into the cottage.

'Thanks,' Maeve said. 'He's a holy terror, so he is. Thcy all are.'

'How many?'

'Six of us altogether, I'm the only girl. And the oldest. How about you?'

'Me? Oh, I ... I'm ... No. No brothers or sisters. There's just myself.'

'God! Wouldn't I love that. No one to drive you mad. The peace of it!'

'It's not all it's cracked up to be.'

'Well, you can take a few of those brats home with you for company, if you want. You're welcome to them.'

Tim grinned. 'I'm sure they're not that bad, are they?'

'Don't get me started. Anyway, you were down in the village, were you? If you'd known, Barry could've given you a lift back up. He's always out and about. But sure you'll know the next time.'

Barry Kilbride wouldn't be offering Tim a lift back from the village or anywhere else for that matter. He'd probably run him down just as quick. 'Yes,' Tim said. 'I'll look out for him.' He thought for a moment. 'Barry, he's ... I mean, he doesn't look old enough to be driving.'

'Ah, sure no one round here cares. He has an uncle a sergeant over in Carlow who knows full well. And if he lets him away with it no one else is going to say anything.' She peered up the road, as if expecting to see him coming round the bend. 'And if it wasn't for Barry I don't know what we'd do. Hauling messages up from Kavanagh's is no joke.'

Tim took another look through the gate towards the cottage. The dog was still tied to the post but had wandered deeper into the yard where Declan and one of his brothers were teasing him with another bamboo cane. A woman appeared at the open front door, arms folded tight across her chest. She wore a faded flowery nightdress and a scruffy brown cardigan. Her hair was long and black with curling ends and a thick stripe of grey running along the centre parting. She raised a hand and waved when she noticed Tim at the gate.

'That your mum?'

'Yeah. That's Mammy.' She kicked a stone into the ditch. 'She's not the same as she used be. My dad left her, you know. Left all of us. Fecked off to Liverpool. Least, that's what Mammy wants to believe. But sure he could be anywhere, couldn't he? Timbuktu for all we know. Not that I've any idea where that is but sure it doesn't matter where he is – the fact is he's gone and as I said to—'

'Left?' Tim managed to interrupt her. 'You mean just ... left?'

'Yeah. Went out for a pint of milk and a batch loaf and never came back. Middle of January it was. And the place only covered with snow. More than six months now and not a word.'

'No letter? No phone call?'

'Nothing. Not that we have a phone, mind. Wish we did but Mammy says we've enough bills already.'

Tim glanced at her mother again. She was calmly watching the boys whip the dog's back legs hard with the bamboo. She stared, glassy-eyed, as if nothing she saw or heard was reaching her brain.

'Shouldn't they ... shall I ... ?' The poor dog. It yelped and barked, trying in vain to escape.

Maeve shrugged. 'If it wasn't the dog, it'd be me or Mammy. Since he left, they've gone wild. I think Mammy's given up. I do my best but they're like something out of the zoo, they are.'

'But how do you ... ? I mean, if your father's gone, what do you do for ... How do you afford ... ?'

She made her way back through the gate, resting her arm on the post as she leaned in close and whispered, 'Mammy had to apply for the deserted wives.' Tim gave her a blank look. 'You know? The government gives it to you when your husband runs off. Deserts you, like.'

'Oh. I see.' The dog was growling at Declan now, teeth bared. Still his mother did nothing.

'It's not much but we have enough to get by.'

Tim nodded, but didn't really understand. How could a father leave a wife and six children? In practically the middle of nowhere. With nothing.

Maeve narrowed her eyes. 'What part of England are you from?'

'Grimsmede.'

'That anywhere near Liverpool?'

'Well, it's not too far from Chester.'

'That near Liverpool?'

'Not a million miles.'

She thought for a moment. 'You could've passed him on the street, so.'

'I . . . I doubt it. They're not that close at all. And it's not like here. I mean, the amount of people, you wouldn't—'

'But you could have. You don't know. I mean . . . it's possible.'

No harm in agreeing with her. 'I suppose so,' Tim said. 'Anything's possible.'

'If he's even there at all, that is,' she said solemnly, the brightness fading from her eyes. 'Sometimes I think Mammy just says that to make us feel better. So we wouldn't be thinking the worst. How would she have a clue where he is? I mean, he could be . . . He could've driven into the sea. Or jumped off the rocks. Or gone someplace and got knocked down or—'

'Maeve,' her mother called lazily. 'Tell that pair to stop, will you?'

Maeve straightened herself. 'Declan! Fintan! Leave Scamp alone this minute or I'll bloody well strangle the pair of you, do you hear me?'

Declan made a face and gave her the two fingers. The dog

leaped at him, sinking his teeth into the boy's calf. Declan roared. Fintan laughed. Their mother stared at her sons before disappearing back into the shadows behind the front door.

Maeve raised her eyes to heaven. 'Second time this week.' Declan was writhing on the ground. 'Serves you right! Do you hear me?' she shouted, tramping over. 'Jesus, Declan, how many times do you have to be told?' She sighed as she got down on her hunkers to have a look. 'This one might need a stitch. That's all we need. A trip to the bloody hospital.' She called over to Fintan, who hid behind a half-empty bag of coal. 'You'll have to run over to Kilbride's. Ask Barry can he give us a lift.'

Fintan, a smaller, carbon copy of his brother, slapped his knees. 'Why do I have to go?'

'Just do what you're told,' Maeve yelled. 'Go on! Go across the fields. You'll be there in no time.' Fintan dragged himself up and shuffled around the back of the cottage. 'Hurry up!' she shrieked. 'Do you want your brother to bleed to death?' Fintan groaned loudly but took off on his skinny legs.

'Is it far?' Tim asked. 'I mean, if you like, I could—'

'Don't mind him! You'd swear it was a marathon he was being asked to run. Five minutes is all it'll take.'

'Do I *have* to go to hospital?' Declan whined. 'Will I have to get a needle?'

Maeve wagged her finger at him as she stood up. 'Stop your moaning. Don't move. I'm going to get something to wash that out.'

'Where would I be going?' Declan snapped. 'I can't fucken walk, can I?'

'Stay with him, would you?' she asked Tim. 'I'll only be a sec.'

He watched her running into the cottage, head down, arms stiff by her sides. Just before she got to the door, a curly-haired toddler, clad only in a pair of red underpants, burst out. She scooped him up deftly without even breaking her stride.

Barry Kilbride was there in ten minutes. He screeched to a halt on the road outside, music blaring, sending a cloud of fine dust into the air. Maeve and Tim half carried, half dragged a struggling Declan to the waiting car. Fintan sat in the front passenger seat, fiddling with the knobs on the radio. 'Would you stop!' Barry told him, pushing him back roughly. 'And have you no manners? Get out and let your sister sit up front.'

'Go on back inside,' Maeve told Fintan. 'There's no need for you to come. Stay and help Mammy. There's a good boy.' Fintan sulkily did as he was told. Tim stood at the gate, feeling awkward.

'Thanks for coming,' Maeve said to Barry. 'I wouldn't have asked only . . .'

'No sweat,' Barry replied, rubbing her knee with a huge hand and making sure to catch Tim's eye. 'Honest, it's grand.'

Maeve turned in her seat. 'Oh, sorry. Barry, this is Tim. He's from England. Staying with Mags for the summer, so he is. She's his auntie.'

'Howya, Tim,' he said, with a false smile. 'Heard you were visiting us right enough. Enjoying yourself so far?' Tim longed to say something smart but he didn't dare in front of Maeve. And Barry knew it. He was the hero come to save the day. 'Jesus, he's a quiet one.' He laughed, giving Maeve a nudge. 'We'll soon knock that outta him, what?'

'Come on, you,' Maeve said. 'It'll be the mortuary we're heading to, if you don't hurry up.' Declan let out an extra loud moan.

Barry revved the car. 'Be seeing you, Tim!' he shouted, above the engine's roar and sped off, tyres screeching.

Fintan stood, dejected, by the gatepost, kicking at some loose dirt. 'Barry Kilbride's a fucken eejit,' he said, before turning into the yard.

'Not again,' Mags said, when Tim got back and told her what had happened. 'Why Tess doesn't get rid of that animal I don't know. Nothing but trouble.' She was lying stretched out on a plastic recliner in the yard, an open magazine resting on her mountain of a stomach. 'It's another mouth to feed and sure she has enough on her plate already with that gang. Especially now that . . . well, that . . .' She trailed off.

'It's OK,' Tim said. 'Maeve told me about her father.'

'Did she now? Poor mite. Terrible close to her daddy she was. Is, I mean.'

'Why do you think he left?'

Mags sighed. 'Lar Mooney wouldn't be the first man to go out and never come back.'

'Maeve thinks something might've happened to him. Something bad.'

She manoeuvred herself into a sitting position, shielding her eyes with her magazine. 'And where would she get that idea from?'

'It's been more than six months and they haven't heard from him.'

She shook her head and tutted. 'Awful imagination she has. Anyway, you got your letter sent off, did you? I suppose Katty had the ear bent off of you?'

'Oh.' Tim reached into his pocket. 'She gave me this.' He

handed her the envelope, thinking she'd changed the subject of Lar Mooney rather quickly. 'It's a job for PJ.'

She ran her eyes over the note. 'She's good like that is Katty. Taking phone messages for PJ.'

'She said to tell you she heard you'd be waiting more than a year. For the phone, I mean.'

'Ah, for God's sake. Where are they going with that sort of carry-on at all? You'd swear we were living in the Stone Age.' She leaned back again. 'Isn't that a glorious day?' She tilted her face to the sun. 'Anyway, you never said what you thought of Maeve.'

Tim swallowed hard. 'Wh-what do you mean?'

'Oh, come on now. Pretty girl. Good-looking boy. That's what I mean!'

Tim's insides began to heat. The sun seemed even hotter on his head. 'I . . . she's . . . I mean . . .'

'Ah, I'm putting you on the spot, amn't I? Don't mind me. Awful cruel, so I am. Did you meet any other locals on your travels? I'm sure the whole village knows you're here by now.'

'Um . . . Father Coffey. He stopped to talk to PJ on the way to the village.'

'Dinny? Asking you all sorts, I'm sure. Anyone else?'

'Barry Kilbride,' Tim mumbled. He didn't even want to say his name.

'What's that?'

'Barry Kilbride,' he said, louder this time.

'Ah! Barry. Now there's a pal for you while you're over. Good lad, he is. Helpful, like. Hard worker. Doing deliveries for Kavanagh's for the summer. Up at Maeve's, was he?'

'Yeah.'

'Has his eye on her, so he does. Competition for you.'

Was it possible to hate someone so much so soon after meeting them? This Barry Kilbride had it all worked out. Tim knew his sort. Some of the biggest bullies in school were teachers' pets. Able to continue their reigns of terror by keeping the adults on their side.

'But sure he's not a patch on you in the looks department, isn't that right?' Mags continued, opening one eye. 'If anyone's going to be turning her head it's you.' She moved over and patted the space beside her legs. 'Come here and sit down.' Tim perched himself on the edge, afraid the recliner wasn't up to the weight. 'Feel that heat,' she said. 'I'll have a great tan by the time this one's ready to come out.'

Whatever about how she'd appeared earlier, when PJ had told her not to be fussing, she seemed in fine form now. Tim fiddled with a loose thread on his jeans, winding it tight around his finger. His eyes wandered over the landscape behind the house. Pylons like mini Eiffel Towers sprouted from a perfect green pasture where glossy black and white cows were grazing. Beyond them, he could see a field of shimmering grain. On the right, ragged hedgerows bordered a large patch of rough grass that led to a group of tall trees.

'When will that be?' Tim felt able to ask the question now. 'I mean, when will the baby be born?'

'Round the fourteenth of September the doctor said. But sure, you never know.' She took a sharp breath. 'The Lord save us! He's kicking like billy-o!' Excited, she grabbed Tim's hand and placed it on the hard, rounded swell, holding it down with her own. 'Can you feel it? There!'

He could. Beneath the thin covering of her tartan dress,

the warmth of her skin found its way into his own. And underneath that, under the layers of flesh and muscle, he could feel the strength of the life inside, squirming like a fish in a bucket. He was reminded of the ship. The ship in his dream. Pitching and tossing on the waves.

She stroked his hand. 'I'm just hoping this little one gives me plenty of notice.' She laughed nervously. 'It's a fair enough drive to the hospital.'

'Would you like a boy or a girl?'

She looked into Tim's face with her deep, dark eyes. 'As long as it's alive and kicking. That's all that matters.'

Tim tried not to think about the whole process. About how scary it must be. 'Will PJ be with you when it's being born?' he asked. 'I mean . . . to help you.'

'Help me?' She frowned. 'Sure it's me who'll be doing all the work.'

'But . . .' Tim pictured scenes of births in films and TV programmes – it always looked very painful '. . . you know, just to be there. Wouldn't you like him with you?'

Her face hardened. 'I'm sure I'll be well able to manage on my own if it comes down to it,' she snapped.

Tim froze. He felt stupid. He hadn't meant any harm but his silly questions had probably reminded Mags of what was ahead of her. Things she was trying not to think about.

She turned her face and stared out over the fields, her mouth in a tight line, her breath rushing hard in and out of her nose. 'It won't be the worst thing I've ever had to cope with,' she said, after several moments of silence. 'I don't need anyone to be holding my hand.'

'I . . . I'm sorry,' Tim said. 'I just thought you . . . well . . .

that you might be scared. Something could happen. The baby might . . .' He couldn't say it. But Mags knew what he meant.

'Sometimes it's only yourself that you need. You can't be relying on other people.' She was looking hard at him now. 'And, anyway, there's things worse than death, Tim. The day will come when you figure that out for yourself.'

'Maybe he's just some random kid. Some total stranger who happened to be passing.' Luke kicks off his shoes and stretches his long legs. 'Why does he have to be . . .' he air-quotes his next word '. . . significant?'

I take the photo from the coffee table and study it again. 'I'm not sure Mam would put her arm around a stranger like that.'

He sinks back into his chair. 'Not now, maybe.' He yawns. 'She might've been different then.'

Monday evening and Luke has called in to my place. My place – another privilege I've Dad to thank for. Back when the Celtic Tiger was just a cub, he bought two apartments in this development from a builder pal, who offered him the chance to get in on phase one. Mam thought he was crazy. 'The docks? Not the best part of Dublin, is it? Don't know that anyone would want to live down there.' Shrewdly, Dad sold one at the height of the boom, pocketing almost four times the amount he'd paid. The other, he said, was mine to live in as long as I liked, allowing me to move from the dated Churchtown semi I'd shared all through college. It's not even worth its original price now that the property market has collapsed. But Dad's not worried. 'It'll come round again. And sure didn't I make enough off of one of them? You can't have your cake and eat it.'

I like it here. It's bright and clean and a handy straight run down to the courts. It's relaxing to sit on the balcony and watch the activity on the Liffey – the river traffic, the odd cruise liner in the summer. And it's handy for Luke to drop by on his way home. In theory he still lives with his parents in Clontarf, but he spends more nights here than there. He cracks open a can of Coors. 'Look, I wouldn't worry about the photo. It was years ago. Before you were even born.'

'Only just.'

'But still before.' He takes a long slug, his soft brown eyes searching mine. 'Determined to make a mystery out of it, aren't you?'

'I'm not *making* a mystery out of it. It *is* one.'

He reaches into his trouser pocket, finds his iPhone and waves it in the air. 'See this? It's called a . . .' he enunciates every syllable '. . . *tell-eh-phone*. A handy invention.' He holds it up to his ear, mimicking my voice. 'Eh, hi, Dad. How're you? Just wondering, who's the curly-haired little fucker in the photo?'

'I'm not doing that! I mean, I might mention it next time I see him but I'm not going to call just to ask him.'

'Don't see why you wouldn't. I would.'

'I know. You'd just storm in. All guns blazing.'

He drains his can. 'A lot to be said for it.'

'What if Mam was there beside him when I called?' He

gives me a quizzical look. 'He obviously doesn't want her to know he gave it to me. I know the way he works.'

'If he meant to give it to you at all.'

I shake my head and reach for my wine glass. 'Oh, he meant it all right. The more I think about it, the more I'm sure. That stuff I told you he was talking about. Trying to explain why Mam's the way she is.'

'And failing, by the sound of it.'

I shrug. 'There has to be a link. It can't be a coincidence.' I examine the photo again. Mam's smile. Her obvious happiness. It fascinates me.

'You sure the boy can't be a relative?' Luke asks.

'Definitely.' I give him the family history, as much to inform him as to remind myself. 'Dad had two sisters. One's a nun somewhere in South America. Sister … Mary? Maureen? Can't remember. A good bit older than him, she was. Is? Don't even know if she's still alive. The other one died when I was about seven, as far as I know. Nancy. Wasn't married. Cancer, I think.' He reaches his foot over and strokes my shin with his toes. I frown. 'Luke. I'm trying to be serious.'

He pulls his leg back and sits upright. 'OK. I'm sorry.' He puts on his courtroom face. 'Continue, Miss Hyland.'

'Mam had a gang of older brothers. All went out to Canada. In the late sixties, I think. She was the only girl. That's about as much as I know.'

'Maybe he's a kid of one of the brothers, then. They ever visit?'

'Some of them might've come over for my grandparents' funerals. But that was in the seventies. Well before I was born. She definitely hasn't seen any of them since. I think there was some kind of rift.'

Luke reaches out. He takes the photo from my fingers. 'Curly Boy. Looks a bit geeky. A *University Challenge* type.'

'He's about fourteen!'

He sits forward, looks straight ahead. 'Hi. I'm Granville Wetherington. I'm immensely intelligent. I'm from Milton Keynes and I'm studying for a PhD in metaphysical biodynamics. Or something.'

I give an exasperated sigh. 'Anyway, whoever he is, he must be at least forty now. Bit old for *University Challenge*.'

'Oh, I don't know. Eternal student?' He tosses the photo back on the table and pulls another can from the pack. 'And he couldn't be a neighbour?'

'I've been thinking about that. But ... no. Not any I'd be aware of. There was a family who used to live near. Mooney, I think their name was. Lots of boys, they had. But I'm fairly positive none who'd have been that age.'

'What about that fella we saw on the news that time? Something about the local elections. Lissenmore's answer to Donald Trump, you called him.'

'Barry Kilbride, you mean? Or Councillor Barry Kilbride, I should say. Better give him his full title.'

'Couldn't be him, no? From what you said, he sounds like he was always the kind up for a photo opportunity.'

'Round about the right age, all right, but he looks nothing like Curly Boy here. Even allowing for the passage of time.' I tuck my legs up under a cushion. 'Anyway, how did it go today?'

'It didn't.' He sighs, loosening his tie. 'Odds are she'll be deported.'

'But the child was *born* here?'

He shrugs. 'The senior hammered it all home as best she

could but . . .' he slithers his tie from his collar and lets it hang down the side of his chair '. . . no mercy.'

'When's the decision?' I ask tentatively.

'Third of Feb.'

'Anything else that could be done before then?'

'Doubt it.' Elbows on knees, he rests his chin in his cupped hands and stares at the table. He's clearly upset about the case. To those who don't know Luke, he might appear cavalier. But the banter that peppers his casual conversation belies the fact that he's conscientious in the extreme. After a long moment of silence he laughs. 'What about the way your dad looks?' He angles his head to peer at the photo. 'The big bear face on him!'

I hadn't noticed it before. How fierce Dad looks. Furrowed eyebrows, tight mouth set hard in his beard, like a knife wound in fur. 'The hairiness doesn't help.'

'Certainly doesn't look happy. Compared to your mother and the boy.'

He's right. Dad looks a bit stormy. 'It's weird. I mean, it's definitely Mam and Dad but . . .'

Luke gets to his feet and walks to the window. 'It's only a snapshot. I'm sure they were both the very same as they are now. It's just the way the camera caught them.'

I untangle my legs and slip over to join him. We stand together, gazing out at the night. An orange and purple sky. The dark green waters of the Liffey, its rippling surface reflecting the glitter of glass office blocks lining the quay. A spectacular canvas I never grow tired of.

I lean my head on his shoulder. 'I wish I could go back in time. Right there to that moment. I want to know what it's all about.'

His arm ropes tight around my waist. 'Jesus, you have me all fired up about it now. If you won't call your dad, why don't you just text him? Go on. Ask him who the boy is.'

'You know he doesn't text. He can't manage it. Those giant fingers of his. And, anyway, with Dad, well, it's more about what he doesn't say than what he does. I'm sure that's why he gave me the photo. He has something to tell me. He just can't find the right words to use.'

Dear Tim,

So glad you arrived safely. I hope you're enjoying yourself. Give Auntie Margaret a hand while you're there, won't you, love? And PJ too. And be careful with your money. That was a lot Dad gave you. Make it last the length of your stay. Try not to spend too much of it on sweets.

Dad's ankle doesn't seem to be as painful now. At least, he's not complaining as much! Going a bit crazy being around the house all day, though. Uncle John's coming up for the weekend to see him, so that'll be nice.

Look after yourself.

Love, Mum

PS Don't forget to do your art project.

Tim sat at the kitchen table to read Mum's reply. It was the first letter he'd ever received from her. As his eyes wandered over the few lines, this crazy image of her – and Dad – appeared in his head. A bird's-eye view of the two of them clambering out onto the red-slated roof of their house, hanging onto the chimney pot and peering across the horizon as though somehow they might catch a glimpse of him and what he was up to.

'Mum says I've to give you a hand,' he said to Mags.

'Chance'd be a fine thing.' She laughed, flicking a tea towel at his head and catching the back of his ear. 'I've a good mind to let her know you haven't done a tap.'

Mags was in good form. At least, she seemed to be. It was difficult for Tim to know. Some days they might be getting along fine and then, without warning, her breathing would become heavy and she'd walk out of the room. She'd disappear upstairs or out to the yard, and Tim grew to understand she wanted to be left alone. When she emerged again, she'd be quiet for a time, usually holding her hands on her tummy as though she might be in pain. Often she stared at Tim in a daze, her eyes glassy, her cheeks high with colour. He learned to be on his guard, always mindful that her mood might suddenly change.

She leaned down to check on the brown bread she had baking in the oven, a soft grunt escaping from her throat.

'Let me have a look,' Tim said. 'You probably shouldn't be doing things like that.'

Her hair blew out from her head with the blast of heat from the oven. 'Well, would you listen to him?' she said, slowly straightening, her hand pressed into the small of her back. He didn't know what she meant and he couldn't see her face. He held his breath, biting his lip, afraid he might have said the wrong thing. 'You sound like an old man, so you do.'

She was smiling. Phew! He sighed in relief and grinned back at her.

'And as for helping out, don't you be worrying about it. If I need a hand, I'll ask. But I didn't invite you over to be doing housework.' She rooted through the vegetable rack beside the dresser. 'What your mammy doesn't know won't hurt her. If you're writing back, tell her you're helping out good-oh. That'll keep her happy.' She set a turnip down and began to hack at its gnarled skin with a large knife. 'It's about time Joan let go of the reins. She can't keep control of things for ever. You're not a baby any more.' *Thwack!* The blade came down hard on the chopping board.

Tim jumped. 'But she let me come, didn't she?' he said, more than a little scared at the way she carelessly – it seemed to him – skinned the turnip.

'She did. I'll give her that. But you're only here on your own because of your dad's accident.'

'Would you prefer if Mum had come too?'

She gave him a high-pitched laugh. 'Well, I bet *you* wouldn't! You wouldn't be getting away with murder if Joan was here, I can tell you! She wouldn't be letting you skive off the way I do!'

'But I don't *mind* helping! I—'

'Ah, don't be going all defensive on me. I know you don't. I'd probably have you scrubbing floors and the like if you lived here, so I would.' Holding her tongue at the corner of her mouth, she leaned heavily on the knife and brought the shiny blade down hard again and again. Concentration showed on her face as she sliced and Tim was a little unsettled at the fierceness that showed in her eyes. There was something ... on edge about her, as though he could sense another of her walking-out-of-the-room episodes coming on. He ran his fingers over the smooth oilcloth covering the table, tracing its swirling pattern of fruit and leaves as she deftly diced the slices into neat, evenly sized cubes.

'What was it like growing up?' he asked. 'With my mum, I mean.'

She swiped the orange chunks into a big metal saucepan and hefted it onto the electric ring. She directed her answer to the kitchen wall. 'Have you never asked your mammy that question?'

'Mum doesn't talk much about Ireland.' Mags turned to the table. She kept her eyes on it as she vigorously wiped it down but made no comment. Tim pushed a little further. 'Why do you think that is?'

She was agitated, rubbing so hard he thought she might wear a hole in the oilcloth. 'Sure no one would want to let on they're Irish over there,' she answered eventually. 'Asking for trouble, you'd be. What with all that stuff the IRA are up to.'

She was right on that score. He'd learned that lesson himself only a few months ago. He'd joined the camera club at school and had been trying to impress its president, a popular senior called Geoff Hardcastle, who called himself 'U2's Biggest Fan'. 'My mum's from Ireland too,' Tim had told him.

U2's Biggest Fan had sneered, 'I wouldn't boast about it if I were you.'

Later, Mark had told Tim that Geoff Hardcastle's cousin had been badly injured by flying shrapnel in the Hyde Park bombing. When Tim mentioned this to Mum, she'd frowned. 'Probably best not to be saying too much about the Irish thing, love.'

'But she's my mum!' Tim said to Mags. 'She doesn't have to keep quiet about being Irish to me, does she? Or not talk about where she grew up?'

'Look,' Mags said, clattering knives and forks onto the table. Her cheeks had reddened and she was getting flustered with the cutlery, setting the places all wrong. 'Never mind why your mammy does or doesn't talk about where she came from. You've . . . you've more important things to be worrying about.' Her tone was softer now, more light-hearted. She was trying to change the subject.

Tim was puzzled. 'I have? Like what?'

Mags pointed a fork at him. 'Like Maeve Mooney for one,' she said, smiling now and doing her best to distract him.

It was Tim's turn to blush. He couldn't hide the fact that he liked Maeve, and Mags gave him plenty of opportunity to see her. She sent him down to Mooneys' most mornings. To bring down a freshly baked loaf or apple tart; to collect a pile of clothes Mags had offered to iron; to give Tess a copy of yesterday's newspaper. In the afternoons, he always found another excuse to wander back down – 'I told Maeve I'd show her how to use my camera, let her take a few snaps', or 'I might see if Maeve would like a walk to the village.'

'Don't be trying to let on you don't know what I mean,' Mags said. 'I can tell! Sure aren't you only dying to get down there every chance you get?'

'I . . . um . . . I . . .'

'You'll have to win her mammy round first, though,' Mags continued, as she lifted the saucepan lid and looked at the turnip through the rising steam. 'She's a scary one is Tess when it suits her.' That much was true. Tess didn't say much but when she did speak she was direct and to the point. 'Suppose she has to be, with that gang of hooligans to control. Always been good to me, though, so she has. Didn't know a soul when I moved here after I got married. Tess is a blow-in herself so she knew what 'twas like.' She opened a cupboard. 'PJ was born and reared in this house. Did I tell you that? Born and reared. And weren't we lucky his mammy left it to him when she died? But for it, we might have been on the streets.' Handing Tim the butter dish and the salt cellar to place on the table, she kept talking, spewing out words to fill any spaces he might find to ask questions she clearly didn't want to answer. She couldn't have made it more obvious if she'd tried. 'Met him the winter before Mammy and Daddy died,' she was saying now. 'Came up to the farm to mend a few fences in the back field. Took his time, let me tell you!' She laughed. 'Had the road between here and there worn out, so he did. 'Tis lucky we are that PJ makes his own work. Not dependent on some factory or wherever, like Lar Mooney was. Let go from the granite quarry after twenty years and straight onto the dole.'

Tim's ears pricked at the mention of Lar. 'He was fired, you mean?'

'Ah, the Lord save us, no. Place closed down, so it did,' Mags answered, taking the bread knife and sawing the fresh brown loaf into crumbly slices with exuberant relish. 'Tess could've been a bit easier on him, though. Not her fault, I suppose. Worried, she was.'

Tim imagined what it must have been like. He had a little more sympathy for Maeve's dad now. 'But still,' he said, 'running off like that? Just disappearing and not even writing to say he's OK.'

'Awful woody that turnip,' Mags said, poking at the chunks in the saucepan. 'Be a miracle if I can get it to mash so 'twill.'

'Tess thinks he's in Liverpool,' Tim said. 'Why would she think he's there?'

'Hmm? Sure didn't the guards tell her a fella looking like him and driving the same type of car had taken the ferry to Liverpool the next day? Can't be sure 'twas him mind but . . .' She slapped four chops on the grill. 'Now. PJ'll be in soon. Enough chatting. I've a dinner to get ready.'

Tim went upstairs to the bathroom, wrinkling his nose at the smell of the grilling chops that followed him. It seemed Mags was as unwilling to talk about growing up as Mum was. Maybe it was just that their parents were dead, that their brothers had all left. Or could it be something else? And what about Lar? Could he really have left his family and be living a different life in Liverpool or wherever? Maeve didn't think so. She couldn't accept that he didn't want anything more to do with them all. That he didn't care what happened to Tess, to the boys, to Maeve herself. She couldn't imagine he'd be so heartless. That was why she was so sure there must be some other explanation. That something bad must have happened to him. And Tim was inclined to agree.

On his way back downstairs, he could hear voices. PJ was home. He and Mags were whispering, but loudly, and Tim could hear them if he strained. He paused on the last step to listen. 'Haven't you enough on your plate without taking all that on as well?' PJ was saying. 'Can't you let her sort it out on her own?'

'It's hardly the end of the world,' Mags said. 'And Tess has always been good to me. I don't mind.'

PJ grunted. 'Only encouraging it, so you are. You know right well how I feel about it.'

Mags clattered about the kitchen, making more noise than she usually did. 'You made it perfectly clear before. You needn't be reminding me.'

'Then why has nothing changed?' He pulled a chair out from under the table. Tim could hear its legs shuddering across the lino.

'Would you stop. We're all only trying to do the best.' Tim couldn't make out what PJ's next comment was, but it annoyed Mags. 'Ah, don't be rocking the boat,' she said. 'Leave well enough alone. You know I don't want any upset at the moment.'

'Maybe you should've thought about that before you got involved,' PJ said. 'I've a good mind to—'

'Are you determined to ruin this time for me or what?' Mags snapped. 'I can't be dealing with any commotion, do you hear me? God knows how I'm going to feel come the middle of September. I might . . .' She paused. When she spoke again, she sounded a little less angry. 'Look, I know it mightn't seem so to you, but this is the perfect time. And I don't want it destroyed. I just wanted this summer for . . . Well, you know what I wanted it for. And you agreed. All that other stuff, just let it be. It'll work itself out.'

The middle of September. She must mean the baby, Tim thought. But what about all the rest of it? Whatever it was, PJ wasn't happy. And, by the sound of it, it was something to do with the Mooneys. Tim stood as still as he could, hoping they might continue their conversation but there was no sound except, after a moment, Mags calling, 'Tim! It's on the table.' He waited a few seconds then stepped into the kitchen. Mags smiled at him when he sat down. 'Tim got a letter from his mammy today. Isn't that right, Tim?' she said. 'Tell PJ all about it.'

'There's not much to tell,' Tim said. 'Dad's ankle isn't too bad, she said.'

'That's good news,' PJ replied, showering his dinner with salt. 'Anything else?'

'Not really. Just that my uncle John is visiting at the weekend.'

''Tis nice she wrote all the same.'

Tim nodded. 'It's the first letter Mum's ever written to me.'

'Is that so?' PJ said, glancing at Mags. 'I suppose there's never been any call for it before.'

Mags looked away from him. As the minutes passed, her face grew cloudy and she only picked at her food. Tim could sense another of her episodes coming on. He tried extra hard to eat his turnip. 'It's all right,' she said, when it was obvious he was having trouble. 'You can leave it.' Then she was on her feet and she was off, straight out of the back door and into the yard. PJ shook his head, got up from the table, sank down in an armchair and hid behind his newspaper. Tim sat staring at the orange mound on his plate, feeling thankful he wasn't expected to eat it but guilty because Mags had put a lot of effort into preparing it. When she returned after a few minutes, she held a hand over her eyes, saying she had a headache and needed to lie down. Tim saw her ankles were red and swollen and he could tell from the sound of her steps that it took her ages to climb the stairs. He was surprised PJ didn't go after her, even if they'd been snapping at each other earlier. He was probably well used to her moods but surely he'd want to check she was OK? With Mags not there to object, Tim cleared away the dishes and did the washing-up. What was going on? What argument or disagreement had he overheard? Whatever it was, it was nothing to do with him so it was probably best, he decided, to forget all about it. With everything dried and put away, he sat back at the table and did some work on his art project.

'Don't be minding her,' PJ piped up from behind the newspaper, after a long silence. 'Women's stuff so 'tis. The baby and all. She'll be grand.'

Next morning, after Tim had finished his breakfast, Mags asked him to shoot down to Kavanagh's for some cream crackers. 'You wouldn't mind, would you? Don't feel like eating anything else,' she said, rooting in her purse for some money. She looked tired. Puffy, purplish half-circles sat under her eyes. She threw a glance out to the yard where PJ was loading the van with supplies for a job – coils of heavy grey cable and huge, chalky sheets of plaster board. 'And here,' she said, wrapping half a brown loaf in a chequered tea towel and popping it into a plastic carrier bag. 'Drop that into Tess for me, would you? There's a good boy.'

Outside, PJ nodded at Tim. 'Can't give you a lift. Not going through the village this morning.'

'That's OK.' Tim clutched the bag close to his chest. 'I don't mind the walk.'

'Don't mind calling in on the Mooneys, you mean.'

'I, um . . . No, I . . .'

'Go on with you.' He slung some lengths of copper piping into the van, raising his voice over the clatter. 'I know Mags has you doing deliveries for her. You needn't be pretending otherwise.'

And what harm was there in that? Tim didn't understand why helping Tess was such a crime. *You know right well how I feel about it.* That was what PJ had said last night. Did he not like the Mooneys? Surely he'd be sympathetic seeing as the father had disappeared? It was all very strange.

The morning air smelt damp. Mags had said a downpour was due. As Tim walked, great puffy clouds began to tumble up from the horizon, swallowing huge tracts of blue sky. As he approached the pebble-dashed cottage, sure enough, there was Barry's car, pulled in at a slant across the gateway, engine running noisily. Maeve was chatting to him through the open window while Declan and Fintan were busy tying their whingeing younger brother, Donal, to the gate with a length of washing line. Tim noticed the wound on Declan's calf. It was dark and bloody. The dressing that had covered his stitches had long since fallen off. No one had bothered to apply a new one, even though Tim knew they'd been supplied with extras. Maeve had given him a detailed account of the hours they'd spent at the hospital and how wonderful Barry had been. *Barry waited with us the whole time . . . I don't know what we'd have done without him.* She straightened as Tim came close, tucking her hair behind her ear.

'Want to walk down to the village?' Tim asked, trying to sound carefree and natural in front of Barry. Maeve opened her mouth to answer but Barry deliberately revved the car, drowning her voice. She rolled her eyes, and made a face. Tim lifted the plastic bag and shook it. 'Just giving this to your mum,' he shouted. 'Be back in a minute.'

Scamp rushed at Tim as he neared the front door. Since Declan had been bitten, the dog's tether had been switched from the gate to the trunk of a straggly cedar that grew in an un-concreted corner of the yard. He'd already worn a track in the dry dirt that circled the base. He yapped hysterically at Tim, straining at the length of rope that contained him. Tim felt sorry for Scamp. It was cruel to keep him tied up like that.

The Mooneys' cottage was small and dark, single-storey,

with one main living room leading to three bedrooms, a bathroom, and a poky, scullery-type kitchen. Tim thought it felt unfinished, uncared-for. The doors were half painted, the floors bare. It smelt of vegetable peelings, raw meat, damp turf – things that were on the way to becoming something else. When Tim walked in, Tess was standing at the front window, looking out over the yard and beyond through the greying web of lace that covered the glass. Tim had never seen her in anything but her night clothes and that morning was no different. He coughed.

'I . . . No, I mean, Mags . . . She gave me some bread to give to you.'

Tess chewed at the insides of her cheeks and continued staring out of the window. Tim felt awkward, standing there, holding the bread, not knowing where to put it. The table was the obvious place. But it was covered with messy piles of unironed clothes and a flattened-out newspaper spread with potatoes, some peeled, some still in their mucky skins.

Without turning, she spoke: 'What do you suppose is going on there?' She lifted the curtain to one side. 'Do you think he has designs on her?'

Tim felt heat rush to his head, burning under his skin. Maeve and Barry. That was who she meant. Why would she ask a question like that? Was she deliberately trying to embarrass him? Seconds passed in silence, though it felt to Tim like hours. The two youngest boys – twins Ciaran and Cormac – waddled from a bedroom in a trance, each dragging a filthy, fraying blanket. Both had plumes of matted candyfloss hair that stood out stiffly from the backs of their heads. They clambered onto the brown corduroy couch, covered themselves with their blankets and sat staring at Tim.

Tess turned her head when she heard them but it was Tim she focused on. 'Hmm?' she said. 'What would you say, Tim?'

'I don't know. I . . . I've no idea.'

'You should be making it your business to know. If you've any balls at all, that is.'

Tim was on fire now, wishing the scuffed boards on the uncarpeted floor would separate so he could fall between the cracks.

'Well? You like her, don't you? And you'll be gone without even a kiss to remember her by if you don't get a move on.' She reached out and took the bag, pulled the bread out and, as she did, the tea towel loosened. A small white envelope, slit open at the top, fell from its folds. She didn't hesitate for a second, bending to pick it up almost before it hit the floor and pushing it hastily into her cardigan pocket.

'Ah, don't mind me,' she said, pulling herself up. 'Only acting the maggot, I am.'

What did that mean? Tim didn't know. But he was sure of one thing. The envelope – which could only have come from Mags – had been stuffed full of cash.

She gave Tim a glare, her cheeks reddening. 'Will . . . will you tell Maeve I want her to go down the village for a few things? Tell her not to worry about the spuds. I'll finish the peeling.'

Tim was glad to get back outside. He ran across the yard, hands in his pockets. At least he was getting his wish of a walk with Maeve. 'Your mum wants some things in the shop,' he said, when he reached her. 'We can walk together.'

Barry leaned his head out of the window. 'I'll drive you down. Looks like rain.' He smiled at Tim. Far too widely. 'I'll have us there and back in no time.'

Tim felt his shoulders slump. What fun would that be? He'd been hoping for a long walk, a slow pace, arms swinging. His hand might brush against Maeve's. She might curl her fingers round his . . . He bit his lip.

Maeve looked skywards. 'You could be right. Thanks, Barry.' She began to walk back across the yard. 'I'll be out in a sec.'

'Take your time,' Barry said, looking straight at Tim and smiling. 'We'll be waiting.'

Shit. Barry *bloody* Kilbride. Tim was fuming. He climbed into the back of the car, sinking into the fake-fur seat covers and getting an instant headache from the stink of spicy pine air freshener. Barry turned the radio up – 'Crazy Little Thing Called Love' – his fingers hammering out a beat on the steering wheel. Tim caught his eyes in the rear-view mirror, quickly looked away and prayed Maeve wouldn't be long. Mercifully, she skipped back in seconds, letting out a sigh of relief when she flopped in beside Barry. 'Thank God for that! I was nearly having to take one of the twins.' She tapped Barry's arm. 'Go on! Get going. In case she changes her mind.'

Barry took off, speeding down the narrow road and laughing his stupid head off when he nearly had a head-on collision with an oncoming tractor. Maeve giggled but, all the same, she threw Tim a nervous glance. He pretended not to notice, wishing she hadn't agreed to the lift. Though they were outside Kavanagh's in minutes, he'd gladly have walked. Barry stuck his head out of the window when Maeve and Tim hopped out. 'Hey, Tim Boy. Get us a cauliflower while you're in there, yeah?' Tim shrugged when Maeve gave him a puzzled look. Then the radio was turned up full blast and Barry was mouthing the words to 'Too Shy' by Kajagoogoo, staring hard into Tim's face.

'Did you say something to Mammy?' Maeve asked, as they walked along the aisles in Kavanagh's. 'She's in an awful good mood. She's after telling me to buy chocolate fingers. And a swiss roll. Raspberry ripple, if you don't mind.' She waved a ten-pound note in Tim's face.

He shook his head, picturing the wad of notes in the white envelope. 'I don't think so.'

'*And* some penny jellies for the lads,' she continued. 'Weird.'

'Well, it might be . . .' He stopped himself. He wasn't sure if he should tell. If Mags was secretly helping Tess, perhaps it should remain just that – a secret. If he did say something, could he be sure Maeve would keep it to herself? What if it got out and PJ heard about it? Mags sending his hard-earned cash down to the Mooneys'? He was sure to go mad. Much as it might be nice to have a shared secret with Maeve, he didn't want to get Mags into any trouble or maybe send her into one of her weird moods. He picked a packet of cream crackers from the shelf.

Maeve stepped in front of him. 'What? It might be what?'

'Nothing. It's nothing. I—'

'You coming Saturday night or what?' It was Tommy Kavanagh, pushing his chubby self between them. Tommy was another who was clearly in love with Maeve. His approach was far from subtle but, for once, Tim was glad of his muscling in.

Maeve took a step back. 'Saturday?'

'Youth club summer disco.'

'Oh. Yeah. I mean . . . I don't know. I'm not sure.'

Tommy turned his pinprick eyes to Tim. 'You going?'

'Me? I don't know. Should I?'

'Dunno. Just asking.' He reached under his AC/DC T-shirt and scratched his wobbly stomach.

Tim glanced at Maeve. 'Maybe.'

Tommy stretched over to a display of fresh cakes and took a jam and cream doughnut. He pushed one end into his mouth, bit down, chewed it a little then worked it into his cheek. 'When will you know?' he asked Maeve.

'I'll have to ask.'

He crammed the rest of the cake into his mouth and his eyes rolled back a little in his head. 'Probably see you Saturday so.' He grabbed a chocolate éclair as he walked away.

'God, would he ever leave me alone,' Maeve said, under her breath. 'It's not as if I've ever shown the slightest bit of interest.' Tim understood Tommy's pain. It was obvious he was aching. The way he'd looked at her . . . 'If Mr Kavanagh knew he was at those cakes there'd be war. Still, must be nice when your dad owns the shop.' She tossed a box of chocolate fingers into her basket. 'Not having to pay for stuff all the time.'

'Has its disadvantages, though,' Tim said. '*Tummy* Kavanagh might be a better name for him.'

Maeve tried hard not to laugh. She bit her lip, then covered her mouth. But as they made their way to the counter, she couldn't hold it in any longer. Mr Kavanagh – an intense string of a man who wore a buttoned-up sparkling white shop coat and was known for his complete lack of interest in anything other than his cash register – appeared not to notice. He expertly packed Maeve's items into a plastic bag and counted out her change, all the while unaware she was almost choking. Outside, they both exploded.

'What's the joke?' Barry wanted to know when they got back to the car.

'Ah, it's nothing,' Maeve said. 'Don't mind us.'

He flicked his fringe from his eyes with a jerk of his head, trying to make it look like he wasn't bothered, but Tim sensed he was rattled.

On the way back, a shower started – a scattering of fine drops that quickly turned to a deluge. The only sound was the *whish, clunk* of the windscreen wipers sweeping away the rain that snaked down the glass. The air inside the car grew muggy. Tim rubbed the misted window, peering out at the sodden landscape and thinking that by rights the weather should've had him feeling pretty miserable. But something about the set of Barry's jaw, the tension in his shoulders, caused him to sink back into the fur-covered seat with satisfaction.

Barry dropped them at the gate without a word, performed an elaborate U-turn and sped back towards the village.

'Do you think you'll go?' Tim asked Maeve. 'To the disco, I mean.'

'Maybe. But I'll have to ask. What about you?'

'I'll go if you're going.'

'Will you be allowed?'

Tim was about to say, 'Of course, why wouldn't I be?' but then he paused. There was no telling what mood Mags might be in. He'd have to pick his moment. 'Probably,' he said. 'But . . .'

'But what?'

'Well, sometimes Mags . . . she's kind of moody, you know? Have you ever noticed?'

The rain was getting heavier. Maeve's hair had darkened, and her face was spotted with drops. 'Mammy says she's fragile. Had a hard life, she said.'

'In what way hard?' Tim's heart speeded up a little. 'Did she ever say?'

'Not sure she knows exactly. Just has some idea that she didn't have an easy life before she met PJ.' She gathered her bag to her chest. 'You could come in out of the wet but I've loads of work to do and I—'

'It's OK.' Tim tried not to sound disappointed. 'Mags'll be waiting for her crackers anyway.'

'Going fruit-picking up in Crowe's farm tomorrow, if you want to come? Pay's not much. But we might earn a pound if we're lucky.'

Tim smiled. 'Sure. What time?'

'Early. Seven o'clock OK?'

'I'll be ready.'

The rain was pelting down even harder now, great splashy drops that stung Tim's face and trickled in under the neck of his T-shirt as he walked the short distance back. Mags was waiting for him at the door, towel at the ready. She hurried him upstairs to change his clothes and they sat at the kitchen table afterwards drinking hot, milky tea and eating cream crackers spread with blackcurrant jam.

'You gave Tess the bread?' Mags asked him.

'I did,' Tim answered, through a mouthful.

'Good. I like to help out. It's the least I can do.'

The *least?* There'd been a *lot* of money in that envelope, Tim knew that much. And maybe it wasn't the first time. Maybe she'd given Tess cash before and PJ had found out about it. Was that why he didn't seem too keen on the Mooneys? Supporting all those kids when their own father had fecked off to England? And PJ and Mags with one of their own on the way. It'd be enough to make any man mad.

'They can't have much money, can they?' Tim said. He watched Mags carefully.

'They're surviving.'

'Maeve came with me to the village. She bought cakes and biscuits in the shop.'

Mags stopped nibbling at her cracker. 'What of it?'

'And jellies,' Tim added.

'No crime against that, is there?'

He shrugged. 'No, but . . .'

Mags stiffened. 'But what? A few treats now and again? No one'd begrudge them that, surely.'

Tim crunched methodically. The back door was open and the rain splashed in, speckling the lino with spray. 'PJ doesn't like the Mooneys, does he?'

Mags's eyebrows bunched in together. Two lines, like a number eleven, appeared in the middle of her forehead. 'And what in God's name makes you think that?'

Tim gulped. 'Just . . . I don't know. A feeling.'

'Ah, you know PJ,' she said, the lines disappearing. ''Tis easy enough to be getting the wrong idea off of him.'

'So, he doesn't mind me going down there? And you helping Tess out? With the bread and all, like today?'

'A bit of bread is hardly the end of the world, is it?' she said, swiping crumbs with one hand into the palm of the other. 'Or the odd apple tart. I'd like to think Tess would do the same for me, if the shoe was on the other foot.' Tim had thought she might confide in him. That she'd come clean about the envelope. But that wasn't going to happen, it seemed. She pushed herself up and shuffled over to her favourite spot by the sink. 'And sure what does it matter what PJ thinks anyway?' she said to the window. 'You have to paddle your own canoe in this world, Tim. If you listen to what everyone else thinks, you'll end up doing things you'll always regret.'

Dad calls before eight on Friday morning, shouting into his ancient Nokia as usual. 'Be on the road by ten, so I will. Should be finished at the site by half twelve.' I struggle to catch his next few sentences – a combination of bad signal and Luke asking if I want coffee.

'Look, Dad,' I cut across his indecipherable words, 'I don't have much on today. I'll head out to Dún Laoghaire. Be easier than you trying to park that monster jeep in the city centre.' I throw back the duvet. 'I'll find somewhere nice for lunch and text you.'

He says something about making it somewhere near the ferry port. 'That's the part I know,' he yells, before the connection dies.

I head for the bathroom. 'God help him, finding the place where he's pricing the job.'

'Google Maps?' Luke suggests, deadpan. 'Satnav?' We both laugh. I picture Dad driving along the Dublin road in his own individual way – treating the wing mirrors as decorations and swinging around corners without applying the brake. He never sat a test. He let that nugget slip when I was applying for mine. Dad was one of thousands who availed themselves of the famous driving licence amnesty in the late seventies, brought in to clear the backlog of applications in the test centres. I'm well used to his technique, though. Growing up, he must have clocked up thousands of miles ferrying me here and there in the beat-up old Hiace that doubled as a storage-shed-cum-office-on-wheels. Mam never learned to drive. I often wonder why she's never struck out on her own, become more independent, less reliant on Dad. It's as though she was – and still is – tied to that house. Wary, somehow, of the world beyond.

Once out in Dún Laoghaire, I realise it'll be a waste of time trying to explain the name, location, and noticeable features of a café to Dad. Chances are he'll never find it. So in my text I tell him we'll meet at the Victoria Fountain. Even if he has to do the unthinkable and ask someone for directions, at least it's a well-known landmark. The town hums with the expectation that, despite the recession, always comes with a Friday. I park in the shopping centre car park and, out on the street, jostle my way past wax-jacketed blonde mummies pushing red-cheeked babies in buggies the size of small cars. Throngs of uniformed schoolgirls with heavily kohled eyes and bird's-nest hair skip down the street, yapping into mobiles, throwing their arms around the floppy-haired boys they meet outside a deli. School lunch breaks are obviously serious social occasions nowadays. I feel old.

I see them waiting for me as I cross the road. Them. Mam has made it too. She stands beside Dad, her arm linked through his, her sheepskin-gloved hands pulling her woollen scarf up over her chin.

I smile, give her a hug. 'You look like you're dressed for the Antarctic, Mam.' I kiss her cheek. She's shivering. 'You never said you were coming.'

'Only decided at the last minute, so she did,' Dad answers for her, with a note of tetchiness.

We start walking. Mam being here has thrown me a bit. Her non-committal 'We'll see,' as I'd left on Sunday evening had made me sure she wouldn't come along. It's not that I'm unhappy to see her, it just puts a different complexion on things. And, if I'm not imagining it, Dad's a bit put out too. It's not only that tone in his voice, it's the way he strides ahead of Mam and me, hands thrust deep into the pockets of his anorak.

We head for the nearest coffee shop, a generic type of place serving cellophane-wrapped snacks: blueberry muffins; Smartie-studded cookies; toasted ham and cheese sandwiches labelled 'Croque Monsieur'. It's busy, but I spy an elderly couple just leaving and I guide Mam to the table – a corner one, beside the window. 'You sit down,' I tell her. 'We'll sort it.' She settles herself in, sheds her gloves and unbuttons her coat. Then she begins piling up the used coffee cups, plates and cutlery. 'Leave it, Mam. They'll be over in a minute to take care of it.'

'It's fine,' she says, mopping a puddle of coffee with a wad of paper napkins. 'Makes it easier for them when they come to clear it away.' A knife slides to the floor, clatters across the tiles. She jumps. 'Sorry,' she says, bending, contorting herself to scrabble for it on the floor. 'Sorry, sorry.'

I lean down, whispering, '*Please*, Mam. It's OK.'

'There. I've got it,' she says, pulling herself up. She's breathing heavily, gripping the knife so tightly her knuckles look like they might burst through her skin.

I leave her and join Dad in the queue. As soon as I appear beside him, he grabs my elbow hard and hisses in my ear, 'Not a single word to her about that thing in the envelope, do you hear me? *Nothing.*' I take a step back, shocked at the ferocity in his voice. He locks his eyes on mine, his fingers digging into my arm. 'Not a *single* word.'

I swallow. *Jesus, Dad*, I'm thinking. *What the hell?* 'OK, OK. I won't. But—'

'Just forget about it. It's ... Just give it back, all right? It's not of any concern.'

'I don't have it with me.' I throw a glance over my shoulder. Mam's oblivious, staring out of the window as the table is cleared by a young girl in a pink apron. 'It's in the apartment.' I squeeze my bag tighter under my arm. The photo nestles there, in the pocket of my wallet.

He moves along, fiddling hurriedly at the baskets of food on the counter, flinging things onto the tray. 'Well, keep it safe,' he mutters. 'Bring it with you next time you're home.'

'But ... but what's it all about? Who's that boy? What's he—'

'I said it's not of any concern. Your mother, she ...' His voice lightens as he orders: 'A pot of tea for two and a ... a ...'

'An Americano,' I say.

'Right, right, one of those.' Flustered, he pats his breast pocket, then all his pockets.

'It's OK, Dad. I'll get this.' I reach into my bag, my fingers slicing along the stiff edge of the photo as they rifle through my wallet. I push my Laser card into the machine, leaning in towards Dad as I do. 'What about Mam? You were about to say something there.'

'No. No. Nothing. Nothing at all.'

'Is it because she came with you?' I whisper. 'You were all set to talk to me about the photo, weren't you?'

He lifts the tray and strides towards our table, leaving my question to hang in the air.

He sits beside Mam and I take the chair opposite. The sharp winter light coming in from the coast exposes lines on Mam's face that the dim interiors back in Lissenmore keep hidden. Makeup is a virtual stranger to her although, today, she's dragged a cakey tan powder over her skin – one probably drawer-bound for decades – and has accentuated her sparse eyelashes with filaments of an obviously dried-out mascara. I look at her and I see it again. The great, yawning gap that follows her wherever she goes. The deep, dark hole that waits to swallow her. She's on the edge of it now. Teetering.

'Hope this is all right,' Dad says to her, unloading the tray. But she doesn't appear to hear him, she's so far removed from the 'now'. Eyeing the food he's selected, I know she'll eat not a bit of it. I sip my coffee, slice a corner from my rubbery carrot cake. 'How did you get on pricing the job?' I ask Dad.

'Grand,' he says, chewing.

'Is there much in it?'

'Good bit.'

'When do you expect to hear?'

He shrugs. 'Dunno.'

It's like wading through mud. I think about making some inane observation about the weather when my mobile rings from the depths of my bag. The noise brings Mam back to the present. She watches me fumble for it, her dark eyes fixed in a stare, as though she can sense what's hidden in the folds of my wallet. I read the caller ID. 'Sorry, I have to take this.' I make an apologetic face. 'Work.'

The café is even more crowded now. The chattering lunchtime hordes. Instead of squeezing my way past the tightly packed tables and coat-draped chairs to go outside, it's easier to take the call in my seat. It's Eamon Carty, a solicitor who instructed me in an unfair-dismissal case – I've been waiting to hear from him for weeks. I hold a hand over one ear, his nasal drone feeding into the other. But I can't exclude completely the clatter of cups, the snatched conversations of the crowd – *Nasty bitch, I only asked ... Yeah, got it last week, d'ye like it? ... You coming tonight or what?* – that whirl around the room. And then Mam's voice. Her panicky whispers filtering into my ears: '*... mistake ... shouldn't have come ... hate this place ...*' I can't help allowing her words to get the better of the legal facts I should be concentrating on. I presume at first she's referring to the café. Then I hear more: '*... boat ... time ago ... the sea ... thought it'd be all right but ...*' Dad mumbles something I can't make out. I allow Eamon to continue while I half listen, straining to catch more of what Mam is saying: '*... what he ... night ... wish we hadn't ... why didn't he ...*'

I finish the call. I spin back around. Mam jerks her head away the second I catch her eye. But it's too late. I've already spotted it. The unmistakable glitter of tears. 'Is something wrong? Are you all right, Mam?'

'She's grand,' Dad answers for her. He takes her hand in his. 'Aren't you, Mags?'

Mam nods, but unconvincingly.

'Are you sure?' I persist. 'Is there something you're not telling me?'

'Ah, lookit, Orla, didn't I tell you she's grand?' Dad snaps. 'What more do you want me to say?' He gives me a knowing look, raising his eyebrows and widening his eyes.

'But I was only—'

'Let's leave it now,' he cuts me off. 'We didn't come up expecting to be quizzed like we're on trial.' He glares at me and I feel guilty, though I'm not sure what for.

He stays pretty much silent for the rest of our time together. I try hard with Mam, but it's mostly small talk. They walk me to the car park entrance when we're finished. Mam's hug goodbye is loose and her smile, when I pull away, looks forced. Dad squeezes me extra tight and, as he does, he whispers in my ear, 'We'll leave it now. We're agreed on that.' I watch until they disappear around the corner, Mam's arm linked through Dad's, her steps unsure, a little wobbly, like a small child's.

As I drive back to the city, Dad's last words repeat in my head. *We're agreed on that.* You might be, Dad, I think. But I haven't agreed to a thing.

When the alarm clock rang at half past six next morning, Tim was already awake. He'd developed a bit of a cold after the soaking the day before and hadn't slept too well. He sneezed into his pillow, successfully smothering the noise. If Mags heard, she was sure to put a stop to him going out. He got dressed, crept along the landing and tiptoed downstairs. He was surprised to see her in the kitchen. 'I didn't think you'd be up,' he said. 'It's so early.'

'Woke up once it got bright out, so I did. Egg and fried bread all right for you?'

'Yes, please.' Tim sat down at the table, eyeing her closely, trying to gauge her frame of mind.

She knifed a wedge of butter into the frying pan, threw on two slices of bread, then cracked a brown egg on the edge, hissing something under her breath when most of the yolk ran down the side. ''Tis an early start for you, right enough,' she said, taking another egg from the blue bowl on the countertop. 'Looking forward to it, are you?'

'I'm not sure what to expect. I've never gone fruit picking before.'

'You'll have a great time. There'll be loads of lads up there, so there will.'

'Is it far?'

'A good two miles, I'd say.' She cracked the second egg, making sure this time that all of it ended up where it was supposed to. 'But sure haven't you the legs of a racehorse on you? You'll be there in no time at all.' Two miles. He didn't care how long it took. Two whole miles with Maeve by his side. He'd gladly have walked ten. 'Made a bit of lunch for you, so I did,' she told him. 'You'll need more than strawberries in your belly to keep you going.' The eggs began to sizzle and pop. Mags knew by now how Tim liked them – turned over, the yolks hard, his bread crispy on both sides. 'What's this?' she asked, when she set the food in front of him. She'd noticed his camera stuffed into the pocket of his T-shirt. 'Planning on taking a few snaps? Of a certain young lady, no doubt. Well, I hope you're not too busy to actually pick some fruit. I'd like to make jam with whatever you bring home.' She smiled and sat down, pouring herself a mug of tea.

'I'm . . . glad you're feeling better,' he said.

'Better? Sure what was wrong with me?'

She hadn't reappeared after she'd gone for her lie-down after dinner the night before. 'Last night. Your headache. You said—'

Her gaze wandered over his face. She swallowed. 'I'm grand, so I am. Don't you be worrying about me.' He rushed his food, eager to get going. The last forkful was still in his mouth when he stood up to leave. 'Come here to me,' she said.

He stepped towards her and she patted his chest. 'You're a good lad, Tim, do you know that? A good lad.'

He was out on the road before he realised he'd forgotten his lunch. Doubling back, he sped across the yard and skipped through the door into the house. After the brightness of the morning outside, the room was dim as a cave and, for a split second, he couldn't see Mags. Then, as his eyes adjusted, he made out the shape of her slumped over the table, her head half buried in her arms. 'Um ... I forgot my lunch,' he said, lifting the bag from the dresser. She looked embarrassed when she sat up, smoothing down her hair and patting her mottled cheeks with her palms. Tim felt awkward. She was trying to pretend she hadn't been crying but there was no disguising it. She nodded as he backed out of the door, staring at him as though he reminded her of someone she couldn't quite place.

Nearing Mooneys', he spied Maeve walking towards him. She could see from his face that something was wrong. But he denied it when she asked. If he told her Mags was upset, she'd ask why and he wouldn't be able to say. And she might suggest they go back and see if she was OK and Mags might get annoyed. Best to leave it, he thought. It was probably as PJ had said. That it was women's stuff. That she'd be grand, and not to be worrying about it at all.

The more immediate worry was that Maeve wasn't alone. Declan, Fintan and Donal were in tow. The three of them were already scrapping, belting each other's backs, their yelps rising high and clear in the morning air. 'Mammy made me bring them,' Maeve said. 'I couldn't get out of it.'

'It's OK,' he lied, for the second time in as many minutes. 'I don't mind.'

'You don't have to pretend,' she said. 'I know how you feel. I have to put up with them all the time.' He felt bad then. Selfish. They walked without speaking, the boys following and providing a soundtrack of shouts and curses. After ten minutes, Maeve indicated a break in the hedgerow to the right that led to a narrow dirt track. 'Shortcut,' she said, herding her brothers in front. 'Go on. Run. Last one there's a rotten egg.' They galloped off, disappearing around a bend.

Maeve plucked a long blade of grass from the ditch. 'What's it like, being the only one? Sometimes I try to imagine it, but I can't.'

Tim half suppressed a laugh. 'It's hard for me to imagine the opposite.'

She waved the grass in the air. 'Never satisfied, are we? Always want what we don't have.'

'Do you really think that? I mean, you're saying you don't want what you have. Your family. The boys.'

'No. Don't mind me. I'm not saying that at all. The boys ... well ... you've seen what they're like. But I wouldn't be without them. It's just since ... since Daddy's gone.' She sighed. 'It's hard. That's all.'

'That's something else I can't imagine. Someone disappearing. It doesn't make sense.'

'You're right. It doesn't.'

'Do you think ... do you think he'll come back?'

She snapped a twig from a tree and swiped it through the air as she ran ahead. 'Come on. We'd better catch up with the lads and see what they're up to. If they haven't beaten the daylights out of each other, that is.' Tim's heart felt heavy as he followed her.

The farm was owned by the Crowe brothers. The older

two, Mossy and Barry, were badly shaven, heavy-set men with sharp slits of eyes peering out from under tweed caps. The younger one, Wishy – Aloysius – wore glasses with cracked lenses and an ugly raised shoe on one foot to compensate for a short leg. Wishy was, Maeve whispered, 'not the full shilling,' and Tim watched him, limping aimlessly around the farmyard as though he was trying to prove he could walk as well as anyone else. By eight o'clock, enough pickers had gathered and Wishy handed out buckets and plastic containers. 'No scoffing. D'yiz hear me?' he shouted, clearly enjoying his small bit of authority.

Declan laughed and sang out, 'Wishy Crowe, he's awful slow. Wishy Crowe, he's—'

Maeve elbowed him in the ribs. 'Shut up. Or you'll be sent home.'

It started out as a perfect day. The sun was warm, the sky was pure blue, the strawberries were the sweetest Tim had ever tasted. (No one took any notice of Wishy's warning – far more berries were eaten than went into the buckets.) The boys ran off to the upper field to pick, keen to keep as far from Maeve's watchful eye as they could, so Tim had her to himself all morning. He worked quickly, figuring out the biggest clumps of berries could be found hiding under the leaves. His first bucket was full in minutes. He didn't need the pocket money: he just wanted to impress Maeve. It was around half past ten when they broke for lunch, but they were both starving. Tim shared the ham sandwiches and fruit cake Mags had packed for him; all Maeve had brought was a packet of crisps. He thought about Mags as he ate, hoping she was all right. And he thought about Mum and Dad, wondering how much they missed him.

When they'd finished eating, Tim pulled his camera from his pocket and asked if he could take Maeve's picture. She pretended to be shy at first, slouching down and hiding her face behind her hair. Then she sat up in an exaggerated film-star pose: shoulders back, eyes wide, pouty mouth stretching to a smile just seconds before he snapped. He took some of the landscape then, shots of the wide-open green fields topped with blue sky and a couple of close-ups of strawberries, thinking he could use them for his project. Later, he sneaked some of Maeve as she worked, her body bent over, her ponytail a golden-brown stripe along her back. They didn't talk much as they worked: the heat and the effort sapped their energy. But Tim didn't mind. It was enough that she was there. Beside him. Beside him and nobody else.

And then *he* had to arrive. Just as Maeve and Tim were carrying the last of their buckets to be weighed. Not to pick fruit, of course. Oh, no. Barry wouldn't want to get his hands dirty. He was there to collect and deliver it to shops and roadside stalls in the surrounding area. A role he considered far more significant, judging by the way he strutted around the farmyard and spoke down to poor Wishy.

He strolled over to them. 'Can give you a lift home if you like?' he said to Maeve. He glanced at Tim. 'No room for Prince Charles, though. Sorry.' He indicated the crates of strawberry punnets lining the back seat of his car. Tim dug his nails into his palms.

Maeve smiled. 'Ah, Barry, that's good of you. But I have the boys with me. Thanks anyway.' She walked over to join the queue for weighing.

Tim gave Barry a satisfied smirk.

'Something funny?' Barry asked, his voice low and

menacing. 'I'll wipe that smile off of your face for you, so I will. Just you wait.' Sauntering over to Maeve, he leaned down, laid a hand on her back and whispered in her ear, leering back at Tim while he did.

'What was Barry saying to you?' Tim asked Maeve, as they walked home across the fields. He hated himself for being curious. It was exactly what Barry wanted.

'Ah, nothing,' Maeve answered. They were each bringing home two large buckets of berries in part payment for the amount they'd picked. She took a big strawberry from hers and bit into it. 'Nothing to be worrying about anyway.'

But Tim did worry. He couldn't help it.

And he had plenty of time for it. It rained without stop the next day. Mags insisted he stay indoors. She'd discovered him sniffling and warned him he'd be staying put come Saturday night – disco or no disco – if it got any worse. He tried everything to get down to see Maeve: 'I have a rain jacket'; 'PJ can give me a lift'; 'I'll run, I'll hardly get wet at all.'

Mags stood her ground. 'It's not just you getting wet, it's the damp air going into your lungs. Your mammy wouldn't thank me if you came down with pneumonia.' She was going way over the top but Tim couldn't persuade her. She did her best to keep him occupied. From somewhere upstairs she produced a jigsaw. Five hundred pieces. A landscape of fields with a castle on a cliff edge and foamy waves licking the rocks below. He worked on it for more than an hour until he realised at least fifty pieces were missing. Mags felt guilty then and brought him a mug of hot chocolate and a plate of biscuits. She was making the strawberry jam and the whole house was filled with the sugary-sweet smell of boiling fruit.

Tim turned on the TV, hoping for once there might

actually be something interesting on. But he was doubly disappointed. Not only was it some stupid kids' programme with a red-haired wooden puppet speaking a weird mix of English and what he supposed was Irish but, as usual, the picture was fuzzy and kept fading in and out. He switched it off with a sigh. He should've brought some books. He'd meant to, but his rucksack would only hold so much. He'd presumed Mags might have some but all he'd managed to find on the dresser shelf were some of her women's magazines, a thick paperback called *The Thorn Birds* that had a half-inch section of pages missing, and a leather-bound Bible. There was nothing for it but to take his art project out again. The berries came in handy – he sliced some open in different ways and spent ages drawing the patterns he found inside. But his mind kept wandering to Maeve. And Barry. He doubted there was anyone who could stop *him* going out and about. He was probably down at Mooneys' this very minute. And here was Tim, stuck inside with nothing to do but his stupid art project. Still, it was better than nothing, he supposed. For the briefest of moments, he actually felt grateful to Miss Thistle.

He worked away, sketching, colouring and writing notes about the patterns he found while Mags continued the jam-making in the kitchen. After some time, he became aware she'd gone silent and he turned around, curious. There she was, gazing at him, her eyes glassy as she stirred the jam mixture round and round, methodically, like a robot. It was dangerously close to the top of the pot. 'Mags!' he called out. 'It's going to bubble over!' She smiled at him. A big broad smile that told him she hadn't heard him at all. He jumped up, sending his pencils rolling across the table and clanking onto the floor.

Too late.

The sticky pink goo rushed over the rim of the pot, like molten lava. Down the sides and onto the cooker top where it pooled in a steaming, frothy lake. Mags woke up from her daze and shoved the pot away from the heat. Tim expected she'd be angry. Instead, she wrapped her arm around his shoulders and laughed. 'An awful eejit I am.' She pulled him tight. 'That's a right mess I've made of it. A right mess.'

'I'll help clear it up,' Tim said, squirming a little under her grip.

''Tis grand, so 'tis. No hurry. Best to let it cool a bit first anyway.' She kept her arm around him as she steered him over to the table. 'Now, show me all these lovely drawings you've been doing.' She made Tim explain everything he'd done so far, all the while holding him close, though he wriggled to try to show her he was a bit uncomfortable. He only managed to extract himself from her grasp by pretending he needed to go to the bathroom.

She was humming along to the radio when he came back downstairs. ''Twasn't that bad after all,' she said, wiping the cooker top. 'Only lost about half a jar.'

'Would it be OK if I took some home?' Tim asked. 'Mum loves strawberries.'

'Home? Ah don't be talking about going home,' she said. 'Not yet anyway.' She rinsed the cloth under the tap. 'But all right. I'll put a jar aside. Now, would you have a look in the dresser drawer for me? There's a good boy. I'm sure I've a packet of jam-pot covers in there somewhere.'

Tim pulled open the drawer. It was full of all sorts of stuff – boxes of matches, loose coins, buttons, rolls of Sellotape. He rooted around and found what Mags wanted, stuck right in at the back. As he pulled the packet out, with it came a piece of folded notepaper. He didn't mean to be nosy but he couldn't help taking a look. The paper held some old black and white photos.

'What're you at there?' Mags walked over. 'Did you find them?' Tim handed her the jam-pot covers.

The door opened. It was PJ, home earlier than expected, his jacket soaked and his hair haloed with a mist of fine raindrops.

'Put all those back now, do you hear me?' Mags told Tim. 'Only rubbish, so they are.'

'What's only rubbish?' PJ asked. He glanced over. 'Family pictures.' He looked at Mags. 'You'd hardly have kept them this long if they were only rubbish.' He peeled off his jacket and sat down at the table, lifting a foot onto his knee to untie his bootlace.

'Come on now,' Mags said to Tim. 'Put them away. You can see them some other time.'

'Let the lad have a look,' PJ said. 'Isn't he entitled to?'

Mags bristled. 'What for? Sure what interest would he have?'

'Isn't it part of the family history? Have you ever seen any pictures of your uncles, Tim? Or your grandparents?' Tim shook his head. 'And would you like to?' Tim nodded. 'There you are now,' PJ said to Mags.

She scowled, folding her arms and biting her bottom lip. She wasn't happy. That was pretty clear. She watched Tim closely as he examined the first photo. It showed a couple walking along a city street. A stern, tiny woman in a smart belted coat, a hat as flat as a pancake nestled on her tight, fair curls; and a huge rock of a man with slicked-down, side-parted hair, wearing a dark, double-breasted suit and a thin tie knotted high up on his neck.

'Are they my grandparents?' he asked. Mum didn't seem to have any pictures of them. At least, if she did, Tim had never seen them.

Mags nodded.

'I don't think I ever met them, did I? I mean, they never visited us, did they?'

'No,' Mags said quietly.

Tim chewed his lip. He knew nothing about them. And all those other relatives – the uncles in Canada, their wives, their children – they were all strangers. He hadn't known his other grandparents either. Dad's father had died young and his mother – Nana Swift – had lived in a creepy seaside nursing home somewhere near Cardiff for the last few years of her life. Dad had taken him to see her a few times, but when he complained about the smell of boiled chicken and wee, and the way she talked nonsense and kept poking her bony fingers hard into his chest, Dad said he didn't have to go again.

'Did they know about me?' Tim asked.

Mags's features twisted. 'Of … of course they did. Just because you didn't know much about them doesn't mean … No, no, of course they knew about you. Don't be silly.'

'Are these … your brothers?' Tim asked, pointing at another photo. It showed a group of young men sitting on a stone wall, and another astride a bicycle in front of them. They all wore heavy boots and had their shirtsleeves rolled up to their elbows.

'They are,' Mags replied.

'What are their names?' Tim wanted to know.

'Mikey, Paddy, Tommy, Jimmy, Francie,' she rhymed off. 'Now, I think that's enough. Come on. You can help me label the jam jars.'

'That's only five,' Tim said. 'There's six boys in the picture.'

'That's just a friend of theirs.'

'Christy,' PJ said. 'Wasn't that his name, Mags?'

'Yes,' she said matter-of-factly. 'He went with them to Canada. Your mammy was friendly with his sister.'

'When was the last time you saw any of them?' Tim asked.

'They came home for the funerals. Mammy's and Daddy's. I haven't seen any of them since.'

PJ stood up. He stuffed his wet boots with newspaper and placed them by the back door. 'Is there any food going?' he asked Mags.

She took the photos from Tim and pushed them to the back of the drawer. 'I've no dinner made, if that's what you're wondering. How was I to know you'd be home at this hour?'

'I was only asking. I can fix something up for myself.'

'That you can,' she said. 'Because as soon as I've covered the jars I'm going for a lie-down. Every part of me is aching.'

Tim could hear them late that night as he lay in bed trying to sleep. Their words reverberated through the floor, high-pitched and questioning. He couldn't make out what they were saying but it was clear they were having an argument.

The torrent dwindled to a trickle, and next morning a rather sorry-looking sun managed to melt a hole through the dense covering of grey cloud. Tim wrote to Mum before he went downstairs for breakfast.

Dear Mum

I'm having a great time. I went strawberry picking. I brought some back and Mags made jam. Mags showed me some pictures of my grandparents and my uncles. Maybe you can tell me about them when I get home. I've made friends with a family called the Mooneys. They live on the way to the village. There are five boys and a girl. I might be going to a disco at the youth club on Saturday night. Mags said it's OK if I do.

I hope you and Dad are well.

Love from

Tim

He could have told Mum about Mags's moods and how he wasn't sure from one hour to the next what kind of humour she'd be in. But that might only worry Mum and she had enough to be dealing with at the moment, looking after Dad. It wasn't as if she could do anything about it anyway.

He was going to call in on Maeve on his way to the post office but he spied Barry's car parked in the yard. Its doors were open; Declan and Fintan were monkeying around in the front. Tim's insides burned. If Barry was there, he'd rather press on to the post office in the hope he'd be gone by the time he got back.

Katty yelped in excitement when he opened the door. An actual customer! She was all questions about his stay – what he'd done so far, who he'd met, how did he like the place. Tim answered as best he could while, at the same time, trying to back out of the door. Once he'd escaped, he slipped the letter into the postbox and made his way to Kavanagh's, where he bought some chocolate, a bottle of Coke and a large bag of pink and white marshmallows. Don't waste your money on sweets, Mum had said. But in a place like Lissenmore, there wasn't much else to buy.

When he reached Mooneys', Barry was gone. Maeve was in the yard, pegging wet clothes on a slack line that stretched from the cedar tree to a metal hook attached to the gable end of the cottage. 'Saw you passing earlier,' she said. 'You went to the village?'

'Posting a letter to my mum.'

She grinned. 'Have you told her all about me?'

Here it came – the fire creeping up his neck. 'I . . . I . . .'

'Ah, I'm only messing,' she said, touching his arm. An electric fizz ran through his body. 'Sure you've more to be talking about to your mammy than me.' She plucked a peg from the row she had clipped to the front of her oversized navy T-shirt. 'What about tomorrow night? You're coming, aren't you? I'm allowed go.'

Tim nodded. 'Mags said it's OK. Hope she doesn't change her mind.'

'Why would she?'

'She's a bit . . . unpredictable.'

'Probably the baby. Mammy was like that with the twins. All over the place she was.' She flung a white sheet over the line. 'I'm sure it'll be fine. She'd hardly stop you going if I'm allowed. We'll call down for you about eight.'

He gulped. 'We?'

'Me and Barry.'

'Oh. He's coming?'

'No way of getting there without him.'

'We have to drive? I thought it was near.'

'Ah, it's not that far. Only down the road. But too far to be walking.'

Was there no escape from him? Nowhere free from Barry Kilbride?

The youth club disco was held in a hall on the outskirts of the seaside town of Faranboy. Hardly 'down the road', it was five miles away by car, but less than half that distance if you walked across the fields. Mags seemed to be even more excited than he was, fussing about and insisting on ironing his T-shirt and jeans, despite his protests. 'Sure you want to look smart, don't you?' she said. He was going for a casual, couldn't-really-care-less look, but her careful 'pressing' destroyed that hope. In front of the bathroom mirror, he tried to beat the curls out of his hair, but, as always, they sprang to attention seconds after he'd slapped them down.

Mags beamed when he came downstairs. 'Would you look at yourself,' she said. 'Isn't it only gorgeous you are?' She tugged at his T-shirt, pulling down the sleeves he'd carefully rolled up to his shoulders. 'There now. That's better.' She stepped back and looked him up and down. 'What about a photograph? Go and get that camera of yours.'

Tim groaned and tramped upstairs. As he took his camera out of the drawer, he heard the sound of an engine revving. Looking out of the window, he saw Barry's car in the yard and Mags leaning through the passenger-seat window.

'There you are, Tim,' she said, when he returned with the camera. 'Stand over by the door. Maeve's going to take it for us.' Tim blushed as Maeve climbed out. She looked beautiful.

Pale pink shirt, the tails hanging out over her dark jeans, the late evening sun picking out golden highlights in her hair. 'Come on out, PJ!' Mags yelled. 'Picture!'

PJ ambled out, blinking against the strong light. Things had been frosty between himself and Mags since the episode with the photos. Mags was doing her best to cover it up and be cheerful but PJ couldn't hide his bad form. He stood stiffly on one side of Tim, Mags on the other. She snaked her arm around Tim's shoulders, pulling him close to her side, her other hand resting on the rounded swell of the baby. Tim was mortified. There was Barry, smirking out at him.

'Everyone say cheese!' Maeve said, pressing the button.

Mags didn't release Tim immediately. Once again, he had to wrench himself out of her grip.

'You be careful now,' Mags warned Barry, when they were all in the car. 'You're sure you don't want PJ to bring and collect? I'd be worried about the way back. It'll be closing time. There'll be all sorts of eejits out on the road.'

Barry laughed. 'It's PJ's driving you should be worried about. Not mine.' He had a point. Given the choice, Tim wasn't sure which of them he'd pick.

Either way, it didn't really matter. He ended up walking home on his own.

Tim was stuck in the back, squashed in with Tommy Kavanagh and his scatterbrained chatterbox of a younger sister, Sinéad. She asked Tim stupid questions he found impossible to answer, and giggled her way through one boring story after another. Tim made a few smart comments, hoping she'd get the hint, but short of telling her to shut up, there was no let-up to her babble. It meant Tim couldn't hear what Barry and Maeve were talking about up front, only mumblings and laughter. Barry rubbed it in, leaning over to Maeve and whispering, while throwing sidelong glances at Tim. Tommy just stared out of the window, slyly fishing in his pocket for sweets, popping them into his mouth, trying to eat them without chewing, hoping no one would notice and he wouldn't have to share.

Music was booming from the dome-roofed, windowless hall when they pulled up in the car park. Phil Collins, 'You Can't Hurry Love' . . . Hordes of teenagers milled around in small groups outside. Girls linked each other, shrieking and laughing loudly enough to attract attention. Boys smoked cigarettes and pretended not to notice them.

They piled out of the car and made their way over to the wide-open doors of the hall. Several boys made eye contact with Barry, faintly twitching their heads in greeting. A few girls waved at him – 'Howya Barry!' – before falling in towards each other in a giggling heap. It was obvious he loved it, stretching himself up to his full height and sauntering across the tarmac as if he owned the place. Maeve kept up with him, the loose spirals of her hair swaying from side to side as she walked. Tim watched, deflated, as Barry's arm circled her waist and they disappeared inside.

What a joke. How had he ever thought it might be any different? He hadn't a hope against Barry Kilbride. He slunk around the side of the hall and leaned against the wall, looking down over the town, out to where the blue-green sea glittered and shone in the distance. The pale shape of a ferry moved slowly along the horizon, on its way in or out, he wasn't sure. It made him think of home. What would Mum and Dad be doing now? Saturday night. Chicken Maryland in front of *The Paul Daniels Magic Show*. A box of Terry's All Gold. They'd both fall asleep after the first layer. He missed them. As he pictured them dozing off on the couch, he wondered why Mags had asked him over. It was hardly the best time, what with the baby and everything. But, he supposed, it was better than waiting till after. This way, at least, she had time for him.

'There you are! I was wondering where you'd got to.' Sinéad popped her head around the corner. She skipped over, arms swinging, smiling stupidly. She'd re-glossed her lips and tied the tails of her neon-yellow shirt in a knot, showing off her belly button. 'They're after leaving me on my own,' she moaned. 'Tommy's bet in to some young one already and Maeve and Barry are all over each other.'

Tim felt his skin prickle, as if he'd been stung all over with nettles. He bit down on his lip. Hard. Harder. He needed the firm distraction of a sharp pain.

'Are you coming or what?' Sinéad took his arm and pulled him away from the wall.

What was it Tess had said? . . . *if you've any balls at all . . . gone without even a kiss to remember her by . . .*

Inside, the hall was packed, the music so loud Tim's chest throbbed. Pulsing beats sent shivery shots up his legs. Coloured beams criss-crossed the room, spinning and flashing like searchlights in the dark. The air was musky, moist and hot – how he imagined the air in a jungle – and he found it hard to breathe. He pushed his way in, squeezing past backs, rubbing against shoulders, quickly losing Sinéad in the heaving throng. It was Barry he saw first, a flash beam highlighting the iron-on Irish flag on the back of his denim jacket. Maeve was beside him, swaying to the music. Tim shoved his way over. *You're not going to have it all your own way, Barry Kilbride. Not tonight.* But then, as though timed to perfection, the DJ announced he was going to 'slow things down a little'. Barry draped his arms around Maeve's neck and pulled her close. Her face was only inches from Tim's but she didn't see him. Her eyes were tightly closed.

He pushed his way out through the crowd, handing over the price of a can of 7Up at the door and gulping it down as he walked across the car park. He stopped at the edge, gazing over the fence to the green and golden fields that led to Lissenmore. The sun had almost disappeared, the sky feathered with pink. He crushed the can in his fist and flung the crumpled metal into the air.

There was no way he could face the drive back. He'd rather walk home on his own.

In mid-vault over the fence, he heard someone call his name. *Maeve?* For one sweet second he hung there, a leg on each side, his heart soaring ... only to see Sinéad rushing across the car park, tugging down her tight stretchy skirt as she ran. 'Tim! What're you doing? Are you not coming back inside?'

'I ... I'm not feeling too good. I don't want to wait for the lift home. Won't take me long to cut across the fields.'

'Sure you could be an hour walking.' She put her head to one side. 'I'll come with you, if you like. Keep you company.'

'No. I'll be better on my own.'

She tossed her fair curls. Her earrings – gem-studded silver crescents – twinkled in the last of the evening sun. She was quite pretty, really. But he didn't change his mind. 'Besides,' he said, 'you'd never manage it. Not in those shoes.'

She looked down at her shiny white stilettos. 'All right so.'

She sighed. 'I'll tell the others.' Then she grinned. 'If I can tear them apart, that is. Did you see them? Maeve and Barry? Didn't I say they were all over each other? That's the start of something. I just knew this was—'

'I have to go.' Tim finished climbing over the fence. 'I'll see you later.' After a few moments, he looked back. There she was. Making her way towards the hall. Arm-in-arm with a ponytailed boy wearing a black leather waistcoat.

It wasn't yet dark and, though Tim couldn't be completely sure of the way, he trusted his sense of direction. The first field he crossed was a huge square of stony, bare earth, squelchy and mucky in parts after all the rain. After twenty minutes or so, he was sweating. He stripped off his T-shirt and marched, bare-chested, through a golden sea of waist-high grain – barley? He wasn't sure – that left red weals striped across his forearms. After that, it was a clamber through a tangle of thorny brambles and a trek across a meadow flecked with grazing sheep. From there, he saw the pylons that weren't far from the house. They looked like metal monsters close up. Soon, he was tiptoeing through the pasture filled with the shiny-flanked cows and, before long, the whitewashed walls of the house shone out through the falling dusk.

He tried not to think about Maeve and Barry, forcing himself to figure out calculations so that he wouldn't start picturing the pair of them dancing so close together. Estimate the area of the grain field, he told himself. How many steps will it take to cross? How tall is that pylon? How many cows in that herd? He was still counting – how long have I been walking? – when he made his way through a gap in the hawthorn hedge that bordered the back of the yard. He almost didn't see the car parked at the side of the house. If it had been anyone else's, he might not have noticed it in the growing darkness. The light that fell from the kitchen window made the highly polished paintwork of Father Coffey's Fiat gleam.

When he thought about it later, lying in bed and listening to Mags's and PJ's muffled whispers, he wished he'd had the sense to hang back at the door a while longer. Perhaps then he'd have had more of an idea of what was going on.

'Sounds unbearable.' Luke scrutinises an affidavit. He chews a biro as his eyes swivel from left to right. I've been describing the lunch in Dún Laoghaire. How everything between Mam and Dad had been so … tense. How there was clearly something wrong. 'I honestly don't know how you managed to get through it.'

It takes me a moment to realise he's joking. 'You really shouldn't bring work home. Messes with your head.'

'Home? Really?' He looks up with a grin. 'And there was me thinking this was just a place to lay my head now and again.'

'You know what I mean.' I lean into the fridge and root for a tomato. 'And it's not funny.' I find one that's just about still firm and place it on the chopping board. 'I'm concerned about Mam.'

'Why don't you just talk to her? You're both adults, for God's sake.'

I sigh. 'It's not that easy.' I pick up the tomato. 'I might as well be talking to this.'

'Maybe I could speak to her. I could use a . . . particular line of questioning.'

'A cross-examination, you mean? Can you imagine where that'd get us?' I slice the tomato into quarters. I talk to her in my head: The answers have to be inside you somewhere, Mam. It's just a matter of finding a way in.

Luke decides not to stay over. His own mother has been complaining she's hardly seen him since Christmas. A complete exaggeration but, nevertheless, he chooses to pacify her rather than listen to me wittering on about the photo. I can hardly blame him. It's got to the stage where I'm annoying myself.

After he leaves, I stay up late, flicking through the channels but finding nothing I can focus on for more than a couple of minutes. I go to bed, exhausted, but sleep won't come. His face keeps appearing in my head. The boy in the photo. I want to find out who he is, why he's there. Why Mam has her arm so tight around him. I'll call Dad tomorrow. Just before lunch. The likeliest time he'll be out of the house. Less chance of Mam overhearing. He might not want to talk about it but I'm not going to let it rest.

All next morning, I'm fidgety. Ciara, the other junior I share the office with, has noticed there's something up. 'I've a new name for you,' she says, the second time I drop an entire file and scatter papers all over the floor. 'Orla Hyland-Fling. Describes you perfectly. At least today.'

'Sorry, I'm . . . Don't mind me. Late night.' She gives me a smirk. 'No, actually. Luke didn't stay. I just . . .' But there's no point. Not with Ciara '. . . couldn't sleep. That's all.'

She totters off to her desk, her six-inch heels leaving tiny indentations all across the carpet. Ciara and I were called to the Bar at the same time but she flounces around like she's been qualified for decades. Since she caught the roving eye of the effusive Garret Lord SC, she's become insufferably cocky. That she is, apparently, the third in a line of attractive juniors who've become 'close' to Mr Lord is, as she would say, 'of no moment'. She's been spending weekends at his Ballsbridge penthouse since the start of the October term. 'He's separated. Marriage over. Who cares?' she protests. Luke says he'll give it till Easter.

She leaves for lunch at twelve forty-five. I'm alone. I dial the number without hesitation. 'Where are you, Dad?'

'Up above in Faranboy,' he shouts. 'Just after parking here at Lidl's. Have to go and get some messages for your mother.' There's no trace of the tone he used in the café. 'Was out and about, so I was. She gave me a list.'

'Well, make sure you stick to it. You know how she gets if—'

He doesn't allow me to finish. 'Indeed and I do. You don't have to be telling me. The last time I—'

It's my turn to interject. 'Dad, what was all that about in Dún Laoghaire?'

Silence.

'There was clearly something wrong with Mam.'

More silence.

'It was something to do with the picture, wasn't it? The photograph.'

Nothing.

'Look, Dad, there's no use denying it. You've stirred something up, whether you like it or not. I know you want me to give it back – you made that pretty plain – but I can't just pretend I didn't see it or that you didn't go to the trouble of giving it to me in the first place.'

'What's that? Signal's not great, it's—'

'Don't give me that, Dad. You're in the best place for a signal for miles. Even with that brick of a phone of yours.' I stand up from my desk, wander to the window. A crisp, clear day. Brilliant blue sky. Hungry seagulls swooping low over the soup-like Liffey oozing its way up the quays. 'Come on, Dad. Tell me. Who's the boy in the photo?'

'Didn't I already ask you to leave it? Didn't we agree? Can you not just drop it now?'

'No! I can't just drop it. And I didn't agree to anything.'

'Look. I made a mistake. I shouldn't have given it to you. Just after . . . well . . . after what we were talking about when you were down that day, I thought—'

'*Talking* about? We weren't talking about anything! That's the point, Dad. There *is* no talking. It's all ssh this and don't-say-anything that. There has to be some reason Mam's the way she is. And it'd be a lot better if we tackled it head on.'

'It won't do any good, Orla. Even if . . . No. I've decided. Just leave it.'

I spot a pink-tracksuited teenage girl pushing a child in a buggy alongside the river. Her jet-black ponytail swishes from side to side. Huge gold hoops hang from her ears, glinting in the sun. 'It was the year I was born, wasn't it?' My eyes follow her determined stride. 'That summer.' She stops suddenly, reaching down to tuck the red blanket tighter round the child. 'I'm right, amn't I? Mam's pregnant in that photo. Expecting me.'

'Look,' he says, after a long pause, ''twas a long time ago.

What's done is done. It's no good—'

'Who is he, Dad?' My heart goes into overdrive. 'Who is he? Did I ever meet him? And the way Mam's arm is around him. Whoever he is, he meant something to her.' My gaze bounces dizzyingly all over the view – from path to sky to river to rooftops – and when my eyes settle, I look for the girl. She's gone. Bizarrely, I start to panic. Where could she be? How could she and the child have gone so far as to disappear in just a couple of seconds?

'He stayed with us,' he says. 'That summer.'

What? Have I heard him right? '*Stayed* with you? Why? Who was he? A . . . a foreign student? Someone you found on the side of the road? Who, for God's sake?'

'Look, I've said too much already. I—'

'You've said hardly anything! That boy, he means something. All this is about him. Tell me, Dad. Please. Just tell me what it's all about.'

'Forget it. There's no use. I told you. I made a mistake.'

'Jesus, Dad. This is crazy. Maybe I'll ask Mam about it, then. Maybe she'll—'

'Don't dare. Don't say a single word. I'm warning you. No good will come of it.'

I lean my forehead against the cold window. 'It's obvious there's something about him. You wanted me to know, then Mam found out you gave me the photo – quizzed you about it, I don't know. Got angry. Then you got cold feet. I'm not stupid, Dad.'

He sighs. 'I'm done talking about it, Orla. Just leave it now. I have to go and get the messages.'

'His name, even. Just tell me his name. You don't have to say anything else about him, if you don't want to.' My mind is working it out. I could try tracing him. He mightn't be that difficult to find. If he's still alive, that is. Unless . . . I wonder if something bad happened to him. Could that be the reason for all this secrecy?

'I have to go,' Dad says. 'I don't want any more said about it. You can tear up that picture, do what you like with it. Your mother . . . Neither of us . . . We . . . I have to go. All the best. Bye-bye now.'

He's gone.

I pull my head from the chilly, damp glass. Before I turn away, I catch a flash of bright colour. The girl in the pink tracksuit. On this side of the road now, chatting to another young mother, right underneath the window. I thought she'd disappeared because she'd gone so far away. The reason I couldn't see her was because she'd come so close.

God, he's exasperating. I feel like flinging my phone at the wall.

'Christ, Orla,' Luke says, seeing my face when we meet up after work. 'Is it worth getting into such a state?'

'I'm not in a state. I'm just annoyed. He can't give with one hand and take away with the other. It's not fair.'

'Then do something about it.'

How would Tim explain being home early from the disco? And on his own? He didn't want to say anything about Maeve being with Barry. He'd never hear the end of it. The only half-decent explanation was the one he'd given Sinéad. He hadn't felt well and didn't want to wait ages for a lift. As it turned out, he could've said anything at all: no one seemed too concerned that he'd come home early. Or why. Or even how he'd got there. At least, that was the way it appeared.

He tugged his T-shirt back on as he crossed the yard. Mags might be embarrassed if he walked in half dressed in front of Father Coffey. Rapping lightly on the back door before he pushed it open, he called out, 'I'm back.' There was a scuffle. A scramble? Definitely a movement of some sort. Four pairs of eyes rounded on him when he stepped inside. PJ and Father Coffey stood stiffly beside the dresser, hands behind their backs. Mags sat on the couch. With Tess. No one said a word. Tim gulped. Why were they all staring? Had he put his T-shirt on inside-out? Back to front? Were there ears of barley caught in his hair? Cow shit on his jeans?

Father Coffey was the first to speak. 'Tim! There you are now and we only just talking about you saying what a great lad you are weren't we PJ?' he said, taking no breaths between words.

PJ nodded. 'Aye. We were, Dinny, we were. A great lad is Tim. A great lad altogether.'

Then Tess said brightly, 'You're home early. Did Barry drop Maeve off too? Didn't think she'd be back till after twelve.'

'I . . . I wasn't feeling well. I walked back by myself. Over the fields.' He waited for Mags to comment. Are you all right, Tim? Can I get you anything? But she said nothing. Instead, she continued to stare, though he wasn't sure from the glazed look in her eyes whether she could see him.

Something was up.

'Is . . . everything OK?' he asked.

'Course it is!' Father Coffey said, beaming. 'Just a routine parish visit. A friendly chat. Met Tess out on the road, so I did, and I brought her along. Kill two birds with the one stone – isn't that what they say, what?'

A parish visit? This late on a Saturday night? And what would Tess have been doing out on the road? Mags sat rigid as a statue, still staring at Tim, as though a spell of some sort might be broken if she took her eyes off him. Beside her, Tess fidgeted with her wedding ring. Tugging at it and twisting it round and round her finger. The lines on her forehead seemed to cut deeper into her skin and the bluish circles beneath her eyes were darker than before.

'You must be tired, Tim,' PJ said, laying a hand heavily on his shoulder. 'After walking all that way.' He steered him towards the stairs and Tim climbed them without argument. Whatever they'd been discussing, it wasn't for his ears. They'd made that much plain.

He got ready for bed. Before he hopped in, he went to the window and peered out into the darkness. He couldn't see it, but the sea was out there. Only a short distance away in Faranboy. Knowing it was close made him feel safer somehow. He lay awake a long time. Maeve. Barry. How late did they stay? Were they together all night? Had they ... kissed? Of course they had. He'd been stupid to think he had a chance. What hope did he have against someone like Barry Kilbride? He was older, taller, better-looking. And then there was the car ... Tim was just a schoolboy. A stupid English schoolboy, who'd be gone in a few weeks. Maeve needed someone who could be there for her. Tim understood that. With her father gone, there was protection in someone like Barry. He couldn't compete with that. Tess had been having fun at his expense that day. Telling him he should get a move on if he wanted so much as a kiss. She'd probably said it to Mags. He pictured them both. Having a good laugh about it.

But the way they'd all been when he'd walked in tonight ... It was like every ounce of humour had been sucked from the air. The grave tone in PJ's voice. Father Coffey's pretend smile. Mags's vacant stare. Tess worrying the ring on her finger ...

He didn't want to think about it.

About him. Lar Mooney.

But maybe Maeve had been right. Maybe something *had* happened to him.

He woke in the dead of night to the woolly murmur of whispers. Mags and PJ talking. Were they arguing again?

Their voices emerging out of the silence. Coming and going. Like the steady hum of the sea.

Next morning, Mags insisted they go to mass. The previous couple of Sundays, she'd told PJ to go on his own while she stayed at home with Tim. She knew it wasn't something he was used to and didn't want to force him to go. Mum went to mass every Sunday. But not Dad. He'd told Tim he'd 'converted' when he got married but that was as far as it had gone for him. 'Don't have much faith in religion,' he often said, with a laugh. Tim wasn't sure how it came about that he got to stay at home with Dad while Mum went to mass but, whatever the reason, he was glad. She'd brought him along once, when Dad was away visiting Nana Swift in Cardiff. They'd sat in a freezing, marble-pillared church, Tim's nostrils tingling with the scent of incense and beeswax, his eardrums ballooning with echoing coughs and sniffs and mumbled prayers. And the sermon that dragged on and on. Tim couldn't understand a word. He was stunned when Mum told him that the priest was actually speaking English.

The church was in Faranboy. On the way, they passed the hall where the disco had been. Now, a heavy chain and padlock secured the doors, which were squiggled with spray-painted graffiti – fuzzy scarlet letters that said 'UP THE IRA'. Tim sat between Mags and PJ, trying to keep himself upright as PJ hurtled over bumps and potholes with his usual flair. Mags was being all bright and breezy. But to Tim she was trying a little too hard. It had to be something to do with the night before. The more he thought about it, the more convinced he was that Maeve's instincts had been right, that something had happened to Lar. They'd all looked so suspicious. And why else would Tess have been there? It was a priest's job to impart bad news and Father Coffey wouldn't have wanted to say anything in front of Declan and his brothers. It made sense that he'd tell Tess while she was in the company of friends who could look after her.

The mass was long and boring. Mags leaned in to Tim a couple of times while Father Coffey delivered his sermon. She took deep, shuddery breaths every few minutes and seemed relieved when Father Coffey announced, 'Let us pray,' covering her face with her hands.

It was after, when it was over, that Tim saw Maeve. And Barry. As he made his way down the central aisle, flanked by Mags and PJ, he caught sight of Declan and Fintan jumping up and down on a pew. Maeve was trying to keep them in order. Unsuccessfully. She grabbed at them but they dodged her, vaulting neatly onto the next pew. Tim was about to go over and help but then, of course, Barry came to the rescue, catching both boys by their wrists and dragging them outside, followed by a red-faced Maeve.

Father Coffey stood in the porch, nodding at the mass-goers as they slowly filed past. He briefly laid a hand on Tim's head and gave him a straight smile, one that didn't reach his eyes.

'You two go on,' Mags said to PJ. 'I'll be there in a minute.'

As they walked down the steps, Tim glanced back over his shoulder and saw her, deep in conversation with Father Coffey.

It was a blustery day. Snow-white clouds raced across the sky and the tall poplars on each side of the church swayed in the wind. Tim wasn't in any mood to talk to Maeve after what he'd seen in the disco. He hoped she wouldn't notice him but, as she turned her head to toss her hair from her eyes, she spied him and waved.

'Where'd you get to last night?' she asked, as she ran over. 'Sinéad said you were sick or something. Walked home by yourself, she said.'

PJ fumbled in his jacket pocket for his keys. 'Getting into the van,' he said. 'Follow me over. Don't be long.'

Tim nodded and watched his uncle's trouser legs flapping about his ankles as he strode across the churchyard.

Maeve touched Tim's arm. 'She likes you, you know, Sinéad. Asking me all about you, she was. Didn't know what to be doing with herself after you left.'

'Didn't look that way to me,' Tim said. 'I was barely gone a minute when I saw her paired off with someone else.' He zipped up his jacket and sank his hands into the pockets. 'Seems she wasn't the only one either.'

Straight away, he was sorry he'd said it. He shouldn't be sniping at her when her father could be ... Well, who knew what had happened to him? It didn't feel right. If Maeve preferred Barry, then maybe he should let them get on with it. She deserved to be happy, didn't she?

'What do you mean by that?' she asked, pushing her hair back from her eyes.

'Nothing. I didn't mean anything.'

She shot a look at Barry, who was using his knees to shove the two boys into the back of his car. 'I'm not doing a line with him, if that's what you think. I mean, I'm not going out with him.'

'It's your own business. You can do whatever you like.'

'I'm serious. Barry's a good friend to us. And ... well ...' she leaned in close '... promise you won't tell? He's going to bring me over to Liverpool. We're taking the car on the boat. We're going to look for Daddy.'

Tim swallowed hard. 'But you don't know . . . I mean . . .' He had to ask. 'Did your mum say anything when you got in last night?'

'About what?' She laughed. 'She said loads of things.'

'Did she say she'd been down with Mags? And that . . . and that Father Coffey was there too?'

'No.' She frowned. 'She didn't. What of it?'

'I think something's going on. Something they don't want us to know about.'

Her face fell. 'Like what?'

'I'm not sure. But I think . . . I think it might be something to do with your dad.'

'What do you mean?'

'Come on, Tim. Let's get out of this and home to our dinner.' It was Mags, hurrying towards them, her head dipped against the wind.

'I have to go,' Tim said to Maeve, his voice low. 'Don't say anything. Not yet. I'll see if I can find out any more.'

Mags went to a lot of trouble with dinner that day. Juicy roast chicken with carrots and mashed parsnip. Potatoes, too, of course. Not her usual floury ones, boiled in their skins, but crispy ones, roasted in the oven. As they ate, Tim's thoughts went to his conversation with Maeve, to what could have happened to Lar. If something *had* happened it was surely bad news. He could be in trouble. With the police. Maybe he was in prison. Or he could be ill. Seriously ill.

Maybe he was dead.

He had to do his best to find out.

He yawned. Loud and wide.

Mags took the bait. 'Tired?' she said. 'Must be that big walk you did last night.'

'Suppose so,' Tim said. 'Though I didn't get to sleep for ages. And then I woke up in the middle of the night. I could hear the two of you talking.'

'You could?' She cut through a potato. 'I'm sorry, love.'

'It's fine. I understand if you've . . . important things to talk about.'

PJ shifted in his chair. He scratched his beard, then reached for the salt and shook far too much of it on his food. Mags loaded her fork with a chunk of chicken, carefully added a layer of parsnip, and popped it into her mouth. She chewed for ages. Tim waited patiently. She was thinking.

When she spoke, it wasn't what he'd been expecting.

'I thought we could go off somewhere nice today. What do you think?' She looked at PJ. 'A walk on the strand, maybe. We could get ice-cream. There's that little place does ninety-nines.'

'Aye. We could,' PJ said. 'Fair breeze out, though.'

'We'll be grand. Be a bit of fun. Would you like that, Tim?'

He couldn't make them tell him what they'd been talking about. But it was more obvious now it was something they didn't want him knowing. Mags was being far too cheerful – Tim could see it was forced. 'I won't tell!' he blurted. 'I'm able to keep a secret. It's about Lar Mooney, isn't it? Something's happened.'

Mags took a deep breath and slowly got up from the table. She came around and stood behind Tim, tousling his hair with her fingers. 'Now, listen to me. There's nothing to be telling about Lar Mooney, Mr Two-and-two-make-five.'

'But Father Coffey . . . and Tess. Why—'

'Father Coffey and Tess nothing,' she said, cutting him short. 'Letting your imagination run wild, so you are.' She hooked a finger under his chin and pulled him round to face her. 'So you needn't be going and filling poor Maeve's head with any rubbish, do you hear me?' She smiled but Tim didn't buy it. 'Now, hurry up and finish that dinner while I go and get myself ready.'

They were trying to distract him, Tim knew. Taking him to the seaside, like he was a little kid. Pretending nothing was wrong when it was obvious something was up.

Pebbles and shells crusted the sloping curve of Faranboy strand and rough waves left a frill of lacy foam where the water met the land. Great gusts buffeted their bodies as they walked and Mags clung to PJ for fear she'd topple over. They walked the length of the beach, all the way to the dead end of a sheer cliff face where fat seagulls circled, squawking. PJ bought ice-creams and they sat down on a cast-iron bench on the promenade to eat them but a shower began. It grew heavier as they headed back, turning to a downpour just after they got into the van.

'That's the day over,' PJ said, turning the key in the ignition.

As they passed the church on the way home, Mags blessed herself, then took a tissue from her sleeve and dabbed at her eyes. 'No, no,' she insisted, when she caught Tim looking. 'I'm not crying. It's just the wind after making my eyes water.'

Tim stared straight ahead. Did she really think he'd fall for that? Whatever all this was about, she'd hardly be able to hold it inside for ever.

Sometimes, in the night, my brain seems to figure things out. Or at least find solutions to problems in places that, awake, I'd never think to search. I've often discovered the legal weak spot in an opposite number's case papers when on the cusp of sleep. Something I've read, over and over, in the bright light of day, reveals its flaws only in the darkness of night. After the phone call to Dad, it comes to me just before dawn on the Saturday morning.

Barry Kilbride.

If the boy stayed that summer, then surely Barry will remember. He would've been a teenager himself back then. He's lived his whole life in Lissenmore. There's not much about the place he doesn't know. Always had political ambitions, did Barry. A man with a finger in every pie, he does his utmost to solve every problem that lands on his doorstep. The local population – the old, the young, students, mothers, workers, the unemployed, immigrants, emigrants – they all know who to call on when they need something sorted. There was never a doubt he wouldn't be elected to the council and, to be fair to him, he puts the work in. He makes it his business to know everyone else's and, after many years of dedicated service, next step is a seat in the Dáil. At least, that's what he's hoping for. Come the next general election, Councillor Barry Kilbride's pudgy face will be looking out from every lamppost and telegraph pole in the area.

I fall asleep again, waking to the sound of Luke asking if I want a coffee. I give him a thumbs-up and open my eyes. He's pulled back the curtains. The window frames a dripping grey watercolour view of distorted buildings, leaden river and concrete sky. Typical. Stuck in the office all week when it's dry. Once the weekend comes it's lashing. 'And bring me the laptop, would you?' I ask him. 'I want to look something up.'

I do a quick search online. Barry has a website, albeit a rather rudimentary one. The home page shows a picture of the smiling man himself ('Barry Kilbride – Your Voice Is Mine'), which looks as though it might've been Photoshopped – his teeth are far too white and even, and his skin is definitely not that tanned in reality. The way the content is presented, it seems as though Barry Kilbride is single-handedly putting the world to rights. Luke returns from the kitchen with the coffee, settles himself back on the bed beside me. '"Road repairs after recent bad weather essential, according to Barry Kilbride,"' he reads. '"Job creation top of agenda, agrees Kilbride." "Loss of local garda stations – Barry lobbies minister." And listen to this one. "Barry kicks up a stink over proposed septic tank charges."' He laughs. 'What are you looking at that for anyway?'

I explain. 'He might know something. It's possible.'

'Suppose so.' He peers at the screen again. 'Jesus, it's a different world down there, isn't it? Another country.'

I pretend I'm insulted. 'I hope that's not the sound of condescension I hear. There is life outside the Pale, you know.'

'If you say so.'

'How many times have you actually been outside Dublin?'

'Plenty! Via the airport.'

'Exactly. You haven't a clue.'

'Why not show me around, then? About time I met your parents.'

I've been reluctant to introduce Luke to them. Not that I think Mam and Dad won't like him, it's just with Mam being so low this past while, I'd hate him to get the wrong impression. Much as I've explained what she can be like, I'd still prefer her to be in good form when they meet. But he's probably right. It's about time.

'Hmm? What do you think?' He sits up straight. 'Why don't we go today? Stay the night somewhere around there. Make a weekend out of it? You could try searching out the Kilbride fellow too, ask him a few questions.'

'I don't know.' I'm already picturing us stepping into the kitchen back home. Mam staring at Luke. Dad being over-friendly. All of us making small talk about the journey down. Then Mam asking worriedly about our New York plans.

'Come on! Live dangerously!' He drains his mug and stands up. 'And we might put an end to this mystery once and for all.'

'You're serious? You actually want us to drive down now?'

'Why not?'

'Because – because it's raining. It might get heavier. There could be flooding, we might—'

'Come on, Orla. We don't have anything else planned. And eff the weather. It's not like we'll be walking.'

'I'll have to text Mam. Let her know. And what if we can't find Barry Kilbride? If he's away or—'

'Jesus, Orla! You either want to be proactive or you don't. If he's not around, so what? We'll deal with that if it arises. You want to try getting to the bottom of this photo thing, don't you?'

'I suppose so. It's just – I don't know – involving someone else. I'm not sure.' I close the laptop. 'Maybe I should just keep it in the family.' I take his extended hand, let him pull me from the bed.

'I'm involved and I'm not family. Not properly anyway.'

Luke and I have never had any serious discussions about any future we might have together. We've gone as far as the New York Bar plan. But after that? It's pretty much 'wait and see'. There's never been a mention of anything long term, anything that might involve either of us having to admit our relationship might actually *be* long term. But I'm not worried. I'm happy for things to keep going as they are, content that we'll more than likely continue on this route until one day we'll realise our paths have permanently merged and that we're destined, in fact, to be together for ever. I am who I am with Luke. When I'm with him, I don't have to be someone I'm not just to please him. I've experienced those who've brought out the worst in me. He tends to bring out the best.

'OK, then.' I manage a smile. 'I guess it's meet-the-parents time.'

I book us into Castlefox Manor for the night – a country-house hotel about a half-hour's drive out of Lissenmore. I text Mam, tell her we'll call in tomorrow lunchtime. I don't want to land in today. She's not great with last-minute stuff. She'll need time to prepare.

We take Luke's car. We're well on our way by midday. 'At least the wipers work in mine,' he says, flicking them on to full speed. 'And there's less chance of a breakdown.' He constantly makes fun of my Micra – ten years old and looking every day of it – but I take it good-naturedly, the way it's intended. 'Any idea where to look for Kilbride?' he asks. 'Where would he be if he's around?'

'Counting his profits in one or other of his businesses, no doubt. I'll nip into Kavanagh's in the village first. Well, the place Mam still calls Kavanagh's. She has me doing it too. Barry took it over a few years ago. Turned it into a Spar. If he's not there, we can try the Haven House in Faranboy.'

'The Haven House. Sounds cosy. Log fires, friendly barman, country cooking?'

'That sort of thing. Gastro-pub. Used to be a hole. Everyone said he was mad but he turned it into a goldmine. No recession in that place.'

'Liking the sound of this Barry Kilbride.'

'He's not the worst, I suppose, but . . .'

'But what?'

'Don't know. Always feel a bit uneasy around him. Like he has something on me.' I look out at the damp landscape flying by. 'Can't really explain it.' Away to the left, I glimpse a sliver of grey sea, almost imperceptible against the dirty white sky. The old road – the one that narrowed to a thread through one-street towns and villages – showed more of the coast. I preferred it. This newer route cuts straight through the countryside, slicing precious minutes off our journey but bypassing civilisation in the process.

'What's so funny?' After a while, Luke catches me smiling.

'Gastro-pub. Always makes me laugh. Dad's reaction when

he heard what Barry was doing to the Haven. "*Gastro-pub?*" he said. "And what's that when it's at home? Some class of a disease, is it?" He's priceless.'

Lissenmore village is dead. Not a soul on the street. Hardly surprising, given the weather. I recognise no one working in Spar. There was a time I would have, but now it's staffed by unfamiliar, bored teenagers, furtively scrolling their phones behind the cash register. Offspring, no doubt, of parents priced out of Dublin during the boom. Families occupying shoddily built estate houses worth less than half the amount they forked out for them.

'The boss around?' I ask a fake-tanned blonde, with obvious hair extensions, petrol-blue nails and a face that says, 'I don't belong here.'

'Just missed him. Gone up to the Haven for lunch.'

I thank her, contemplate buying a newspaper just to give her something to do, but decide against it when Katty Hackett pushes open the door, her bony frame shrouded in a dripping, hooded plastic mac. I put my head down – I'll be trapped here for ever if she catches me. Over eighty now, Katty ran Lissenmore's post office for about half a century, finally closing it after she'd been robbed for the third time in eighteen months. A photo of her brandishing the axe she kept under the counter, which she'd used to try to scare the raiders, made the front page of the national papers. The post office – a room to the front of her house – has never reopened. Unprofitable and downright dangerous, who in their right mind would want to take it over?

I hurry to the car. 'Quick, let's get out of here.'

'You're that scared of her?' Luke laughs.

'It'd just be a barrage of questions. The same ones she

asks me every time. Her brain's a bit confused now. Human equivalent of CCTV she was, back in the day. Whatever was happening, Katty knew about it.'

'Maybe you could ask her about Curly Boy. She might remember something if she's been around that long.'

'Hmm. Possibly. Though getting sense out of her these days isn't easy. Last time she managed to waylay me, she told me how lucky I was to have a husband who was so handy. "PJ was always a great worker," she kept saying. "Blessed you are. Blessed." God love her. Never found a man herself. Married to that post office, she was.'

I point out our house as we speed past. Smoke flying up from the chimney in a steady stream. Dad's jeep parked round the side.

'The old homestead,' Luke remarks. 'Pretty much as I imagined it. Actually looking forward to meeting your mum and dad.'

I tell him to take the next left towards Faranboy and the town reveals itself as we round a bend. Forlorn. Dejected. Like all seaside towns in the middle of winter. We clunk into and out of a pothole. My head slaps back against the headrest. 'Keep your eyes on the road, you idiot. Or you'll never get to meet them. Today or any day.'

He does as I say with a smile and we carry on through the rain. It's pelting down in sheets now. It couldn't be more miserable. What a day for a wild-goose chase. That's what this may well turn out to be. One part of me sees the sense in what I'm trying to do. The other thinks I'm nuts. But I have to get to the bottom of it. Have to find out whatever it is that photo is hiding. Dad's doing his best to keep the truth about it from me. But he was the one who gave it to me in the first place.

He dangled that carrot in front of my nose, then withdrew it. It's maddening. But he did it because he knows me. Knows how resolute I am when it comes to solving puzzles, to finding gaps and filling them in. 'Always knew you'd be one for the law,' he'd said, when I made it my choice of career. But I know him too. He won't betray Mam. Wants me to discover this truth, whatever it is, for myself. That's all very well but, really, does he have to be so stubborn?

'Scene of many a teenage romance,' I tell Luke, as we pass the Lidl supermarket.

'Strange place for it, I would've thought.'

'Youth club socials. Discos, as Dad used to call them. There was a hall there once. Burned down ten years ago. There weren't any funds to do it up. You-know-who snapped it up for a song.'

'And, let me guess, made a killing selling the site to the Germans?'

'Got it in one.'

'Sounds like a man with his eye very definitely on the future, this Councillor Kilbride.'

The view out to sea is misty and grey, the rain relentless, as we pull into the car park in front of the Haven House. I open the door and we make a run for it. 'Well, let's hope he can help cast some light on the past.'

I spot him as soon as we walk in. On his own at a round table opposite the door, shoulders hunched over a bowl of soup. A newspaper is spread out before him but he's not reading. His true mission is the covert surveillance of his territory. At every sound, his head twitches; at every flash of movement, his eyes swivel to its source. The comings and goings of patrons, their average spend, the most popular orders, his staff's attitude and behaviour – nothing escapes the attention of Barry Kilbride. He catches my gaze, holds it for a second, registers a flicker of recognition. Barry knows well who I am, though there's always been a coolness there that's hard to explain. Mam's never been overly fond of him for some reason and Dad can take him or leave him. Their feelings go against the grain: most of the locals think the sun shines out of his rear end.

'Leave everything to me,' I whisper to Luke. 'I know how I'm going to handle it.' He orders food and drinks at the bar while I choose the empty table to Barry's right and sit down. The place is busy enough for a dreary Saturday afternoon. A handful of muscly lads are glued to the football on a huge flat screen hanging in an alcove; three small girls in glittery pink outfits dance around a cast-iron mermaid fountain in the centre of the floor; black-clad staff zip between tables, serving food on square slates to chatting couples and families with young kids.

I shoulder off my damp jacket and drape it over the back of my chair. Barry's eyes are aware as he sips from his soup spoon, watching, but not conspicuously so. I nod at him. 'Business is good by the look of it,' I remark.

''Tis not bad. Considering.'

'You've done a great job on this place. Big changes.'

'Oh, aye, big changes indeed. Um . . .' he clears his throat '. . . home for the day, is it?'

'Ah, you know. Thought we'd take a spin down.' I smile when Luke appears and I introduce him. 'Never been outside the Pale, this fella,' I say. 'Had to show him how the other half of the country lives.'

Barry chuckles, his belly straining at the buttons of his striped shirt. Hard to believe he was considered a bit of a looker back in the day. Full of himself he was. Driving around the place in one fancy car after another. Forever on his way to or from somewhere, sorting this, arranging that, finding opportunities to make ready cash. He was always a bit of a nationalist – nothing wrong in that – but since becoming a councillor, he's played it down a little. Seems to be keen to be all-inclusive. All things to all men. He even arranged an 'Integration Evening' last summer for the East Europeans – mainly Polish and Romanian – who've moved into the general area in recent years.

'And what do you think?' he asks Luke. 'Good enough for you, is it?' Luke grins, makes a face, says something about not having seen enough of the place yet. A pot of tea and an over-garnished club sandwich are delivered to Barry's table by a nervous young girl, her pink cheeks deepening further when she almost drops his empty soup bowl. 'So,' Barry says, eyeing a middle-aged couple in matching navy anoraks coming through the door, bringing a blast of cold air behind them, 'what has young Miss Hyland been saying about us? All positive, I hope?'

'Oh, of course,' Luke answers, trying to keep a straight face. 'Never stops going on about the place, how much she misses it, how much she'd love to move back.'

'Is that so?' Barry says, scraping rocket leaves and cherry tomatoes to one side of his plate. ''Tis a good time, right enough. Have you had a look around? Plenty of cheap property to be had.'

I give Luke a glare. 'Well, I . . . No, not yet.'

Barry carefully extracts the little wooden stick that holds

his sandwich together. 'Well, don't be leaving it too long. Prices'll only fall so far before they start rising again.'

'That's what I keep hearing,' I say. 'Not sure how much truth is in it.'

'Ah, now,' Barry says. 'Things'll come round again. Recessions come and go, so they do. Never seen one last for ever.' He bites into his sandwich.

Here it is. An opening I can exploit to my advantage. 'You'd hardly remember the last one?' I ask. 'Back in the eighties?'

He nods as he chews. 'Indeed and I do. A lot tougher back then, I can tell you.'

Our food arrives. I stir my soup, dissolving the blob of cream that floats on top. 'So I believe. If the things Mam and Dad tell me are anything to go by.'

'A different world, by all accounts,' Luke says, copping on to what I'm doing. 'Only talking about that on the way down, weren't we, Orla?'

'I mean, I'm too young to remember,' I say to Barry. 'But whenever I look at, you know, photos and stuff from back then, it's like an alien planet.'

Barry shifts in his seat and pours himself more tea. 'Don't know I'd go that far but, well, there's been a fair few changes right enough.'

I slip my hand into my bag, feeling for the by-now familiar hard edge. 'Take this, for example. Found it last time I was home.' I hold the photo under his nose and give him a broad smile. 'Gas, isn't it?' He jerks his head back a little in order to focus. 'Look at the two of them,' I joke. 'What are they like? Would you even recognise them?'

He turns away from the photo, directing his attention to

his food. 'Of course I would. I'd know Mags and PJ Hyland anywhere.'

'I'm in it too. Would you believe that? Mam's pregnant with me. Nineteen eighty-three. Can't have been taken too long before I was born.'

'Is that so?' he says distractedly, nodding a greeting to a man carrying a sleeping baby.

I pretend to examine the photo. 'Not sure who that young lad is,' I say, as if I've only just spotted him. I hold it under his nose. 'Any idea?'

I count in my head as he contemplates the image, watching his face for any trace of recall. He sits still and silent. A full ten seconds pass. Finally, he breathes heavily and blinks as though roused from a daze. 'No. Not a clue.' He shakes his head. 'Wouldn't know him at all.' Then he's on his feet, bumping against the table, knocking cutlery to the floor. 'Nice talking to you,' he says. 'Call in again next time you're around.' After a swift, quiet word to the barman, he's gone.

We say nothing for a moment. I wait for Luke to react. After sipping his coffee he turns to face me, tells me what I already know. 'He recognised Curly Boy, all right. Couldn't have made it plainer if he'd tried.'

Mags came into Tim's room early next morning. 'Tim, come on. Get up, love.'

He opened his eyes. She pulled back both sets of curtains and leaned down, gently shaking his shoulder. 'Get yourself dressed. PJ's starting a new job and he's taking you with him.' She left him no time to ask questions. It seemed he was going. Whether he liked it or not.

After a rushed breakfast, Mags hurried him out of the door. PJ was waiting in the van with the engine running. He grunted a greeting when Tim hopped in. Before they pulled away, Mags thrust a bulky tinfoil-wrapped shape through Tim's window, along with a plastic beaker filled with milk.

'Couple of ham sandwiches,' she said. 'And a few slices of brack.'

'Thanks,' Tim said. 'We'll be gone for the day, then?'

'You will. Do you good.' She yawned. 'I'll see you tonight, all right?' There was silence between herself and PJ. No goodbyes. After they'd come back from Faranboy, they'd practically ignored one another all evening. Tim had felt awkward, sitting in the charged atmosphere, eventually heading up to bed earlier than usual. He'd kept an ear cocked, expecting to hear their voices drifting up through the ceiling but had fallen asleep to the sound of silence.

PJ revved the engine. Mags stepped back and the van lurched forward. They were off. Through the gate, left onto the road and on past the turn for Faranboy. Further on, a right at a crossroads brought them onto a clear, wide stretch that cut through miles of flat, open countryside. There wasn't another car to be seen. Tim settled back in his seat and watched out of the window. There was no sun. Thick white cloud covered the sky. Everything looked dead. After a while, they passed a lake, its gun-metal surface devoid of life or shine. Tim's thoughts began to wander. Why now? Why today? Was it just a coincidence that he'd been whisked away? It felt forced. Like they wanted him occupied. Out of the way. Were they trying to keep him from Maeve? Mags's insistence that he was wrong about Lar Mooney rang hollow. *Mr Two-and-two-make-five* . . . He took a sideways look at his uncle. PJ sat forward in his seat, his back straight, his skin stretched white over his knuckles as he gripped the steering wheel hard. He drove fast. Faster than he normally did. It made Tim nervous. A yellow road sign came into view, indicating a sharp bend to the left. If PJ saw it, he ignored it and didn't adjust his speed. God must've been looking out for them, Tim thought, when PJ took the bend and had to swerve wildly to avoid a pair of cyclists. 'Bloody tourists,' PJ muttered, still on the wrong side of the road. Tim saw them, reflected in the wing mirror, a bearded man and a blonde woman with rucksacks strapped to their backs. He kept his eyes on them till they disappeared, then found himself studying a spider's web that was strung between the mirror and the body of the van. Its dusty threads, vibrating in the breeze, held trapped a tiny black fly. For one split second something flashed clear and plain in his head – something about the meaning of time and chance and circumstance – but then his brain couldn't fix on it any more and it was gone. He sighed loudly, scratched his head, bit his nails. 'When will we be there?'

PJ kept his eyes on the road, sailing over a hump-backed bridge without slowing down. Tim's stomach did a somersault. He thought he might throw up. Then PJ swung a sharp left through a set of granite gateposts, each one topped with a lichen-encrusted eagle. The van bumped up a straight avenue lined with ivy-strangled trees that grabbed at each other from either side. The dark green tunnel seethed with a leafy dampness that filtered into the van.

'Now. We're here,' PJ finally answered, as he pulled up on a gravelled clearing in front of a huge, stone-built house. 'Castlefox Manor.' It was like something from the Middle Ages. Arch-topped windows, a turret at each corner and battlements running round the edges of the roof. As Tim took it all in, a man appeared from around the side. PJ hopped out and Tim watched as the pair of them chatted, nodding intermittently, hands in their trouser pockets. The man was as tall as PJ but much older, with grey, slicked-back hair and a thick moustache nestling under his nose, like a small, woodland animal. He wore a crumpled but expensive-looking beige suit and carried a brass-tipped wooden walking stick. After a minute or two, he shook PJ's hand, waved in at Tim, then walked away.

'Who was that?' Tim wanted to know.

'Charlie Fox,' PJ said, a little gruffly. 'Lord of the manor.

Wants his stables fixed up.' He hopped back into the van and drove around to the back of the house. 'You think you'll be able for it?'

Tim hadn't much of an idea what it would entail. 'Um ... what do I have to do?'

'Whatever I say. That's what.' He threw a pair of well-worn work gloves at Tim. 'And get those onto you – you won't survive without them.'

And that was how Tim spent the week. Building up crumbling walls, replacing missing slates, stripping out rotten timbers. They left at eight in the morning and rarely finished up before half past six. Coming back each evening, exhausted, Tim was fit only for food, a bath and bed. It was hard work. But satisfying. Mags always had a huge dinner waiting, the bath water heated, fresh towels laid out on Tim's bed. But things didn't seem any better between herself and PJ. She'd dish up his food, clear his plate away, ask him to bring down his dirty clothes for washing. But that was about it. With Tim, she appeared warm and attentive. With her husband, she was decidedly frosty.

Father Coffey's car was in the yard one evening when they returned home from work. PJ mumbled something under his breath as he brought the van to a halt and he slammed the door when he got out.

'Well, I'll take my leave,' the priest said, when they went inside. 'I'm sure the men here will be wanting their dinner. Isn't that so?'

Mags stood up from the couch. 'Thanks for dropping in, Father.'

'You'll think about what I said?'

'Of course.'

Father Coffey fished about in his trouser pocket and produced a string of white beads. He handed them to Tim. 'Take those, lad,' he said. 'Never did anyone any harm to say the Rosary once in a while.'

Tim thanked him. He was unsure what the Rosary was but, not wanting to appear ignorant, he said nothing.

'Prayers? Is that it, Dinny?' PJ said, irritated.

Mags scowled. 'PJ,' she said, 'a prayer never hurt anyone.'

Father Coffey cleared his throat. 'I'll be off so,' he said, staring hard at PJ. 'God be with you.'

After dinner, exhaustion set in for Tim and he lay on the couch to watch a surprisingly unfuzzy TV while Mags tidied the table and PJ followed her around the kitchen. Tim was happy they were talking. But though he could hear only snatches, it was definitely not a pleasant conversation. '... have to ...' he heard PJ saying, '... not fair ... chance ... home ...'

Mags answered, her tone sharp, but most of her words muffled. '... ruin this on me ...' she was saying '... when I'm ready ... difference ... in time ...' The mumbles, in spite of their tone, became like a lullaby and, soon, Tim began to drift. His body ached from the day's work. His palms were calloused and raw, his arms and legs heavy as tree trunks. Sleep came swiftly.

He woke some time later to find he was being steered up the stairs by PJ, his legs jellyish and his head pounding. Mags settled him into bed and sat on the edge, stroking his forehead until his brain closed down again and the night took over.

And then they came home on the Thursday night to find the house empty. Mags had left a note for Tim propped against the stainless-steel teapot on the kitchen table.

Dear Tim,

I'm not sure if PJ will have told you, but I've got to go up to hospital in Dublin for a day or two. Nothing serious. Tess is coming with me for a bit of company. She's going to visit an aunt of hers.

Back Saturday.

Love, Mags

Tim looked at PJ. 'Why didn't you say anything?'

PJ plonked himself down on a chair. ''Tis only a couple of days,' he said, unlacing his boots. 'She'll be back Saturday night.'

'I know, but . . . ' Tim fingered the note '. . . you could've told me.'

'And have you asking questions the whole day?'

'How did she get there?' Tim wanted to know. 'Why didn't you take her?'

'Father Coffey was going to Dublin, so he was. Gave them a lift. Getting the train back, they are.'

Tim frowned. 'But when did she find out she was going? Who told her she had to?'

'A few days back. Nurse called in and arranged it.' He kicked his boots under the chair. 'Let's just have the dinner, all right? This is what I'm talking about. Questions, questions.'

He served up the food Mags had left for them. A stew bobbing with flaky lumps of meat, soft carrot slices and whole waxy potatoes.

'The . . . the baby's going to be OK?' Tim asked, sitting down. 'I mean . . .'

PJ slopped a ladleful onto Tim's plate. 'Nothing serious. Isn't that what she said?'

'But . . . how? . . . I hope . . .' Why hadn't Mags told him?

He knew very little about the process of having babies, apart from the cartoonish drawings in his biology book, so he'd no way of knowing if a hospital stay at this stage was normal. All the friction there'd been between her and PJ these past few days – could that have made her unwell? He popped a chunk of potato into his mouth.

'Look,' PJ said, after a minute, 'everything's grand.' He wiped his mouth with the back of his hand. 'She'll be back before we even know she's gone.'

The next afternoon they finished the job. After tidying up, PJ told Tim to wait in the van while he went to have a word with Charlie Fox. Tim couldn't wait to get back. He was even hungrier than usual. With Mags not around, breakfast had been a slice of brown bread and butter in the van, and the small lunch PJ had thrown together had been eaten before noon. He shuffled his feet around, hoping he might find a forgotten packet of crisps or a chocolate bar among the clutter. All he managed to unearth was a lone digestive biscuit – in an obviously long-discarded packet – that broke into soft, damp crumbs as soon as he touched it.

PJ returned after ten minutes or so, hopped in and switched on the engine. He sat looking out of the window, tugging at his beard and whistling through his teeth. Then, reaching into his jacket pocket, he withdrew a clean, brown envelope. 'There you go,' he said, picking out two twenty-pound notes. 'You're not a bad worker.'

Tim stared at the money PJ had pushed into his hand. 'Thanks. Thanks a lot!' It had never occurred to him that he might actually get paid for the work he'd done. He was shocked.

'Pays fair does Charlie,' PJ said, manoeuvring the van along the avenue. 'Never tries to beat me down. Gives what I ask and no complaint. There's not everyone would do a job for him, mind.' He drove through the gates without looking left or right. 'Suppose he's happy he got it done at all.'

'Why's that?' Tim asked.

PJ gave the gear stick a shove. The van shuddered, then jumped forward. 'Bit of a West Brit is Charlie, but sure that's hardly a crime. Have to take work where you can get it, that's what I say.'

'What's a . . . a . . .'

'West Brit? Well,' he wriggled himself up in his seat, squashing his curls against the roof – he was in a good mood having been paid, 'there's some round here would say it's a . . . it's a class of a traitor. You're Irish but you tip your hat to the Queen, think life across the water is better, that sort of thing.'

Tim nodded. 'Like Katty? She said she'd prefer Maggie Thatcher to be running the country.'

PJ let out a roar of laughter and the van swerved in towards the hedgerow, branches scraping noisily along the side. 'Did she now?' he said, shaking his head. 'That's a good one. Katty Hackett. That's a good one and no mistake!'

Tim liked that he'd said something PJ found funny. He liked it a lot. He was used to the journey now, familiar with the landscape. The miles seemed to roll by quicker than before, each one bringing them closer to food. His stomach was making loud grumblings. He could hear it even above the hum of the engine. He was trying to calculate the number of minutes left till they got home when PJ took a sudden turn at the sign for Faranboy. Tim groaned. What was he doing? Did PJ not realise he was almost dead from hunger? PJ drove all the way to the seafront, pulling up in a parking bay facing the strand. 'Can't be doing with all that standing over a stove tonight,' he said. 'Wait here.'

He bought their dinner at Angelo's Takeaway. Huge fillets of cod in greasy batter, and thick, lardy chips drenched in salt and vinegar. They sat in the van and ate. Tim had never tasted anything quite so delicious before.

'Do you like it here, Tim?' PJ asked after a while, wiping his fingers on his trousers.

The foamy waves rushed to the shore, one after the other, unfurling over the shingle. 'It's nice,' Tim said. 'Beach is a bit stony, though.'

'No. I mean here. Ireland. And Lissenmore. What do you make of it?'

Tim took another bite of his fish. 'It's good.'

PJ pulled a needle-thin bone from his mouth and flicked it out of the window. 'Would you say you'd like to live here?'

'Not sure. Never really thought about it.'

'Bit different to what you're used to, what?'

'More than a bit,' Tim said. 'A lot.'

'But we're not the worst, are we, Mags and me?'

This was the longest conversation Tim had had with his uncle. And the strangest. 'Of ... of course not,' he replied, more than a little uncomfortable at PJ's question.

'Look, I know things haven't been the best this past few days but, well, they'll work themselves out. When Mags comes back we're going to ...' He trailed off.

'Going to what?' Tim asked.

'We're going ... we're going to be grand. That's it. We're going to be grand.' He finished his food, screwed his damp paper wrapper into a ball and tossed it on the floor of the van. When Tim had eaten every last crumb of his own, he did the same.

Not long after they got back to the house, PJ fell asleep in an armchair. Tim turned on the TV but he didn't have the patience to stand twiddling the aerial to tune it so he turned it off again. If Mags had been there, she'd have kept Tim entertained, quizzing him about his day, asking all kinds of questions as she went about serving dinner. Without her, the house felt different, more full of shadow than light, with the space around things more obvious than the things themselves. The table, the lamp, the dresser – they looked strange just sitting there. Purposeless. Without Mags, they didn't make sense.

He considered doing some work on his project but he wasn't really in the mood. He deserved something sweeter after working a full week. He left PJ quietly snoring, his chin on his chest, his arms hanging limp over the sides of his chair, and headed out into the warm, late evening. The sky was still blue, with yellow-tinged clouds, like buttered popcorn, flowering up from the horizon ahead. A cloud of midges zigzagged about his head, dispersing when he waved a hand through them, gathering in front of his face again seconds later. The normally ragged ditches had been tidied, loose piles of newly cut grass and tangled weeds heaped beside the hedgerows. The smell reminded Tim of his back garden on summer evenings. Dad – crimson-faced and breathless – propelling his ancient hand mower over the lawn in neat, up-and-down stripes. The slice of metal through grass. The worry on Mum's face as he came dangerously close to her dahlias.

As he neared the pebble-dashed cottage, Scamp's frenzied barking broke the silence. Arriving at the gate, Tim saw it was the boys' latest exercise in torture that was causing it. The poor dog was tied to the post again. They were teasing him with a strip of uncooked bacon, dangling it tantalisingly just out of his reach and collapsing in devilish laughter each time he strained at his tether, his jaws snapping, his eyes rolling wildly.

'You shouldn't do that,' Tim called out to them. 'It's not a very good idea.'

Declan shouted back, 'Shut up, you. It's a great idea! Isn't it, lads?'

'The best!' Donal agreed, mesmerised. 'Look at his eyes! Raging, he is.' He bolted towards the cottage. 'I'm going in for another rasher!'

Maeve appeared at the door, one twin on her hip, the other by her feet. She straddled the width of the hall, blocking Donal's way. 'You're not going anywhere. Those rashers are for your tea, not for tormenting Scamp with.'

Donal tried to push past her. 'A sausage, then.'

'I said no! Now off you go. Go on.'

He skulked away, shoulders slumped. 'Fat cow,' he muttered.

'What did you say?'

'I said you're a fat cow,' he shouted. 'You won't let us have any fun. Wait'll Mammy gets back. I'm going to tell her you starved us.'

'Tell her what you want. I'm in charge whether you like it or not.'

'And that you beat us black and blue.'

'Well, you'd better give yourself some bruises or you'll have a hard time getting her to believe that one.'

He leaned against the cedar tree, sulking, gouging the earth with his heels.

'He'll be the death of me, that child,' Maeve said, as Tim walked over. She let the twin – Cormac? Ciaran? Tim couldn't tell one from the other – slide to the ground. They both toddled over to their brothers. 'Keep them well away,' she shouted. 'And would you ever stop teasing that poor animal!'

She looked worn out, but no less pretty. Her hair was scraped back in an untidy ponytail. She wore a frilled patchwork skirt to her ankles and a white T-shirt with lines of lace across the front. 'You were working with PJ, I believe?'

'Got paid for it too,' Tim said.

'Lovely. You can buy me a present so.'

'I . . . I . . . What would you like?'

'Ah, Tim, I'm only joking.' She smiled, showing her neat, pearly teeth. Then she stopped, her expression changing, growing darker. 'Do you believe the story about Mammy and Mags or what? Going up to Dublin together. All seemed a bit sudden to me.'

Tim nodded. 'It did seem strange. Just leaving me a note, not telling me herself.'

'A note? Weird. First I knew was when I saw the suitcase sitting in the hall.'

'PJ said Father Coffey gave them a lift.'

'He did. Well, he collected Mammy, and Mags was in the car, but sure he could've brought them anywhere. We've no proof they've gone to Dublin.'

'But Mags said she's going to the hospital. And that your mum's visiting an aunt.'

'Sure how do we know if that's the truth? Do you believe everything you're told?' She lowered her voice, though the boys would hardly have heard if she'd shouted, given the racket they were making. 'Look, I'm not sure but . . .' she leaned in to Tim '. . . Mammy took her good suit.'

Tim shrugged, not sure of the significance. 'What do you mean?'

'Why would she do that if she's only going up to see her auntie Gretta? She only wears that suit for serious stuff. When the headmaster calls her in to have a talk about the boys. Or for funerals.'

She waited for Tim to figure it out, watching his face intently.

All sorts of theories went through his head but none he wanted to put to her. He'd no idea what clothes Mags had taken with her, not being familiar with the contents of her wardrobe. He tried to brush it off. 'Maybe she'd nothing else clean. Or she wanted to impress Father Coffey. Or—'

'We're never done washing in this house! Mammy doesn't have much but she always has something clean. And as for impressing priests – she's no holy Joe. She might push me out the door every Sunday for mass right enough, but since Daddy left, she hasn't gone herself at all.' She looked anxiously at the boys again, biting at her right thumb, tearing off a crescent sliver of nail and spitting it onto the ground. 'It's something to do with Daddy being gone. It has to be. He must be in trouble.'

'The night of the disco. When I got home. I told you Father Coffey was there. And your mum.'

She nodded. 'Did you find out anything else?'

'I asked Mags. She said it was nothing to do with your dad.'

'Did you believe her?'

'Not really. And Mags and PJ have been acting weirdly

since then. Whispering and arguing and then not talking to each other. There's definitely something going on.'

'There you go,' Maeve said. 'I'd bet my life they're not where they're saying they are.'

'So where do you think they've gone?'

'To sort it out. Whatever it is that's wrong with Daddy. Mammy would need a friend, wouldn't she? She'd need someone with her if Daddy—'

At that moment, Donal came running round from the back of the house, galloping across the yard swinging a string of raw sausages like a lasso. 'Lads! Lads!' he yelled. 'One each! Come on! He's going to go mental!'

Maeve sighed. 'They're so much worse because Mammy's away.' Tim watched Donal trying to yank the sausages apart while the others looked on impatiently, Fintan and Declan dancing on the spot, the twins laughing and deliberately bumping into each other. Scamp had stopped barking, probably exhausted. He panted loudly, his long pink tongue lolling out over his teeth. Maeve turned to Tim despairingly. 'You wouldn't be able to keep an eye on them, would you? The twins need a bath.' Tim's face fell. She grinned. 'Just make sure they don't kill each other.' She scooped one twin up in her arms and the other scampered after her back to the house.

The sausages were separated now. The boys had laid them on the ground about a foot out of Scamp's reach and were gradually inching them closer, making bets as to which one he'd snatch first. Tim did exactly as Maeve had asked at first – kept an eye on them, hoping he had the courage to intervene should anything life-threatening occur. Declan, Fintan and Donal were unlike any boys he'd come across before. Though they were brats, they still possessed a certain innocence that made it almost impossible not to like them. 'You know what?' Tim said after a while, trying to sound casual. 'It's not nice to tease Scamp like that. You wouldn't like your sister to do that to you, would you? Leave your food just out of reach and laugh when you got mad.' He moved a little closer. 'He's just a poor dog. He's probably a bit sad, being tied up like that.' Cautiously, he reached out and hooked his fingers under Scamp's collar. 'Not too happy, are you, you poor fellow?' As he scratched the dog's skin, Tim felt him relax. Scamp sat back on his hind legs and stopped straining to get the sausages. 'Now. Look at that,' he said, when the animal lay down on the ground, whimpering softly. 'He likes the attention. See? You're a gentle thing, aren't you, old boy? Going crazy tied up all day.' Slowly, so slowly, Tim began to undo the rope attached to the leather collar, the boys standing perfectly still and quiet, waiting for what would happen next.

The second the rope slipped to the ground, Scamp took off like a rocket.

His feet barely touched the ground as he raced around the yard, circling the cedar tree time and time again, whirling about in a furry, fuzzy blur. The boys pointed at Tim, laughing their heads off. Tim tried to remain calm. 'Here, Scamp. Here, boy,' he called, whistling like they did on *One Man and His Dog*. But Scamp wasn't going to give in easily. He belted around the back of the cottage, hair flying, ears flat against his head. Tim ran to the other side, hoping to catch him when he came around the front, but he slipped on loose grit near the gable wall, sliding on his backside for a few feet to the utter delight of the boys. They could hardly contain themselves, though Tim didn't know then that they were laughing partly out of fear. They were far more familiar with Scamp than Tim was.

They could see what was coming.

'The gate!' Maeve had heard the commotion and was at the door, screaming. 'Get the gate! Quick!'

Declan and Donal raced to do as she said, struggling to lift and push the heavy metal gates. Tim got to his feet and tried to run, but a sharp pain shot up and down his leg and he could only stumble lamely towards them.

Fintan bravely tried to catch Scamp, zigzagging after him across the yard. He managed to grab hold of his tail but Scamp shook him off and, like a bullet blasting from a barrel, burst through the remaining gap in the gates just before the boys heaved them closed with a clang.

It was quick. Immediate.

Knowing that didn't make the fact of it any easier but Tim was glad the dog hadn't lingered, suffering, in pain. It would've given the boys some chink of hope they'd have clung to, then later lost. There was never any way he could've survived the impact. What were the odds that a trundling haulage truck was passing at the exact moment Scamp ran out? Since Tim had been in Lissenmore, he hadn't seen anything much bigger than PJ's Hiace on the road, except perhaps Wishy Crowe in his slow-moving tractor.

The boys saw it happen. That was the worst of it. By the time Tim got out to the road, the truck had disappeared, leaving Scamp lying in a horrible, floppy heap, blood trickling from his mouth. Donal's reaction was heartbreaking. He fell to his knees beside Scamp's body, lifting his head and trying to prise open his eyes.

'Wake up, Scamp! Wake up!' he wailed. 'You can have the sausages. All of them. Just wake up. Please!'

Declan and Fintan stood watching, heads bowed, hands in their pockets. They were old enough to know Scamp was gone. Declan glared at Tim. 'Look what you're after doing.'

'Why did you have to go and take his rope off?' Fintan cried. 'Why else do you think we had him tied up?'

Maeve was shouting for the boys from the front door. The twins stood either side of her, wrapped in striped bath towels, their hair plastered dark against their heads.

'You go inside,' Tim said to the boys. 'Go on. I'll look after Scamp. I'll bring him in.'

Declan's eyes were black slits, his mouth a snarl. 'Don't you dare touch him. Do what you like but you're not touching him, you hear?'

'Just . . . just wait here, then. I'll get your sister.'

Maeve ran out before Tim reached her. 'Mind those two,' she said gravely, barely looking at him as she passed.

Tim felt sick. Not just unwell, but sure he was going to throw up. He was lightheaded too, dizzy, as though his brain was spinning in his skull. He brought the twins inside and sat them on the couch. They fixed their eyes on him, their hair dripping, their cheeks blotched. Tim watched out of the window. It was a pathetic sight. Maeve, Declan and Fintan carried Scamp's limp body between them, the dog appearing bigger in death than he had when alive. It seemed impossible that the ball of energy that had streaked around the yard only minutes before was now just a droopy mass of flesh and bone. Donal followed, face gaunt and streaked with tears.

'Will I run and get Barry?' he said, his voice high and shrill. 'We could bring Scamp to the animal doctor.'

His sister and brothers laid the dog on the ground. Maeve

got down on her hunkers, her face level with Donal's and pulled the little boy close.

Tim gagged. Oh, God. What the hell had he done?

Maeve came inside the house, knelt in front of the twins and began towelling their hair, their bodies. She searched the pile of clothes on the table, found two pairs of mismatched pyjamas.

Tim pinched his arms as he spoke. 'Maeve, I'm . . . I'm so sorry. I—'

'I think it'd be best if you just went now.'

'But I . . . I mean . . .' What did he mean? He'd no idea what to say.

'I've a lot to do,' she said, gently helping the boys into their night clothes. 'It's the twins' bedtime. I have to read them a story.'

'I could do that, if you like. Let me help.'

She stood up and faced him. A smear of blood stained the front of her T-shirt. 'Just go home, Tim. I don't want you to do anything. You've done enough already.' She led the twins into their bedroom, half closing the door behind her.

Tim wanted so much to stay, to try to show her – to show all of them – how sorry he was. She was there, on her own, trying to hold things together and now he'd made everything a hundred times worse. He could hear her voice coming from the bedroom – so animated, so full of fun for the two little boys who didn't yet need to know what had happened. He was such an idiot. He'd ruined everything. He went to leave, turning back before he reached the door to cast the two twenty-pound notes PJ had given him onto the table. He didn't know what else he could do.

After we leave the Haven House we drive down to the strand. We sit in the car for a while, watching the dull silver spread of the sea and the unyielding curtain of rain that hangs over it.

'Maybe I should've mentioned that the boy stayed with Mam and Dad that summer,' I wonder out loud. 'If Barry knew that, he might've been more forthcoming.'

Luke sighs. 'Don't see what difference that would've made. If he really wanted to say something, he would have. Don't torture yourself over it.' He turns on the ignition. 'Now. Where's this place?'

Twenty minutes later, we're sailing up the tree-lined avenue to Castlefox Manor. Owned by the Fox family for generations, I first visited as a child on a school trip. The place had become a bit of a money pit and they'd opened it up to paying visitors to try to produce an income, but the venture wasn't exactly successful. Then old Charlie died and his son had sold it to the current owners. They've ploughed a fortune into it, turning it into the place it is today. Four stars.

Antiques-furnished rooms. Acres of woodland. Gourmet restaurant. There's a wedding reception in full swing when we arrive. Our room isn't in the main house, as I'd hoped, but in the converted stables round the back. Luke moans as we're led through a glazed walkway. 'Fucking fortune to sleep in an outhouse?' he whispers. His attitude changes when he sees the lace-draped four-poster, the glass and marble bathroom, the welcome bottle of wine. I pour us each a glass. 'I think Dad used to do work here on and off at one time. When the Foxes lived here, I mean.' I sit on the bed. 'Used to take anything that was going back then, Dad did. Sort of come full circle.'

'Everything's changed but everything stays the same. Isn't that it?'

I look into my glass. 'Something like that.'

'Not quite as bad now, is it, though?' He sweeps his arm out in a wide arc. 'I mean, look around. Thirty years ago I'm sure this kind of set-up was a rarity. Country house hotels are all over the place now.'

'Legacy of the boom.' I lean back into the pillows. 'Nice to think Dad had a hand in the upkeep of a place like this.'

Luke raises his glass. 'Here's to PJ Hyland. And to Curly Boy. If not for him we wouldn't be here at all.'

It's a strange truth. I put my glass on the bedside table, lie down and stare at the ceiling. 'I wonder did he do something bad. Or if something bad happened to him. I get this sense that . . . I don't know. There has to be a good reason, a good, solid reason, for all the secrecy. Only dark memories are kept hidden. No one buries the good ones.' Luke joins me on the bed. I curl into him and we fall asleep.

I wake first, the sound of roof-battering rain vying with the muffled beat of the wedding band. I reach to turn on the bedside lamp, but before I do, his image flashes before my eyes. Curly Boy. His awkward smile. His white-blond hair. I can't say why but tears sting my eyes as my fingers fumble for the switch. And for that split second, before the darkness gives way, I feel his presence, as though he's right there in the room beside me.

Over dinner, though we talk about other subjects, he's there all the time, hovering, like a sea bird over the waves. Luke tells me again about his asylum case. The decision he's been waiting for is coming up this week and the consequences of failure are playing on his mind. There's a very real possibility that the child involved could be sent, along with his mother, to live in a country where he's never even been. I listen as he sketches some of the details. 'He's as Irish as you or me. Born here, brought up here, going to school here. And *so* smart. Only six but speaks more Irish than I do!' He lowers his voice while the waiter takes our plates away. 'I don't know what'll become of him if they send them back. Probably never see his friends again. His school, his teacher. Everything he knows. Gone.' He runs his fingers through his hair. 'Can't imagine what that'd be like.'

I try to. Try to figure out how I'd feel if I were transported to a place I'd never been before. Strange sights and sounds. Unfamiliar smells. Food. People. Everything different. And I try to picture the little boy Luke is talking about. His face. His confusion. But the other boy keeps getting in the way. Then I hear Luke say, 'What's your take on the whole thing?' and I reply, 'I don't know. We'll just have to wait and see if I can find out any more information,' and I see him flop back in his chair, blank-faced. I lean forward, take his hand. 'I'm sorry. I thought you meant . . . Sorry.' I scan the room. White-clothed tables between murmuring couples, their faces softened by yellow candlelight; glittering crystal, the flash of silverware. I hold the painted eyes of a ringlet-haired girl in royal blue, who stares at me sorrowfully from the gilded frame that surrounds her. 'It's not that I'm not listening. I am. It's just . . . I mean . . . Jesus, Luke, there's more important things to be thinking of, isn't there? Like that little boy in your case. Maybe I should just forget about this. I might never find out the full story. What'll all this become then?' I squeeze his fingers and bring my face back round to his. 'A big waste of time, that's what.'

He grips my hand in both of his. 'But not all this. You and me. Together. I won't ever consider this a waste of time.'

Later that night, in the four-poster's gauzy tomb, though his touch should bring me round, I'm locked in the darkest place. I float, round and round, turning, slithering. His hands are like hands I've never felt before – some kind of alien skin that means nothing to me. I know I'm safe there with him. I have no doubt of our feelings. But something bigger waits out there. Something beyond myself. Beyond Mam. Or Dad. It controls us all from afar. Not in an unkind way, but in a way that scares me all the same. It scares Mam too. I know. It pokes and prods and kicks at her. Pushes and forces and tries to burst out. I don't have any clue what it is, there, as Luke's breath rushes in my ear and his chest presses into my own. But after, in the deepest part of the night, my fingers slide down the side of the bed and into my bag. Feeling, feeling, finding. By the light of my phone, I study myself. The neat, rounded swell that I was. Hidden. But not quite. Her hand held against me, protective, caring. Her arm around him, loving and warm. I can't forget about it. The answers are all there. It's clearer to me now than before. Clearer, but no less indistinct.

In the morning, I'm already awake when Luke opens his eyes. He squints against the brilliant strip of sunlight that bursts through the crack in the curtains. His voice is throaty and dry, carrying with it the remnants of sleep. 'You've forgotten something,' he says, half into his pillow. 'Or we have. Don't know why I didn't think of it before.' He reaches out and touches the tip of my nose. 'And you pride yourself on being thorough, Miss Hyland.'

I screw my face up, puzzled. 'Go on.'

'Well . . . just occurred to me. Have you never been curious about . . .' he pushes himself up on his elbow, resting his chin in his palm '. . . who it was that took the photo?'

When he says it, it seems ridiculous that I haven't thought about it before. I've considered the photo for the image itself and what it might mean. I've never once contemplated the person behind the camera.

Luke yawns. 'Probably not significant at all. Could've been anyone. Not sure knowing who it was would help.'

I slip out of bed, wrap myself in a white robe and pull open the curtains. 'I'm not sure either.' A tiny bird pecks about on the courtyard. 'But it's all about digging, isn't it? Digging and scratching till you find what you're looking for.'

'And a lucky break. Sometimes that's all it takes.'

Poor little bird, I think. You won't find anything to eat there. But then he proves me wrong. He has plenty. The cobbled ground is littered with worms. Countless twisted bodies washed out of their holes by the previous day's rain.

After breakfast, we wander the ordered paths of the formal garden, but the air is cold and damp and we go back inside to the warmth of the oak-panelled library. I flick through a glossy interiors magazine. 'So . . . we're still calling in on my parents, then?'

'You're asking me?' Luke answers. 'Do I need to give my permission?'

'Just making sure you still want to.' I'm anxious about facing Dad, unsure I'll be able to contain my annoyance at the way he's being so bull-headed about the photo.

'Well, you told them we would, didn't you? Can't let them down now. I'm up for it if you are. Best get going soon enough, I suppose.'

Up for it. He makes it sound like a dare. I text Mam and tell her we'll be there in an hour.

While I take care of checking out, Luke wanders about the huge, vaulted hall, inspecting the massive portraits hanging on the walls: bewigged, powder-faced gentlemen in frilly costumes; soldiers in shining armour astride huge, wild-eyed horses. I hear his footsteps click-clack on the stone floor as the guy behind the desk – 'Reservations Manager', according to his badge – taps on the computer and waits for a printout. Probably in his early thirties, balding, and with a neatly trimmed goatee, he surveys the page and asks if we've enjoyed our stay. In a distinct Australian accent, he remarks on the change in the weather and enquires if we have far to travel home. I mention I have family to visit in Lissenmore.

He frowns. 'No way. Used to live there myself, once upon a time.'

'Really? Would I know you? I grew up there.'

'Ah, you wouldn't remember me. You're too young. I was only a kid when we went to Oz. Mooney's the name. Donal Mooney.'

'Mooney. Then I think we might've been neighbours. I'm fairly sure the family who lived down the road from us was called Mooney. I'm Orla Hyland. Would you remember us? My parents? Mags and PJ?' I'm already thinking of showing him the photo.

He shakes his head. 'Don't remember hardly anything from that time at all.'

'Maybe this might jog your memory.' I whip the print from my bag. 'Just came across it the other day. Hilarious, really. The state of my parents! I mean, I know it was the eighties and all but . . .' My attempt to appear casual is failing. I'm babbling, sounding manic. 'And that's me there,' I say, pointing. 'My mother, she was pregnant with me that summer. I was born not long after.' I'm offering far too much detail. But I want to work my way round to asking if he recognises the boy. He seems spellbound for a moment, staring at the image with his solemn green eyes.

'Christ,' he says, under his breath. 'Scamp.'

'Sorry?'

'Just seeing that boy . . .' he frowns '. . . his face, it brought it all back.' He looks up at me. 'Killed our dog, he did. That's it. I remember. Must've been buried in my head all these years and now it's just come flooding back. Incredible the way it happens like that.'

I glance around, suddenly self-conscious. Luke sits in a high-backed wooden chair near the main door, leafing through the visitors' book. A couple pulling wheeled suitcases enter the hall and approach the desk, waiting to check in. I don't have much time: Donal is on duty and under the watchful eye of an officious, smart-suited madam. She stands on the bottom step of the stairs, her steely glare saying 'General Manager' more loudly than if she screamed it.

'Killed your dog?' I keep my voice down.

'Scamp. Don't know how it happened. Can't remember. I mean, might've been an accident, but ...' He laughs. 'No idea who he is, mind. It's just his face, his hair. I think I'd nightmares for years after.'

Madam appears behind the desk, rictus smile stretched across her overly made-up face. 'Everything all right here, Donal?'

'Such a coincidence,' I say hurriedly. 'Neighbours from many years ago.'

'Isn't that nice?' she says. 'Reminiscing.'

'Well, give your parents my regards,' Donal says, making it plain he has to finish up. 'Must take a trip to Lissenmore some time. Only been back in the country a few months.'

'Was there some problem?' Luke asks, as we leave. 'Don't tell me my card wouldn't work. I'll fix up if you had to use yours. I—'

'I'll fill you in in the car.'

'"He killed our dog." That's definitely what he said? You didn't, you know, misunderstand him?' Luke continually glances to his left as he drives, trying to catch my face.

'You make me nervous when you do that. Keep your eyes

on the road.' I rub my hands together against the cold. 'And, yes, that's definitely what he said.'

'But he doesn't know who Curly Boy is?'

'Said he had no idea.'

'And you didn't push him on it? See if he could recall anything else?'

'I didn't want to come across as a complete nut job. I'd already humiliated myself by actually producing the picture. And then there was that witch woman breathing down his neck.'

'You could always give him a call, ask to talk further?'

'There wouldn't be any point. I think it was fairly plain he didn't know who the boy was. He was probably only four or five then – I doubt he's going to remember. He'd blocked out the whole episode. It was clear he was genuine.'

'Well, maybe someone else in his family might remember.'

'Maybe they will, maybe they won't. Who knows?'

'You've changed your tune.'

'I just felt stupid, that's all. I should be able to ask my parents who he is. And anyone with half a brain will wonder why I didn't think of that. And what am I supposed to say?'

'OK, I get you. It's a weird one, all right.'

'And I'm nervous about introducing you, if I'm honest.'

'I'll be my usual charming self. It'll be grand.'

I stay silent till we're almost at the house. Then I announce we should bring something.

Luke laughs. 'A sweetener. Sure.'

'Drive on to the village. I'll run into Spar.'

As we fly past the house, I look to the right. Same as the day before – the chimney smoking, the jeep round the side. But this time Mam's like a statue at the window, arms crossed, a look of longing on her face. I don't tell Luke that I've seen her.

The shop is busy. Men with stacks of Sunday papers, kids with crisps and bottles of fizzy drink, women checking last night's winning lottery numbers. I grab a bunch of pink tulips and a 'homemade' rhubarb tart and join the long queue.

'There's that scary old woman again,' Luke says, when I hop back into the car. It's Katty, hobbling down the path beside us. 'Get out there and show her the picture. Go on. Might be your last chance. She could drop dead any minute.'

'Don't be so mean.'

'It's only a joke.' He gives me a gentle push. 'Go on.'

'We're late as it is. And I don't know what use it'd be. I told you, she rarely makes sense these days.'

'No harm in trying.'

'If Mam and Dad find out what I've been doing there'll be war.'

'Don't see how they could. Barry Kilbride's hardly going to mention it to anyone. It looked like he didn't want anything to do with it. And that Mooney guy? Why would he bother?'

'OK. Just warning you, I may be some time.'

As it turns out, Katty doesn't keep me long. She has on what she terms her 'special' coat – a heather-coloured woolly thing – and is worried it might rain. The coat, she assures me, will be 'fit for the bin' if it gets wet. Fidgety and nervous, she looks at the sky, anxious to be 'in out of it' in case the unthinkable should occur. I want to work my way slowly up to producing the photo but, seeing her agitation, I just go for it. She clasps it in her gnarled fingers, holding it barely two inches from her face.

'What do you think of that?' I ask. 'Do you recognise anyone there?'

'PJ Hyland,' she crows. 'Great handyman. Best worker.' Her head twitches as she tries to focus in on the detail.

'And the boy? Would you remember him?'

She pulls the image even closer, smiling a little, her mouth more full of gaps than teeth. 'Yes. Yes. The hair on him!' Warily, she looks at me, her milky eyes narrowing. 'Never saw him after that.' Then, shaky and anxious, she mutters again about the rain and, pushing the photo back at me, scurries away. I follow her for a few feet, until, sensing I'm behind, she turns and snaps at me. 'Mags Hyland. Her sister's boy that was. Her sister's boy.'

Tim went straight up to bed when he came back from Maeve's, tiptoeing past PJ who was still out for the count in the armchair. He lay awake for ages, consumed with guilt and dreading the prospect of having to explain what had happened. Next morning, he pretended he was still asleep when PJ shouted up the stairs that he was off to Kavanagh's for a few things. When he arrived back, he came up to Tim's room and poked his head round the door. The news had obviously travelled. 'You were in Mooneys' last night?' Tim said nothing. 'Could've told you no good would come of being down there. Wouldn't worry too much about it,' he said, after a pause. 'That hound's had it coming this long time.'

Tim struggled through the day. He kept seeing Donal's pathetic little face in his head, no matter how hard he tried to make it disappear. And every time he heard a car out on the road, he froze, expecting it might be Barry coming to give him a piece of his mind. He was going to love all this. No doubt he was down with Maeve, comforting her after the terrible thing Tim had done.

After lunch, he helped PJ with a long-overdue van clear-out, which, thankfully, passed the afternoon and much of the evening. For their dinner that evening, PJ fried eggs and onions, filling the kitchen with clouds of pungent smoke. Though Tim had thought he was hungry, he managed only a few mouthfuls. PJ read the newspaper while he wolfed the leftovers, along with a tower of buttered bread and a mug of milky tea. 'Mags won't be home till late,' he announced, from behind his paper. 'Don't be thinking you have to be staying up till she comes in.' Tim was grateful for this. He didn't feel awkward escaping to his room.

He had the sea dream when he eventually fell asleep. The one he'd had on the ferry over. But this time, no matter how he thrashed and strained through the waves, he felt something holding him back. He tried, as the ship, to push himself through the deep, and he tried, as the sea, to assist. And he could see his ship-self from up above. A bird's-eye view. A vast turquoise expanse. And cutting across it, taut and scarlet, a line that tied him to the land.

Mags was back. She hugged Tim tightly when he came down for breakfast next morning. 'Oh, I'll be grand,' she said, all bright and breezy, when he asked how she'd got on, if she was all right. 'Nothing to worry about.' She clattered plates out on the table. 'PJ told me what happened. Don't be worrying about it. It's not your fault.' She said it as if it didn't really mean anything. But then, Tim supposed, a dog's death would hardly figure if you had a human being growing inside you and all the responsibility and worry that brings. And, if she really had been in hospital, perhaps there were things, medical things, that were preying on her mind.

There was no mention of mass. Tim was glad. He'd already made up his mind to pretend to feel ill if there was. There was no way he could've faced Maeve or Barry or any of the boys. The way things had gone, Maeve might not want anything more to do with him. He might never see her again. He was thankful he'd already taken some pictures of her. He needed to keep them safe. He went up to his room after breakfast and took his camera out of the drawer. The frame counter read '21'. Only three left till the end of the roll. He went to the window, leaned out and took three shots of the view. Then he wound on to the click, removed the finished film and placed it carefully in the drawer. Whatever happened, Maeve was safe in there now. He'd have the roll developed once he got home. He was sure the wait would be worth it.

He went back downstairs to find Mags had fallen asleep on the couch. Through the open back door, he saw PJ sitting out in the sun reading the Sunday papers. He slouched at the table and laid his head on his arms, trying not to think of Scamp lying dead on the side of the road. Nothing he'd ever done had made him feel so bad. He was utterly miserable.

'Tim.'

Mags had called his name. Tim. Not questioning, like she wanted him, but matter-of-fact, as if she was answering someone who'd asked who he was.

He went over and gently shook her shoulder. 'Mags. I'm here. Are you OK?' But she was fast asleep. He could tell from the depth of her breathing. Maybe she'd been dreaming about him. Maybe that's why she'd called out his name.

He took the plaid blanket she kept folded on the back of

the couch, opened it out and draped it over her, its tasselled edges skirting the floor. He looked at her again and a shiver zipped up and down his spine. Just for a fleeting moment, Mags looked so much more like Mum than she had before.

That night, in bed, in the nameless void you fall through before you hit the soft ground of sleep, the sound floated round his head again.

Tim. The way he'd heard it earlier that day.

He fought against it, tried as best he could to focus on what he'd thought was so clear. But the doubt was like a microscopic worm, burrowing its way under his skin.

He couldn't be truly sure if it was Mags he'd heard calling his name.

He woke next morning with a sense that things had come to an end. He couldn't see any reason why he should stay on. How could he face the Mooneys again? He'd have to spend the time he had left holed up in the house, trying to avoid them, and what would be the logic in that? Everything was ruined. He waited till PJ left for work, then broke the news to Mags.

'I want to go home.'

She put down the basket of washing she was about to bring outside, leaning into it heavily, then looking up into his face. 'Home?' Her eyebrows moved in to meet each other. 'You can't. I mean . . . Not now. Not . . . this early.'

'It doesn't really make any difference when I go. It's not the way it was planned, I know, but—'

'I don't know if it's possible . . . if we can . . . PJ'd have to . . . And the ferries. They're always mad busy in August. People going over and back. You'd have to—'

'I'm sure it'll be fine. Don't worry about me.'

'But no one'd know. When you get to the other side, there'd be no one there to—'

'I've thought about that. I'll walk down to the phone box and call home. I was thinking of leaving on Wednesday. Do you think that'd be OK?'

She'd taken a frilled pillowcase from the basket and was twisting a corner of it round and round the fingers of her left hand, like a bandage. 'Wednesday? The day after tomorrow? PJ's away off in Carlow that day. I'm sure of it. I don't know that he'd—'

'I can always get the train. I wouldn't mind.'

She pulled a chair out and sat down, her breaths becoming deeper, more laboured. 'How about we leave it a few days? What would you say to that? I know you're – you're upset and all about what happened but it's not the end of the world, love. Is it?'

Tim picked at the hem of his T-shirt. He thought he was being reasonable asking to go on Wednesday. If he'd had his way, he'd have gone that very minute. Only a few days ago, the idea that he might never see Maeve again would've been unthinkable. Now it made him feel lightheaded with relief. 'It's not anything to do with you, Mags. I mean, I've really enjoyed being here. But, well, I was always going to have to go home. It doesn't make much difference if I leave a bit earlier.'

And then, as if things couldn't get any worse, Mags's eyes filled with tears. She tried hard to blink them away, but she couldn't stop them falling and she used the pillowcase to wipe them away from her cheeks. 'I'm sorry,' she said. 'Don't mind me. I'm all over the place at the moment.' She rubbed her stomach to indicate she meant because of the baby, then took Tim's hand, kneading his palm hard, over and over. 'It's just . . . well . . . I'd miss you. It's like you've . . . you've been here for ever. I can't remember what it was like before you came, hardly.'

She kept talking, squeezing Tim's hand, telling him the same thing in different words. He felt so awful watching her cry that he found himself saying he'd think about it. Yet, deep down, he was sure he wanted to go. 'I think I'll still phone my mother this morning, though, if that's all right.'

'Of course. If . . . if that's what you want.' She eased herself up from the table. 'Now. Give me a hand to peg these out, there's a good boy.' She winked and gave him a weak smile. 'Might as well get full use out of you.'

In the yard, they stood on opposite sides of the washing line. Tim flung a sheet over the top and together they stretched it out to its full width. It fell, unmoving, a sheer wall that screened them from each other, though they were only inches apart. Tim could see Mags's fingers at the top, clipping the pegs in place, and her slippered feet below, shuffling over and back across the ground.

'Mags,' he said, his heart hammering crazily, like a train gathering speed over tracks. 'Were you really up in Dublin? In the hospital?'

Her feet stopped moving. 'Ah, now, what're you talking about? Sure where else would I have been?'

'I . . . I'm not sure, but . . . Maeve said—'

'Don't be minding whatever she said. I told you, wild imagination she has.'

'She thinks – well, we both think – maybe something happened to her dad. All that stuff when I came back from the disco that night, Father Coffey being here and everything. I know you said it was nothing but I can't, I mean, we can't help thinking . . . And Tess took her good suit. And Maeve said she only wears it for, you know, funerals and things and . . .' He had to do his best to find out. He didn't want to go home not knowing the truth. 'Are you sure it wasn't anything to do with Lar? You would tell me if it was? Maeve should know if there's anything wrong.'

Slowly, Mags pulled the sheet back and looked him straight in the eye. 'I know how much you like her, Tim. But don't think you have to be solving all her problems. All that stuff with Lar, it's . . . not for you to be worrying about. You hear me?'

'I just thought . . . if you knew anything, if . . .'

'Just leave it to them. It's none of our business.'

'But you gave Tess money! I saw it. Wrapped up with the bread.' Her cheeks flushed and she tried hard to stare Tim out while she thought of what to say. 'And you didn't want PJ to see, did you? You didn't want him to know.'

Air rushed in and out through her nose and her chest heaved. 'There's no secrets between me and PJ. And anything I do for Tess, I do because she deserves it. Six kids and no job for Lar to go to and . . . well, you know what happened then. 'Tis no one's fault the way things turned out. Country's in a state, so 'tis. People losing their jobs all over the place.' She snapped the last few pegs to the sheet. 'We do things to help people out, Tim. Sometimes there's no other explanation than that.'

There was a flatness in her tone he hadn't heard before. She'd spoken to him as if he were an adult and he couldn't decide if he liked it or not. She lifted the empty basket and Tim followed her inside. In the kitchen, she was silent as she filled the sink with water and washing-up liquid. He watched her scrub each bowl and plate vigorously with a dishcloth, her movements jerky and mechanical. He stood beside the dresser, running his fingers over the painted grain of the wood. 'I'm going down to phone home now. Do you need anything in the shop?'

She didn't turn around. Just spoke to the window in front of her. 'We're fine for everything,' she said, her voice croaky. 'I'll see you when you get back.'

Before Tim left, he loaded his camera with his second roll of film and slipped it into his pocket. He wanted to take a few more snaps before he left. Not for himself – he certainly didn't need to be reminded of the place – but for Mum and Dad. They'd been good enough to buy him the film and would be looking forward to seeing all the photos of his holiday. He didn't want to disappoint them.

He was dreading having to walk by Mooneys'. He even thought about hitching a lift down to the village but not one vehicle passed him in the time it took to reach the pebble-dashed cottage. He could hear the boys' voices – Declan in charge, shouting orders to Fintan and Donal – and, ducking tight against the hedgerow to keep himself hidden, he could just about see into the yard through the tangle of hawthorn and ivy. Scamp's rope was still tied to the tree, the end of it knotted to Donal's wrist. He ran around the trunk of the cedar, 'barking', while Declan encouraged Fintan to whip him with lengths of white plastic tubing. It would've been funny if it wasn't so sad. And to make it even worse, there, at the base of the tree, was a mound of earth topped with a wooden cross made from a pair of crooked twigs. He had to turn away when he saw that. As he crept along the ditch, managing to dash across the opening to the yard without the boys noticing, he saw the front door was open but, thankfully, there was no sign of Maeve or Tess.

He walked quickly, keeping his head down as he passed through the village. In the playing fields, some boys were practising hurling, the sound of wood on leather like cracks of gunfire. He stopped briefly at the gate, took out his camera, and grabbed a shot of them. Dad would be interested. Then, something for Mum – a bank of wildflowers with a soft ridge of rolling purple mountains in the distance.

Sinéad Kavanagh and a giggly, corkscrew-haired friend were in the phone box when he arrived, both trying to speak into the receiver at the same time. He sat down on the grass verge to wait, sighing when they started making googly eyes and blowing kisses through the door's dirty glass panes. When eventually they fell out of the box, Sinéad tried to start up a conversation with him but Tim shouldered open the door and escaped inside. As he counted out his change, they waved in at him and, for a few awful seconds, he thought they were going to hang around. The last thing he wanted was to be stuck with them all the way back to the village. Then, surprise-surprise, Barry drove past and they flagged him down. Tim turned his face away, though he knew there was little point. Even if Barry hadn't seen him, Sinéad was sure to let him know Tim was there.

The phone box smelt of wee. Why that should be was a mystery – there were open fields for miles around if anyone was caught short. Tim inserted the correct change and dialled the number, remembering the country code from the hours he'd spent studying the telephone book to find silly names. He heard the phone ring. And ring. What would Mum be doing? She might be changing sheets. Or getting the dinner ready. Or maybe she was at the dining-room table, surrounded by a tower of files. Mum did the accounts for a few local businesses. It was what she'd worked at when she'd first met Dad. Tim waited. And waited. Maybe she'd nipped out to the shops. Or was chatting to old Mrs Ball who lived down the road. Dad was surely there. But perhaps he'd hobbled out to the garden and couldn't hear the phone. Eventually, it rang out. Tim pictured Mum coming back into the house from wherever, not knowing he'd been trying to call. Not knowing he wanted to go home.

Walking back, he wasn't surprised when he saw Barry's car driving towards him. He performed one of his show-off U-turns and pulled up beside Tim, radio thumping, arm leaning casually on the open window. 'Hope you know them boys is destroyed after what you done. Destroyed.' Tim continued walking, faster now. Barry rolled along, not caring that he was on the wrong side of the road. 'Fucken hate you now, so they do.' Tim fixed his focus on the sky, trying to put names to the gathering cloud shapes – a giraffe, a teapot, a dancing bear. Barry raised his voice. 'Listening to me, are you? I'm fucken talking to you. Enjoy murdering dogs, yeah?'

No, not a dancing bear. An alligator. Or perhaps a crocodile. Was there a difference? Alligators live in fresh water, crocodiles can tolerate seawater. Tim had read that somewhere. And their snouts . . . something about the shape of their snouts. One was more rounded, the other more pointed. Which was which? He tried hard to remember, all the while walking, walking. Up ahead, he could see the playing fields, could hear the thwacks like exploding fireworks. *Pop*

pop pop. Barry slowed to a stop. Tim overtook the car, feet slap-slapping, shins aching.

'Go back where you came from, you hear me?' Barry shouted after him. 'We don't want your kind round here.' Tim heard the car door open and slam, then footsteps.

Alligator crocodile SHOVE alligator crocodile SLAM alligator . . . DUNT.

Tim reeled sideways and smashed onto the ground, hands breaking his fall, palms scraping across the loose gravel, camera sliding out of his pocket and skittering across the ground.

Barry leered down at him. 'Don't want to see your ugly fucken English face round here any more.' He stamped his foot down hard on the camera. Crunch. 'And another thing.' He rooted in his jeans pocket. 'No one wants your money. You can't buy your way out of it.' He kicked Tim's foot. 'Dirty it is anyway, coming from the likes of Charlie fucken Fox.' As he walked away, the money Tim had given Maeve floated to the ground. Then he was gone, engine roaring, the notes fluttering about in his wake, like leaves.

Tim rolled onto his back, then sat up in the middle of the road to inspect his hands. Sharp beads of stone had gouged into the fleshy parts under his thumb. The left was worst: a mangled pulpy mess glistening with black grit. It hurt. His foot hurt too. He reached for his camera. The plastic casing had caved in, the lens was cracked. He wouldn't be using it again. He looked at the two twenty-pound notes on the ground. It probably hadn't been the wisest move, leaving them for Maeve. What had he been thinking? She didn't want his money. Scamp couldn't be replaced with cash. Though they felt worthless now – just scraps of crumpled paper – he picked them up and shoved them into his pocket along with the busted camera.

Fuck you, Barry Kilbride. Fuck you and everyone else in this place.

He was going. He didn't care. He'd pretend to Mags that he'd spoken to Mum. It's all arranged, he'd tell her. Dad's meeting me from the boat on Wednesday. Yes, the afternoon sailing. And he'd walk to it if he had to. Nothing would stop him from going home. Of course, Barry's car was parked in Mooneys' yard on the way back. Tim didn't bother this time trying to hide himself, just strolled on by as though he didn't have a care. If any of the boys noticed, they didn't react. He planned to pass that pebble-dashed cottage only one more time – on his way out of Lissenmore. For ever.

Mags was watching out for him at the gate. He spied her from a way back, could see the slash of bright yellow – her pinafore dress – against the dark green of the fir tree. Once she saw Tim coming, she waved, then headed back into the yard. He made sure his camera was stuffed deep into his pocket: he didn't want her noticing it was broken. As he came around the side of the house, she was at the washing line, checking if anything was dry. She smiled. A nervous smile, Tim thought. 'How'd you get on?'

'It's all arranged. Dad's meeting me at Holyhead on Wednesday evening.'

A sound escaped her mouth. Not one Tim could easily describe. He went inside and she followed. She stood in the doorway, her body a dark, featureless shape, back-lit by the brightness of the day. She nodded at the kitchen table. 'Look . . . look what came for you.'

It was a postcard, leaning against the teapot, written side facing outwards.

Dear Tim,

Greetings from Cornwall. Just letting you know we've arrived in St Ives. Hope you're enjoying yourself.

Love, Mum and Dad

Tim stared hard at it. *We've arrived in St Ives?* Just like that? Why hadn't she written to him before they left, to tell him they were going?

'They're away on holidays,' Mags said quietly. 'You didn't talk to her at all, did you?'

Tim couldn't bring himself to raise his head. He bit his bottom lip, clicking his thumbnail on a corner of the postcard. He looked at the postmark, tried to make out the date. When had it been sent? How was he supposed to know how long they were staying?

Mags came over, put her arm around his shoulders. 'Listen, we'll say no more about it, how does that sound?' She lifted his chin. 'So now. You'll have to be staying here a while longer, by the looks of it.' Her face brightened. 'That's not so bad, is it? Aren't you enjoying yourself all the same? I know there was all that hullabaloo with Scamp but sure that's hardly the end of the world.'

Tim breathed deep, hard breaths. His hands stung. 'But . . . but how do I know how long they'll be gone? There's no date. I can't even see a postmark.'

Mags's head shook a little and her arm tightened around him. 'We'll find all that out after.'

'Why didn't she write and tell me they were going? It's ages since I sent my last letter. At least ten days.'

Mags took the postcard and stared at it for a long, charged

moment. It wasn't the usual holiday scene – a beach or a harbour, sunset over the bay – instead it showed a sketch of a cute, apple-cheeked boy in a sailor suit, with huge dark eyes and a head of fat curls. 'Looks a bit like you,' she said, her voice thin and whispery.

Tim thought about what it said. *Greetings from Cornwall* . . . It looked like it'd been written in a hurry. But, then, it was just a quick note to let him know. Mum was sure to send more details later, once they got settled in. But Cornwall? That meant they'd be gone for ages. It was too long a drive to go for just a short time. The post took two or three days to get to Ireland. They'd probably arrived last Friday or Saturday. He was stuck in Lissenmore. For another week at the very least. It was almost too much to bear.

Mags uncurled her arm from his shoulders. 'What about a bit of lunch? I could do you a cheese sandwich? Or ham and tomato? How would you like that?' She was delighted. That was obvious. It should've made Tim happy that she was so eager to have him stay longer. But all he could think about were the reasons he wanted to go. 'Now,' she said, taking the postcard from Tim's hands, 'why don't you go and get that school project of yours? It'll keep you busy while I make your lunch.' Then she gasped. 'Lord almighty! Where did that come from?' The postcard was smudged with blood. She stood back and looked Tim up and down. He tried to hide his palms but she'd already spotted them. 'What in God's name happened you? Why didn't you say something?' She took his hands in hers.

'I . . . I just fell over. I'll be fine.'

'No, you will not be fine. Sit down there till I have a look.'

She pressed him firmly into a chair and went bustling

about, gathering together a bowl of warm water, some tweezers, a roll of cotton wool, plasters. 'Not sure if I'm going to be much use here,' she said, splaying Tim's fingers. 'Some bits look deep enough. How on earth . . . ?'

'I tripped. Over a rock. I wasn't looking.'

She arched her eyebrows. 'Daydreaming, more like.'

He winced as she immersed his hand in the water. 'I'm sorry I lied.'

Her mouth curled into a smile. ''Twouldn't be the first one ever told, no more than it'll be the last. Now, you sit back. This is going to hurt.'

He felt stupid. Weak. Barry Kilbride. He should've been able to stand up to him. Should've got to his feet and pushed him back. He pictured himself punching him hard, drawing blood, knocking some of his teeth out.

He'd thought he'd seen the last of him but now . . .

His insides twisted into a knot when he thought about it. Mum and Dad deserved a holiday too, he supposed. But . . .

Mags lifted his hand from the water, patting it dry with a clean towel. The cold metal pinched his skin and she was right: it hurt. 'But, Mags,' he managed to blurt against the pain, 'Dad's ankle. How could they have gone? He wouldn't be out of the plaster yet.'

The tweezers went in deep. Tim flinched and yanked back his hand. Mags grabbed it and pressed his knuckles down flat against the table. 'Your mammy must've done the driving.'

'All the way to Cornwall? Mum *hates* driving. She'd never manage such a long journey.'

Mags leaned in closer, her eyes steady. 'Well, then, maybe your daddy got his plaster cast off earlier than he thought he would. That happens sometimes.' She focused hard, like she was enjoying the whole operation, and tweezed out a big lump of grit. Tim closed his eyes, trying to concentrate on anything but the pain – the radio chattering in the kitchen, the spicy-sweet scent of the apple tart baking in the oven. It made him woozy, off-balance a little, as though the world was spinning too fast. If Dad had got his cast off, why hadn't Mum come over to Ireland, like she'd been going to? Why did they have to go to bloody Cornwall again? Mum and Dad never went away without weeks of planning. Tim wasn't sure what exactly, but something about it didn't seem right.

I needn't have worried too much about introducing Luke to Mam. I can tell she's a bit edgy and her eyes flit about a lot, but she's smiling, which is always a good thing. Dad is another story. It's clear there's a tension between us. Though he welcomes Luke warmly, there's a definite chill to the greeting I receive. Luke notices and squeezes my hand before we sit down. Easy conversationalist that he is, he glances at the headlines on Dad's Sunday paper and starts chatting about the government.

'Shower of messers,' Dad says. 'Have us all on our knees, so they do. Couldn't lead a band, never mind a country. It's an election that's needed. Kick that lot out and bring a new crowd in.'

'All the same, they are,' Mam says, heading over to the kitchen. 'Doesn't matter who's in or who's out. Nothing ever changes.'

'There's an element of that right enough,' Dad adds. 'Promise you the sun, moon and stars when they're looking for your vote. Wouldn't see hide nor hair of them any other time. 'Twould make you wonder about voting at all.'

'If you don't vote,' Luke says, 'you can't really complain about them, can you?'

Dad laughs. 'Suppose you're right there. Though I'll have a quare time figuring out who to go for next time round.'

'What about Barry Kilbride, Dad?' I suggest, catching Luke's eye as I do. 'He's planning to stand, isn't he? And he's an independent. Not allied to any party.'

'Kilbride?' He frowns, wriggling in his seat. 'Don't know that he'd be up to much.'

I decide to push it a little. 'But sure isn't he always doing stuff round about? Do you not think it'd be good to have a local man up in the Dáil?'

'Local he may be but that doesn't mean I've to put a tick beside his name on the ballot paper.'

'What did he ever do to you, Dad?' I ask, trying to inject some humour into my voice. 'You've never been that fond of him.'

He looks me square in the face. ''Tis not anything important, Orla. Nothing you need be concerned about.' He glances at his watch. 'You all right in there, Mags?' he calls out. 'Need any help?'

''Tis ready now,' Mam replies. 'Sit yourselves in.'

Dad jumps up. Luke raises his eyebrows. We both know my question was deliberately avoided.

Over lunch, Mam quizzes Luke about the Bar exam. What are his plans once it's over? Does he think he'd like to live in America? What if he fails? What if I fail and he passes? Luke says all the right things. 'Oh, I'd like to think we're taking a positive view, Mrs Hyland. Neither of us intends to fail.

And I've spent several summers in the States. I'd love the opportunity to live there on a more permanent basis.'

They chat about it further, Dad joining in but keeping it on a superficial level, not probing too deeply. I listen, though I'm thinking only about Katty and what she said. She'd recognised Mam and Dad in the photo, hadn't appeared confused or muddled about that. But then ... *Her sister's boy*. She was mixing him up with someone else. She had to be. Or thinking Mam was someone she wasn't ...

Before Mam serves the rhubarb tart, I run upstairs to the bathroom and afterwards, I don't know why, I creep along the landing into the spare room. I've always felt this room belongs to another time. Over the years, Dad has made several attempts to redecorate it but Mam always resists, saying it's fine the way it is and it'd be a waste of money since it's hardly ever used. I wanted to move into it when I was about thirteen. She wouldn't let me. 'Too cold,' she said. 'Draughty. Your own is much cosier.' And it was. It had been full of junk till I was all of three and Mam finally agreed it was time for me to move out of theirs. Though the spare is bigger, it's at the other end of the landing, and she wanted me in the room beside theirs.

But he would've slept here.

The boy.

If he stayed that summer, like Dad said, then this must have been his room. Is that why it remains stuck in a time warp? Is he – and whatever happened to him – the reason Mam wants it left as it is? Untouched. Preserved. Is it the same reason I've often found her in here, staring at nothing, the window wide open no matter the weather? What is it that she comes in here for? To remember? To forget?

'You all right there, Orla?' I jump. Dad's coming upstairs.

He shuffles into the room, scratches the top of his head, the part that was once thick with those springy curls. 'What has you up here? Are you looking for something?'

'I don't know, Dad. Am I?'

A tight knot of lines gathers in the middle of his forehead. 'What are you talking about? Come back downstairs.'

'He slept here, didn't he? The boy. Whoever he is. When he stayed that summer.'

Dad sighs. 'Not now. Please, love.'

I walk to the back window and scan the landscape, the flat fields melting together under the blanket of sky. I use my serious voice. 'I may as well tell you, I've spoken to a few people. I've been asking around.' Though I have no real information, it's worth seeing how he'll react. 'Barry Kilbride for one.'

He breathes a little heavier, shifts his weight from one foot to the next. 'Kilbride? Sure what would he know?'

'So there is something to know?'

'Ah, would you stop with your smart talk.'

'Funny, Barry didn't want to talk about it either. Took one look at the photo and shut up like a clam. And I happened to get talking to a guy working in Castlefox. A Donal Mooney who used to live down the road and—'

'Lookit. Have you got that picture?' He's angry now.

I can feel my face burning. 'You told me to do what I like with it. Tear it up, you said. But you know what, Dad? You can have it back. I don't care.' I whip it from my shirt pocket and make him take it. He's not to know I've already taken a shot of it with my phone. 'I'll keep asking, Dad. If you won't tell me, I'll find someone who will.'

'Come on back down, will you? Just leave it now.'

'Not before I tell you I had a word with Katty Hackett.' I'm flailing about now, trying anything.

'Ah, Katty Hackett,' he says, shaking his head. 'Sure what sense does she ever make these days?'

'"Her sister's boy." That's what she said. "Her sister's boy."'

He stops dead. Then slowly, slowly, turns and thumps his head against the door frame. Once, twice, three times.

'Dad? What's wrong? Are you OK? Stop that, Dad. Just stop.'

He pulls away, sinks heavily onto the bed, rubbing his hands over his face. 'If I tell you something now,' he whispers to the floor, 'will you promise me that'll be the end of it?' I nod when he looks up. His shoulders rise with the deep breath he takes. 'I'm going to be quick, so I am. Your mother'll be calling up the stairs any minute, even if that lad of yours is charming the pants off of her. I'm only telling you this now because I want an end to it all. I know I was the one gave you the feckin' picture in the first place but that day when you were home after Christmas, I, well, I just thought 'twas time. With you thinking of going away and all. Your mother, she ... Well, anyway, didn't she go looking for the picture the morning we were going up to Dún Laoghaire and 'twasn't where she'd left it and ...' he lowers his voice further '... fierce upset she got. Fierce altogether.'

My heart quickens as I listen. 'What is it, Dad? Just tell me.'

He sighs. Long and loud. 'Katty was right. Your mother, she ... well, she did have a sister. Joan. Oldest in the family. Left for England when your mother was only a child. Got married over there.' My mouth drops open. 'I'm telling you now and then there'll be no more to it. We're after making a promise. The thing is, they ... well ... she fell out with them. With Joan and Edward. And then they lost touch and—'

'Lost touch? How? Why?'

'It just happened. The young lad, he came over that summer and then, well, we never saw him again after that. That was the end of it.'

'The *end* of it? But why not try and find them? It can't be that difficult. They must have a last address, a—'

'It's too deep a scar.' He shakes his head hard. 'No point in it. Your mother, she . . . she won't talk about it. If she finds out I told you, my life won't be worth living.'

'But all these years. What could've happened that was so bad?'

'It's not for you to be trying to understand.' He lifts himself off the bed. 'I'm sorry for . . . for not saying anything before but . . .' he sighs again '. . . these things happen, don't they? Families fall out and then time, it . . . it goes by and it all gets too late. No use in trying to go back. Not a word, do you hear? Not now or ever. That's the last of it.'

His face is flushed deep red. His eyes display a look I've become accustomed to in my work. One that says, 'That's all you're getting, you can take it or leave it,' and I know there'll be no more to be had.

But it's all too cut and dried. Too . . . hasty. And, as I follow him downstairs, his jaunty little steps don't fool me. You might think you've unburdened yourself, Dad, but I know there's a lot more to this than you've told me.

At least another week in Lissenmore. How was Tim going to survive? He could hardly bear to think about it. He wished he could fall asleep and not wake up until it was time to catch the ferry home. Mags said Scamp getting killed didn't mean he had to become a hermit. But she didn't know it wasn't just Maeve and the rest of the Mooneys he wanted to avoid. It was Barry Kilbride as well. 'It's probably for the best that dog is gone anyway,' she'd told him. 'When they start going mad like that, well, there's many would've had him put down ages ago. I doubt Tess'll be shedding any tears over him.'

If that was supposed to make him feel better, it didn't. He felt rotten. She was doing her best to convince him he had nothing to worry about and that it was no big deal that he couldn't go home. But he felt she was going overboard. Trying too hard.

The more he thought about the postcard, the more things just didn't add up.

'Mags, I'm not sure Mum and Dad really did go to Cornwall.'

It was Tuesday morning. Tim was drawing the inside of an apple he'd sliced in half. Mags was washing the kitchen floor. She stopped sloshing the mop around and stood staring at the wet lino for a few seconds before she spoke. 'What are you talking about? Aren't they after sending a postcard?'

'I know, but . . . maybe they were just pretending.'

Her eyes narrowed. 'Pretending?'

'I bet they're planning on coming over here. As a surprise. They could've just said they were in Cornwall to throw me off the scent.'

She started swirling the mop around the floor again. 'I see. And you think they'd go to those lengths, do you?'

Tim shrugged. 'They might. I don't know. I'm sure they miss me. Maybe they can't wait till I'm supposed to be going home. They might arrive any minute. You never know.'

Her head dipped to one side. 'I don't think so.' She came over to him and rubbed his arm. 'Just get on with things for the moment, all right? Don't be thinking too much about it.'

'But I can't *help* thinking about it. I wish they'd let me know what was happening and when I can go home. Wouldn't you like to know too?'

'Sure we don't mind when you go,' Mags said, plunging the mop into the bucket of water. 'You can stay as long as you like.'

How could she be so relaxed about it? 'But school's starting up in two weeks! I have to be back by then!'

'Look, it'll sort itself out. Don't be worrying about it.'

'Unless . . . unless you know more than you're saying you do?' Tim let a smile flicker at the corners of his mouth. 'I mean, did Mum let you in on a secret? I'm sure you're keeping something back.' He wasn't sure at all but it was worth a shot.

Mags dumped the mop back onto the floor and moved it

over the lino in wide circles. 'I know no more than you do,' she said. 'Now, lift your feet while I clean in under the table.' Tim did as he was told. Mags came closer with her movements. Her face was set in concentration and her forehead shone with beads of sweat.

PJ came in from the yard. 'I'm away off now, so I am,' he said, reaching for his keys.

Tim turned to him, biting at the top of his pencil. 'Do *you* know anything?'

PJ stiffened. 'About what?'

'Mum and Dad.'

PJ's hand wavered over his keys. 'You'll have to direct your questions to Mags about that. She's the one in charge. That right, Mags?' Mags continued with her work as if she hadn't heard. PJ leaned down and said, louder this time, 'Isn't that right? You're the one knows what's what.'

Mags straightened her back, grimacing in pain. 'For God's sake, PJ. Isn't it time you got to work? And don't be bringing your big dirty feet in here and I washing the floor.'

'I'm only answering the lad, so I am. More than you're doing by the sound of it.'

Mags's breathing became shallow and she leaned hard on the mop handle as she lowered herself onto a chair. 'I don't . . .' she took a few short breaths '. . . need this at the moment.'

'Isn't that exactly what I've been trying to tell you? It's not good for you. You can't just . . . *Jesus!*'

The back door whacked hard against the wall and Declan Mooney burst in, his words tumbling out in a breathless stream. 'Maeve's gone – Mammy doesn't know where she is she wants to know if you seen her.'

'Hold your horses, will you?' PJ said. 'Slow down. Say all that again.'

Declan inhaled. 'Maeve's gone. She wasn't in her bed when Mammy went in to her.'

Mags rocked in her chair, her arms folded over her stomach. 'I'm sure she hasn't gone far,' she said wearily. 'Probably went down to Kavanagh's.'

'Already been down to ask.'

'Kilbride's, then.'

'That's where Mammy told me to look if you hadn't seen her.'

Mags turned to PJ. 'Do you think you could drop him over?'

'Ah, here now,' he said.

'Go on. The poor mite's already run the legs off of himself. Don't leave Tess worried any longer than needs be.'

PJ rubbed a hand over his forehead. 'Always something with them, isn't there? Aren't we doing enough for them already?'

Mags gave him a stormy look. She lifted herself off the chair and put an arm around Declan's shoulders. She spoke softly. 'I'm sure she'll be in Barry's. PJ's going to run you over there now, all right?' She turned to Tim. 'You go with them.'

'But I . . . I'm not sure I—' Tim stuttered.

'None of your nonsense about not wanting to go out and about,' she said, her raised eyebrows and wagging finger telling him not to object. 'You can't stay cooped up here for ever, avoiding everyone and blaming yourself for what happened. Go on with you.'

Tim did as he was told, albeit reluctantly. Though he doubted he'd have to face Maeve anyway. Or Barry. And he was pretty sure where they'd gone . . . *He's going to bring me over to Liverpool. We're taking the car on the boat. We're going to look for Daddy.*

They bundled into the van. Declan sat in the middle, his feet up on the dash, filthy toes stretching a good half-inch over the ends of his sandals. Once they were on their way, he pulled a couple of sticky Black Jacks from his fist and held one under Tim's nose. 'Want one?' he asked. Tim looked into his pleading blue eyes and could see the gesture was meant as a peace offering. He accepted, unwrapping the sweet and popping it into his mouth. Declan said nothing, but Tim could feel a definite lessening of the tension between them.

PJ turned left before Mooneys', down a treeless lane lined with flat fields of dewy pasture where several sleek horses grazed. The lane curved a little to the right and, after another hundred yards or so, they reached a set of wrought-iron gates, probably eight feet high, topped with gilded spikes. 'I'll wait here,' PJ said, bringing the van to a stop. 'You go and see what the lie of the land is.'

The boys hopped out. Tim began jiggling the hasp on the gate, trying to edge it open but failing. It was no problem to Declan. He had it open in a second, wedging his feet between the bars and taking a ride as it swung open across the oily tarmac driveway. A large bungalow faced them, its diamond-paned windows winking in the morning sun. A pair of fancy white pillars stood at either side of the dark mahogany front door that opened as they approached. A short, girlish woman, with bleached hair cut close to her head, stood on the step. Sheila Kilbride. She took a good look at them, taking a long pull on the cigarette she held between her fingers. 'What is it this time, Declan?' she said. 'Barry's away off, so he is.'

'Is Maeve with him? We can't find her.'

'Wouldn't have a clue, love.' She had a different accent to most people in Lissenmore. Mags had told Tim she was from the North.

Tim stepped forward. 'When did he leave? I mean, what time? Is he gone long?'

'And why should I tell you?' She wrinkled her eyes against the light.

'I . . .' The words wouldn't come. Tim felt his cheeks blush. He tried again. 'I . . .'

She laughed – a wheezy, rasping sound that seemed trapped somewhere deep in her chest. 'Look at his wee face!' she said to Declan. 'Beetroot he is.' She stepped out onto the driveway. 'Och, I'm only pulling your leg, so I am.' Mags had said Sheila Kilbride was a bit of a hypocrite. Suspicious of others but not bothered about anything her son chose to do. Most of the time, she hadn't a clue where Barry was or what he was up to. He had two older sisters but they'd long since left home to work up in Dublin so he might as well have been an only child. 'Don't look so scared, son,' Sheila said, coming closer to Tim. 'I won't bite.' Up close, she didn't look quite so young. Her ink-blob eyes had fans of feathery creases at the corners, and the skin above her top lip was scored with tiny lines. As she bent down to Declan, Tim could see the shadowy grid of her breastbone beneath her open collar. 'You're thinking your Maeve might be gone off somewhere with my Barry? Is that right?' She blew a long stream of smoke from the corner of her mouth. Declan nodded. 'Well, I don't know where he is or what time he left, but wherever that son of mine's got to, he'll be back soon enough for a feed, and Maeve with him you can bet. Tess needn't be worrying, you hear me?' She led the boys back out of the gate and leaned through the window of the van. PJ sat back in his seat, hands behind his curly head. 'Don't be in too much of a panic now, will you, PJ?' she said, laughing in her scrawny chest again.

PJ raised his eyes and sat up straight. 'More to be doing than running round after stray cats like your Barry and young Mooney, so I have.'

'Your good deed for the day,' Sheila said. She coughed hard and tapped the ash from her cigarette.

'Brendan playing last night, was he?' PJ asked, as he started up the engine. Barry's dad was a musician. He played the fiddle in an Irish music group called The Greenfields.

Sheila nodded, taking the last drag and tossing the butt to the ground. 'Mullingar. Must've been four and he getting in. Got up and did a fry for him, so I did, but do you think I could get back to sleep after?' She shook her head. 'And himself'll be dead to the world till dinnertime. No bother to him.'

Tim followed Declan into the van. If Sheila had been awake since four . . . 'You didn't hear anything, then?' he asked.

'Hear what?' she said, through the open window.

'If you've been awake all that time, you must've heard Barry leaving? Or was he already gone by four?'

She cocked her head. 'And what's your name, sonny? Magnum, PI? Is that it?' The crinkles around her eyes tightened and she tried to suppress a smile.

'I just thought—'

'Keep your thoughts to yourself,' PJ said, cranking the gear stick. 'I don't have time for them.' He took off, the rough ground crunching like ice under the tyres.

He let the boys out at Mooneys'. 'I'll let you two break the news to Tess. I'll go back and tell Mags. No doubt she'll be wanting to know.'

Tess called from the front door: 'Well?' Tim was nervous. He wasn't sure he'd be able to look her in the eye. 'Any sign?' Declan shook his head, leaving Tim to explain. 'And Sheila had no idea where Barry might be?' she asked, when he'd finished, pulling her dressing gown tighter round her middle. Tim shook his head. If Tess was annoyed with him over Scamp, she didn't show it. 'Nothing new there, I suppose.' She pulled a ball of tissue from her pocket and blew her nose. 'I'll bloody well kill her when she gets back. Gallivanting off without saying a word. Far too big for her boots, that one's getting.'

Fintan appeared, chewing a slice of burnt toast. 'Maybe Barry's after kidnapping her,' he said. 'Or murdering her.'

'And burying her alive!' Donal piped up from the hall.

'Don't be so thick,' Declan said. 'He couldn't bury her alive if he was after murdering her.'

Donal slunk out from behind the folds of his mother's dressing gown. 'Shut up, you. How do you know?'

'What do you mean, how do I know? If she's dead when he's burying her then he can't be burying her alive, can he?'

'Maybe he might think he killed her but he didn't kill her enough and she'll wake up when he's after throwing her in a hole and—'

'For *Jesus'* sake, will you stop! All of you!' Tess clamped her hands over her ears. 'How can you talk about your sister like that?' Her worried eyes looked out towards the road. Then they lit on Tim. 'She definitely didn't say anything to you, did she?'

'Maeve's not talking to him,' Fintan said. He grinned at Tim, his teeth black with toast crumbs. 'After what he did to Scamp.'

'No, she . . . well, I mean . . . she . . .'

'She what?' Tess rounded on Tim, stepping out from the doorway. 'Go on,' she said, leaning into his face. 'Tell me. She said something, didn't she?'

She was so close, Tim could see the forest of tiny hairs above her upper lip, the rash of threadlike veins on her dry-skinned cheeks, like scribbles of bright red biro. 'What did she say?'

Promise you won't tell . . .

But he hadn't promised anything.

Tim felt the full strength of her stare. He looked away but it was too late. She knew he was hiding something. 'Jesus *Christ*!' He jumped, thinking Tess was screaming at him. Then he saw Fintan had launched himself on Declan's back, latching on with his arms and legs.

'Fuck off, you little bastard!' Declan squealed, wriggling. They both ended up on the ground, Fintan straddling Declan and dribbling a string of black, crumby spit onto his face. Donal started to whine. He tugged at Tess. 'Mammy. Mammy. Mammy.'

Declan had Fintan in a headlock now, hocking gobs of phlegm into his hair. Tess grabbed Tim's elbow. 'Come on. Inside. Can't hear myself bloody well think out here.'

As she pulled him along, he could hear Donal whimpering. 'But how do we know Scamp was really dead when we buried him?'

Once inside, Tess stood in the middle of the room, hands on hips. 'Now. Out with it. Whatever it is you know.' Behind her, on the couch, Cormac and Ciaran lay asleep, sweaty heads protruding from a tangle of twisted blankets and pyjamaed limbs. She glanced at them. 'And don't be minding them. A bomb wouldn't wake them. Up at the crack of dawn, they were.' Tim looked at the two little boys. If he were Maeve, he'd have done the same thing. He'd have taken Barry up on his offer and headed off to look for Lar, regardless of how futile he might've thought it would be. He wouldn't have been able to sit around doing nothing while everyone got on with things, as though it was all right for a man to just walk away from his family.

Tim gulped. 'They . . . they might've gone on the boat.'

Tess swayed a little, then stopped dead, as if she'd been blast-frozen from the inside out. 'The boat? What boat?'

'To . . . to Liverpool. Maeve said . . . she said she wanted to look for her dad. She told me they were going. I mean . . . I mean she didn't say when but . . .'

'And when did she tell you this?'

'The day after . . . the day after the disco.'

Her arms folded across her chest. 'I see.' She looked away, her eyes seeming to focus on the breakfast things on the table – chipped bowls drained of milk and cereal, plates scattered with crusts.

Tim continued, 'I told her you were there when I got home that night. And Father Coffey. And I said . . . I said maybe it had something to do with her dad. That he might be in some sort of trouble or something. That's . . . just the way it looked.'

She dragged a chair out from under the table. 'So you put ideas in her head?'

'No! She'd already told me she thought something was wrong. She was suspicious.'

She sat heavily into the chair. 'Of what?'

'I don't know. She just had a . . . a feeling something wasn't right.'

'Maeve's a good girl.' She traced a finger through the toast crumbs on the table. 'Misses her daddy something terrible, she does. Awful close, the two of them.' She turned to look at the twins. After a long pause she said, 'You'd do anything for your kids. To protect them, like. Anything. Sometimes they don't understand, but then . . .' she turned back to face Tim '. . . they're only kids. You'll know all about it one day, Tim.'

'Do you think they'll find him?'

'How easy is it to find a needle in a haystack? Liverpool's a big place.'

'What makes you so sure that's where he is?'

'It's just what the guards told me.' She got up and began stacking the dirty dishes on the table. 'Someone answering his description seen getting the ferry, they said.'

Tess appeared more dishevelled than usual. Her long black hair – shot through with silver strands – fell in unbrushed straggles about her shoulders. Her fingernails were chewed jagged and not particularly clean. She shuffled a lot, as though her body was something she resented having to move from place to place and her legs were inconveniences that prevented her from spending time sitting down. Tim studied her closely as she cleared the table. She looked pretty miserable. But, then, she'd every right to. Not only had her husband left, she might have news about him that she was keeping to herself. Bad news. That was bound to eat away at her. If Tim's hunch was correct, how long could she keep it up? How long before whatever truth she was hiding found its way to the surface?

He came straight out with it. 'Where did you go with Mags?'

Her hair hung around her face as she wiped crumbs from the table. 'Where did I go with Mags? To Dublin, of course. Where else?'

'What did you do there?'

'Ah, not much. Mags was in the hospital. I stayed with my auntie Gretta in Stoneybatter. Spent most of the time clearing the weeds from her back garden.'

'You didn't get much chance to wear your good suit, then?'

One of the twins thrashed about, kicking at the blanket twisted round his legs. Tess unravelled it, pulling it out from under him. 'You're a cheeky article, you know that?' she said to Tim, slinging the blanket over the arm of the couch. She imitated his accent: '"You didn't get much chance to wear your good suit?" Did you ever hear the like?'

'I . . . I'm sorry. It's just . . . well, Maeve said it was strange you took it, that's all. I think she's just worried something's wrong. With her dad.'

The veins on her cheeks seemed to multiply, the whites of her eyes to bulge slightly. Something inside her was threatening to burst. But all she said was, 'Give me a hand to clear over, would you?'

Tim picked an empty milk bottle from the table. He gripped it tight in his hands, wishing he had the strength to squeeze it till it shattered. He banged it down on the draining board, sorry it didn't smash into a million shards.

Tess jumped. 'Christ al*mighty*—'

'What the *hell*'s going on?' Tim's voice was frantic. Alien. Like it was coming from someone else's mouth. 'You're not telling everything! It's not fair! You're hiding stuff. You and Mags. You—'

'Mammy! Mammy!' Donal shot into the room. 'They're here! Maeve's back! Wait till you see what she has!' He ran around the table twice, ricocheting off chairs and walls, like a rubber ball, before tearing back outside.

Tim was left, open-mouthed, his breath caught high in his chest. He swallowed the rest of his words and stood eye to eye with Tess, the air between them electric. The boys' excited cries rang out from the yard and Tess made for the door. 'There's no more I can say to you,' she said calmly, half whispering. 'You'll have to get your truth elsewhere.'

Tim's heart was pounding a beat so fast he felt his whole body vibrate. Tess hadn't been shocked. There'd been no 'What are you talking about? That's rubbish.' *You'll have to get your truth elsewhere.* What was that supposed to mean?

He followed her outside to see what all the fuss was about. The boys bounced up and down, shouting, squealing, surrounding Maeve. And Barry, of course. They grabbed and pulled like mad things, Donal, being the smallest of the three, whingeing that he couldn't see.

Tess strode over. 'Where in God's name have you been? Worried sick, I was.'

'It's all right, Mammy,' Maeve called from behind the scrum. 'We meant to be back before you all got up but we got a bit lost.' She stepped forward, beaming. 'We wanted it to be a surprise.'

In her arms she carried a tiny black pup.

Tim felt his skin grow cold.

Maeve sank to the ground, keeping a tight hold on the little dog while allowing the boys to stroke its silky coat.

'Easy now,' Barry said, getting down on his hunkers. He gave Tim a satisfied grin. 'Going to take him a while to get used to his new home.'

'About to call the guards, I was,' Tess said. She jutted her chin in Tim's direction. 'He said you were planning to head off to Liverpool, the two of you.'

'Did he now?' Barry said, scratching the pup's muzzle. 'And where would he get an idea like that?'

Maeve said nothing. Tim wasn't surprised. He'd just proven that he couldn't be trusted. There was no point in him defending himself. He felt completely stupid.

'Well, I don't know,' Tess said. 'Very mysterious, that's all I can say.' She was already distracted, being dragged over to the pup by Fintan and getting caught up in the thrill. Tim moved away, sidling off, hoping no one would notice. He was almost at the gate when Declan broke away, carrying the pup in his arms. 'Wait. Do you want a shot of him? Go on. Have a go.' The animal felt warm and solid against Tim's chest, its heart thumping a steady, healthy beat. 'We're calling him Magic,' Declan said. 'It's a deadly name, isn't it?' Tim's lips twitched. It was the best he could do. Fintan came running over, grabbed the pup from Tim's hold and skipped back to Maeve. She turned away when she caught Tim's eye.

'What happened your hands?' Declan asked, noticing the plasters on his palms. Tim toed a stone from the earth and sent it skidding down the road. He walked away without answering.

He could hear voices coming from the house as he went across the yard. Drawing closer he heard PJ: 'You're not thinking straight,' he was saying. 'Didn't Dinny tell you 'twas a bad idea?'

'Sure what would he know?' Mags said. 'A man who's never been married, never had children himself. He hasn't a clue. I'll know when the time is right. Not before. I have to be careful, you understand that, don't you? I'm supposed to be taking it easy. Don't be putting any more pressure on me.'

There was silence for a few seconds and then PJ strode

out, muttering under his breath. 'You're back,' he said, when he saw Tim. 'You weren't long. How did Tess take the news?'

Mags appeared at the door.

'She's fine,' Tim replied. 'Maeve's back. And Barry. They were off getting a new puppy.'

'Is that so? A mountain out of a molehill. Knew it'd be nothing to be worrying about.' He hopped up into the van and drove off, sailing out of the gate without looking left or right.

'Well, thank God she's all right,' Mags said to Tim. 'She's a good girl is Maeve. Wouldn't do anything to upset her mammy.' She put her arm around him. 'And the sky didn't fall down while you were there, did it?' She tried to make him smile, tickling him under his chin. 'All the fuss you were making about facing them and I bet no one said a word, did they?' Tim shook his head, but his lips stayed set in a straight line. What was going on? What was it they'd been talking about? *I'll know when the time is right.* For what? He couldn't explain why, but thinking about Mags's words sent a chilly shiver along the length of his spine.

I can't bring myself to tell Luke what Dad told me. Not yet. I need to come to terms with it first. I feel somehow ashamed. Ashamed to admit that they've kept it from me all this time. That I had no idea. That I wasn't part of the conspiracy. Why is it such a terrible secret that Mam has a sister? That I have an aunt and an uncle and a cousin I knew nothing about.

Why have they denied their very existence? Airbrushed them out of our lives? They don't want me asking questions. Ones that might be too painful to answer. Why did they fall out? Did something happen that summer he was here? I don't even know his name. *Never saw him again after that,* Dad said. Why? Why was it so final? And Katty said the same thing. Whatever caused all this deceit, Mam's been suppressing it for a long time. It has to go some way towards explaining why she is the way she is. To fall out with a sister. To pretend she never existed. That's some secret to keep. I'm angry too. Exasperated. None of this is fair on me. Have they ever stopped to think about that?

'You're very quiet,' Luke says. It's after six now. We've been on the road back to Dublin for half an hour.

'Tired, that's all.'

He glances in the rear-view mirror, indicates, accelerates hard and overtakes the slow-moving truck we've been stuck behind for ages. 'Thanks be to Christ. Thought we'd never get an opening.' He settles down into a steady speed. 'So. What were you doing upstairs that time? Thought I sensed a bit of tension when you came back down. You were talking to your dad, yeah?'

'Just chatting. The usual.' I stare out at the black night and wonder what sort of bond they once had. Mam must be a good bit younger. Ten years at least, if her sister's the oldest.

'You didn't get any more out of him?'

'I'm sure I'll get to the bottom of it in time.'

'So we're no closer to the truth?' Luke asks.

Did Mam resent her sister for leaving? Is that why they fell out? But the brothers left too and she's never kept their existence a secret. It must be something else. Something worse than that.

'Who knows? Time will tell.'

He asks no more for the rest of the journey. He knows when to let me be. Now that the weekend is over, his forthcoming week is on his mind anyway. We drive on through the blackness, the diamond trail of cats' eyes the only light on some of the darkest roads.

I decide I'll wait until he gets judgement in his asylum case before I tell him. He's so caught up in it, so focused, I don't want to distract him. When I wake that morning, I reach out to his side of the bed. It's cold. He's long gone. I text to wish him good luck. He doesn't reply. Not that I'm expecting him to.

I have a frustrating day. The office internet is down. No emails sent or received. It's not until after lunch that it's restored. An afternoon consultation wears me out – a melodramatic woman claiming she badly sprained her ankle slipping on wet tiles at a swimming pool. Her manner makes it hard to be sympathetic. I feel like asking her what did she expect, but, then, it's not my job to be judgemental. Back in the office, I make notes and work on some other cases. Ciara arrives late in the afternoon, cursing the decision she's been given in whatever 'hugely important' case she's had on. Kicking off her heels, she pads around the room, talking animatedly with her opposite number and intermittently leaning over to check emails on her laptop, phone wedged between her expensively suited shoulder and her sharply angled chin. At five, I tidy my desk, give her a nod and a wave, and close the door on her artificially emotional conversation.

I text Luke. I don't ask how it went, just say I'm on my way to his office. He's waiting outside when I arrive. I know from his expression that it's not good news.

'Hadn't a chance,' he says. 'They'll be sent back to Nigeria on the next available flight.'

'I'm so sorry. I know how much it meant to you.' I squeeze his hand.

'Sometimes I hate this fucking country. We expect to be welcomed with open arms all over the world but we throw asylum seekers into shitty accommodation for years, then send them packing.' We start walking. 'And we're blabbering on about the undocumented Irish over in the States? Give me a break.' I listen to him recounting the judge's words. The decision sounds so heartless, so unreasonable.. 'What future is that little boy going to have? Makes me ashamed to be Irish.'

I try my best, reminding him that on another day with a different judge things might have gone his way. They have before. Then I suggest we go for a drink but he's in no mood. The sounds of the city's rush hour reverberate around us as we make our way up the quays. Crossing O'Connell Bridge, we run to avoid a taxi that's taken a red light. Luke swears loudly as it passes behind us. 'What's the fucking point, arsehole?' His eyes follow the taxi to where it joins the long line of traffic waiting at the next set of lights. He shrugs. 'See? Makes no sense.'

Back at my place, he flops in front of the TV, flicking through the channels until he finds something suitably innocuous. I get changed, search in the freezer for a couple of ready meals and throw them into the microwave. I leave the curtains open and stand at the window, watching, as the day falls further into night. I'll tell him my news over dinner; it might take his mind off the day's events. I've cradled it close since the weekend, fallen asleep thinking about it, woken having dreamed about it, and now that I've had time to get used to it, I'm ready to share.

The microwave's ping brings me round. I dish up the food and sit down beside Luke, pouring us each a glass of wine.

'Thanks,' he says, though his tone is without any real depth. 'What is it?'

'Supposed to be chicken korma.'

'Disappointments all round today, then.'

'I just thought . . . something quick. I—'

'It's fine. Don't worry about it.'

I want to say that, actually, I'm not worried. In fact, I'm

quite pleased I've produced food at all. I could've settled down for a bit of channel-hopping myself if I'd felt like it. But instead I opt for 'It's OK if you don't want to eat it. I know it's not the best but—'

'I said it's fine.'

It clearly isn't. In an exercise of pettiness, I begin shovelling forkfuls of food into my mouth to show him how much I'm 'enjoying' it. I know I'm annoying him but I feel justified. It's not my fault things didn't go his way in court. He doesn't have to act like it is.

He plays with the food. 'Looks like the contents of a baby's nappy.'

I let my fork drop noisily onto my plate. 'Thanks for that. Much appreciated.'

We sit, not speaking, listening to the chirpy one-liners and canned laughter of the American sit-com he's been watching. As the mood blackens and the room dims and the silence between us grows, the TV becomes unbearable. I pick up the remote and shut it off.

He drains his glass in one. 'I was kind of watching that.'

I dig my nails into my palms. 'Can't we talk?'

'Don't feel much like it.'

'Well, could you even listen, then? I'll do the talking.'

I take his lack of response as acquiescence of sorts and breathe deeply before I dive in. I'm able to recount the conversation I had with Dad almost word for word. Luke makes no interruptions, no comments. When I'm finished, I wait for him to respond.

He leans forward, pours himself another glass. 'So. You've three more relatives than you thought you had. You don't know where they live and none of them has ever made any attempt to contact you.' His words are delivered in monotone. He turns to me. 'And this is good news, is it? This is the big secret you've unearthed?'

I'm taken aback by his reaction, bad day notwithstanding. But I know he's not feeling sorry for himself. He's troubled about the human cost of the decision that's been made and, because of that, I'm not as angry with him as I could be. 'I just wanted you to know. I didn't tell you on Sunday because . . . well, for exactly this reason. I knew your mind was on the case and I didn't want to trouble you with it. And I needed time to come to terms with the news myself first.'

'And have you?' There's more than a suggestion of condescension in his tone.

'Look, I know this isn't your story. And in light of what might happen to that little boy and his mother, being deported and all—'

He cuts me off. 'Being. Deported. And. All?' He's mocking me now. 'Have you any idea what the "and all" might entail? The child plucked from his school, his friends, the only life he's ever known. His mother is sick! She needs ongoing treatment. She won't be able to afford it over there.'

'You take things too much to heart, Luke. It's not your fault.'

He pours himself more wine, swirls it round in his glass, stares at it intently. 'All that stuff over the weekend. What was it for? Sneaking around showing an old photograph to people you hardly know.' He looks into my eyes. 'All that's in the past, Orla. Ancient history. This is real. Real life. Happening now.'

If he's intending to make me feel guilty, he's succeeding. In the face of the here and now, my quest seems inconsequential. Perhaps not quite meaningless, but not something that should be preoccupying my thoughts. And certainly not Luke's as well.

'I'm sorry,' he continues, his voice a little less sharp. 'It's not that I don't care about your long-lost relations. It's cool. Really. It's just I—'

'No. You're right. Whatever happened back then, none of it's my fault, my doing. I probably need to take a step back.'

'You can't make people get along with each other.'

I know what he's saying makes sense. I'll leave it for the moment. Let it lie. I say nothing about being sure Dad didn't tell me the whole truth, that I've a feeling there's more to it than he admitted. I'll just have to accept that, for the moment, that's all the story I'm going to get.

The days grew thick and heavy. Cloudless skies stretched hazily across the countryside, humid air thickening as the hours ticked into evening until, by the time darkness fell, thunder waited, growling in the distance, and lightning bleached the night in split-second silver strikes. All this Tim knew only from the confines of his bedroom. He'd come down with some sort of fever that sapped his strength and left him pretty much unable for anything.

'Picked up something from that new mutt, no doubt,' PJ said, when it first hit him. 'Jesus knows where Barry got it from.'

'Don't be ridiculous,' Mags snapped at him. 'It's some bug doing the rounds. And, anyway, pup's a pure-bred, far as I know. Got from some breeder up near Ashford. Not some mangy thing they found wandering the roads.'

However much it might've suited Tim to blame Barry for his illness, Mags was probably right. It was a flu-like thing he had – raw, scratchy throat, aching limbs, thumping head. He could barely move. Mags almost went overboard with the attention, checking on him every half-hour, though Tim pleaded with her – in his feeble, invalid voice – not to. He knew how difficult she found hauling herself and her stomach up the steep staircase and felt guilty every time she came into his room – out of breath and red-cheeked – but she insisted. She got tired of asking what he wanted to eat; he didn't know himself. So she took to bringing up plates of things she thought he 'might fancy': cream crackers spread with strawberry jam (no), brown bread topped with processed cheese slices (perhaps – but minus the cheese), banana sandwiches (definitely not). She also thought it absolutely essential that Tim drink enormous amounts of Lucozade. After a few days, three bottles – still in their cellophane wrappers – sat on his bedside locker.

He was glad he was ill. Hidden away in the bedroom day and night. It passed the time until he could leave Lissenmore. He could hardly wait. He slept in fits and starts. Deep, untroubled bouts during the day, where he'd sink into total oblivion for several hours and wake empty, as though his mind had been wiped clean of memory. Then, as soon as life as he knew it began to make sense again, he'd tumble into unconsciousness once more, his head lead-heavy on the foam pillow, the spongy mattress offering no resistance to his stone-boned limbs. At night it was different. Awake, his brain was a glittering trove where jewel-coloured scenes – real and imagined – spun across his mind's eye. Asleep, he had the sea dream over and over, from a different viewpoint every time. Maybe it was the thunderstorms that brought it on, the noise of the rain thrumming on the roof, reverberating down through the walls till the room seemed awash and his bed was the ship he had sailed on. He could hear it in the dream, a wild and whispery lullaby that sent him floating out to sea. Out into the Channel, drifting south along the Cornish coast, trying, in vain, to spot Mum and Dad on the rocky cliff tops of St Ives.

'Has Mum written yet?' he asked Mags, after five days had passed and finally he began to feel he was getting back to normal.

She topped up his glass of Lucozade. 'Oh. Yes. I forgot to say. Another postcard. Not sure yet when they'll be home. But we'll hear again soon enough.'

'What did it say? Can I see it?'

'Of course. I'll find it for you. Not much. Having a good time. Weather changeable.'

'But nothing about going home?'

'I told you,' she said, ruffling his hair. 'Don't be worrying. All that . . . well, all that'll come soon enough. You won't be going anywhere till you're well.' She tucked the blankets tight under the mattress, practically welding him to the bed. 'You've all the time in the world to be thinking about going home. Just concentrate on getting yourself better for the moment.'

He hardly had all the time in the world. School would be starting in little more than a week. Not that he was yearning to get back to class, but he was still planning to leave Lissenmore as soon as he could.

'And what's the hurry, anyway?' Mags continued, pouring him yet another glass of Lucozade. 'Still can't wait to see the back of us?'

Tim laughed at her little joke, just to please her. 'It's not that. I—'

She sat down on the bed. 'It's all right. We'll ... we'll talk about it once you're up and about. How's that?' She laid a palm on his forehead. 'Which won't be for a while yet, by the look of it. Temperature's still a bit high, I'd say.'

'I feel fine.'

'No doubt you do. But you can't be too careful with these things.' She patted the bed, then leaned heavily on the locker to heave herself up. 'Now, I'm going to bring you up some scrambled eggs whether you like it or not.'

When she came back up with the tray, he asked if she'd remembered to bring the postcard. She said she'd looked all over for it but couldn't see it anywhere. 'Do you know what? I'll bet PJ was scribbling sums and the like all over it. God only knows where 'tis now. You eat that up, you hear?' she said, as she left to go downstairs. 'I'll be back expecting an empty plate.'

Was the postcard really lost? Surely she'd have kept it in a safe place for him. Had one even come at all? He didn't like to admit it, but he didn't believe her. The whole thing had sounded ... flimsy. She hadn't wanted him to go home early, that much had been clear. She'd cried when he'd told her he wanted to go. And she didn't seem concerned at all about when he might be going back. There was no doubt in his mind that something fishy was going on. An icy grip seized his insides. Could she have made him ill? To make him stay, for some reason? She might have done something to his food. Don't be stupid, he told himself. All the same, he left his scrambled egg uneaten.

He was out of bed – though still in his pyjamas – and resting on the couch when PJ arrived home that evening. He looked up to see his uncle flinging his keys onto the dresser, his hair and beard flecked with fine dust. Mags was in the kitchen, noisily mashing potatoes for dinner. 'Did you hear?' PJ called. 'Lar's back.'

Tim's heart jumped. Back? He was all right?

Mags stopped what she was doing and turned to face PJ. 'Lar? Are you sure?'

'Amn't I after seeing him?'

'At the house?'

'Standing in the yard with the creatures hanging out of him.'

Mags's gaze darted from the walls to the floor to the ceiling, as if an explanation for Lar's return was hidden somewhere in the room. 'That's that, I suppose,' she murmured, wiping her hands on her apron. 'And the car?'

'Car and all. Though not the old one. Some class of a Japanese yoke, by the look of it.'

'I'll have to go down,' she said, fiddling with her apron ties. 'Tess—'

PJ stretched a hand across her. 'You're going nowhere. It's over now. That plan was never going to last. Just leave it.'

'But I—'

He pulled himself up to his full height. 'I mean it, Mags. Stay out of it now. Just let them alone.' She tensed her body and tried to dodge past him towards the door. He sidestepped and blocked her path, taking her by the shoulders and holding her firm. 'Look, haven't we enough to be going on with ourselves? What with . . .' he caught Tim's eye '. . . you know. And the baby and all.'

'But . . .' She sighed, relaxing her stance. 'All right. I'll leave it for now.' She wagged a finger under his nose. 'But I'm making no promises, mind. If I want to talk to Tess tomorrow or the next day or whenever, then I will. And don't you be thinking of stopping me.'

'What's that I can smell that you're cooking?'

'Burgers.'

'Burgers?'

'Yes. Burgers. I thought Tim might like something ... different. All the kids eat them nowadays.'

'Well, don't be expecting me to like them,' he said, slipping off his jacket. He made for the stairs, shaking his head. 'Burgers,' he muttered to himself. 'Did you ever hear the like?'

So. Lar Mooney had come home. After all the wondering and suspicion. And he was OK. Not dead or injured. But what, Tim wondered, had Mags and PJ been talking about? It seemed they knew more about his disappearance than they'd admitted. *It's over now. That plan was never going to last.* What did it all mean?

He had to talk to Maeve. Despite everything that had happened. He couldn't leave without seeing her again, without telling her how happy he was that her dad was back. He almost felt glad he hadn't been able to go home when he'd wanted to. If he had, he wouldn't have been around to witness Lar Mooney's return and see the Maeve he thought he'd never get to meet. She was bound to be different now – happier – and maybe, just maybe, ready to forgive him for what he'd done.

It turned out she was different, all right. But not in the way he'd imagined.

* * *

She was in the yard when he called down the next day, sitting on the battered old bentwood chair he'd seen the boys use in their games. For once, she was doing nothing more than staring into space and she jumped when she saw him, her back straightening, her hands gripping the seat. 'Tim! I ... How ... How are you?' Her face was hollowed out, grey, her eyes almost hidden under the heaviness of her frown.

'Fine. I'm ... fine. But how about you? Your dad. He's home.'

She nodded. 'Safe and sound.'

'After all the wondering.'

'Yeah.'

'Happy?'

'Of course.'

She didn't sound it. Tim glanced around the empty yard, spotted here and there with puddles of muddy water after the night-time downpours. 'Where is everyone?'

'Faranboy. Daddy took them all to the beach.'

'But not you?'

'It'd be a bit of a squash.'

'Where's ...' Tim hardly dared mention him '... where's Magic?'

She pulled a strand of hair from her eyes. 'Gone with them. Boys want to give him a run on the strand.'

Four or five crows circled the top of the cedar tree, wings flapping, their cries shredding the still air. She got to her feet slowly, all the while seeming distracted, unconnected, like she was only there in body.

'I've been ill,' Tim said. 'In bed for a few days.'

'I heard.'

He waited for her to ask how he was feeling but all she did was look at him. There was concern in her eyes all right, but it unsettled him, made him uneasy. 'Mags ... She seemed a bit shocked your dad had come back. I think she definitely knew more than she was saying all along. Did you find anything out? About . . . about where he'd been?'

She lifted her chin. 'Let's go inside.'

Tim was relieved. He knew he still looked ill. In the bathroom mirror before he'd left, his face had looked washed out and raw. The light inside would be kinder. He followed her into the cottage. A couple of comics – the *Beano*, the *Dandy* – and a small mound of plastic soldiers lay on the kitchen table. 'Daddy brought those back. For the boys.'

'Presents?' Tim said, as he sat down. He was surprised. 'That was thoughtful of him.'

'Daddy didn't want to be away, you know. It wasn't his idea to go. It was Mammy's.' She sat beside Tim and picked up one of the khaki-coloured soldiers. 'I found out the truth. It was all her little plan.'

Tim watched as, carefully, she began standing the figures one behind the other in a line. And he listened to her explain, her voice seeming to come from some other, faraway, place.

Tess had dreamed it all up.

Tired of trying to survive on Lar's weekly dole and with no hope of him getting a job at home, she'd told him to head off to England to find work. She'd waited till the weather had turned, till the ground had frozen and the snow had begun to fall. There'd be more sympathy for the Mooneys, she'd reckoned, if he'd 'abandoned' them in the cold dead heart of winter. When he'd left that night she'd known she wouldn't see him for a long time. Off the boat, Lar had driven to London, found some cheap digs then gone out to search for a job. Meanwhile, back in Lissenmore, Tess was a deserted wife with six children and no income. She'd played the part well; no one had disputed her story. She'd applied for the weekly allowance and, before long, was in receipt of her full entitlements – by no means a fortune, but enough to get by. Lar had found well-paid work on a building site – some skyscraper office block – and as winter had fed into spring, he'd sent home more than half his pay packet every two weeks.

'Posted it to Mags, so he did.' Maeve held one of the soldiers between her fingers and studied its tiny form. 'She knew all about it. And PJ. Couldn't send it here. Katty's eagle eyes would've spotted it. Has a good nose through the post before it's delivered, does Katty. Letters from England for the Mooneys? Sure when did we ever get a letter from England before? But Mags, well, nothing unusual in that.'

'I'm sorry. I should've said something about it before.' Tim told her about the envelope of cash wrapped up with the brown loaf.

Maeve sighed. 'It's OK. I wouldn't have copped on. I'd've just thought the same as you – that Mags was helping us out with her own money.'

Tess hadn't put any time limit on the scheme but she'd bargained on it lasting a lot longer than the six or seven months that it had. All that time and she'd kept it from her children, let them believe their dad had walked out on them.

'So you were right to suspect something was going on,' he said.

'I knew Daddy cared about us. I knew all along something wasn't right. And all she says now is "Stop your moaning. Sure didn't he come back?" He couldn't stick it any longer. He missed us.'

'But at least he's OK. I mean, you were so sure he was in trouble or—'

'I know. And I am happy he's back. It's just . . .'

'And when they went to Dublin? Mags and Tess. They really went over to see him?'

Her eyes settled on Tim's for a pulse, then darted away. She fiddled with a soldier that was out of line, gently sliding him into place with a fingertip. 'Tim, you need to talk to Mags about that.'

Outside, the grating sound of the crows began to fade. Tim imagined their sooty-black bodies flittering away across the leaden sky. He didn't understand. 'You mean they didn't go over to see him?'

'Just ask Mags.'

'What? Is it something to do with the baby? Was she really in hospital? How do you know all this stuff now anyway? About where your dad was and what he was doing.'

She had the table resembling a battlefield now, an army awaiting command. 'Heard them talking, so I did. And rowing. I'm not stupid. They couldn't deny it when I started asking them questions.'

'What's going to happen? Will they get into trouble?'

She shrugged. 'Don't know. Maybe.' Then she took Tim's hands in hers and ran her fingers over the rough, scabbed surface of his palms. Warm tremors zipped up and down his arms. 'What happened your hands?'

'It's nothing.'

'Hardly nothing.'

'Honestly. It doesn't matter.' It seemed insignificant now. She was so close, her face only inches from his. He didn't want to think about Barry Kilbride and what he'd done. Didn't want to think about anything but her.

Her seawater eyes brimmed. 'I thought Daddy was dead. Did you know that?' The tears trickled crookedly down her cheeks. 'I thought he was dead and . . . and Mammy was afraid to tell me. And all the time . . . all the time . . .'

'We both thought he was in trouble.' Tim snaked his arm around her shoulders. 'Don't be sad. You couldn't help thinking the worst.' She leaned into him. 'It's OK.' His fingers stroked her hair. 'It's OK.'

'Oh, Tim,' she sobbed into his neck, 'it's not OK. You have to go.'

Go?

'I know something,' she said, sniffing back her tears. 'I know something I shouldn't.'

'What do you mean? What is it?' He felt her shifting, her body moving closer against his. Though he'd asked the question, he wasn't wondering about what it was she knew. He was only thinking about how it felt to be so near to her.

And then. No. *No!* The sound of a car pulling up outside. They were back.

She threw off his arm and sat bolt upright, wiping her cheeks with the backs of her hands. Tim felt numb and exposed without the warmth of her body against his. And now he was more confused than ever. Lar was home but . . . *I know something*. What did she mean?

He heard the boys milling about outside, their usual high-pitched squealing. Magic yapping like a mad thing. Tess being authoritative for once, telling them to calm down. And the drawn-out commands of a croaky male voice: 'Stop – tormenting – that – pup.'

Maeve jumped up when Lar came inside. 'Will I make some tea, Daddy?' she asked, instantly cheerful.

Lar gave a jerk of his chin. 'Right-o.'

So this was Lar Mooney. Tim looked at him. A plain man, he had a head like a bowling ball, almost perfectly round, shiny and hair-free. His features – eyes like flat blue buttons; squashed, dog-like nose; pursed, pinkish lips – were crowded together in the centre of his face. He stood square, legs apart, hands dug deep into the pockets of his sports jacket. He trained his eyes on Tim. 'Is this . . . is this the lad who's—'

'Biscuits, Daddy! Biscuits,' Maeve interrupted. 'We have Goldgrains. You like them, don't you?'

'Oh. Right-o,' he said again. 'PJ's . . . nephew.'

Tim nodded and stood up. 'Pleased to meet you.' He held out his hand.

Lar gripped his fingers and shook hard. 'Heard all about you, I have. All about you.' He shouldered off his jacket, draped it over the arm of the couch and eased his short, blocky frame into a chair.

'Tim was just going,' Maeve said.

He was?

'Not staying for the tea?' Lar asked.

'He has, um . . . he has things to do, don't you, Tim?' He did? 'Come on, I'll see you out.' She ignored the quizzical look Tim gave her, and took him by the elbow.

Outside, Tess was sitting in the bentwood chair now, a sticky-faced twin on each knee. It was the first time Tim had seen her wearing anything other than nightclothes. She'd brushed her hair, tied it back from her face, and coloured her lips a deep plum colour, which made her look older, though Tim was sure that wasn't her intention. 'Tim!' she said, eyebrows raised, seeming surprised to see him. 'Is . . . Are you . . . ?'

'Yes, Mammy, it's fine,' Maeve said, head down, rushing Tim along.

'What's going on?' Tim whispered, almost having to run to keep up. 'Why the hurry to get rid of me?'

Once out of the yard, standing on the roadside and out of Tess's view, Maeve pulled him round, leaned in and kissed him on the lips. Hard. 'Go home, Tim,' she said, drawing back, her face milky-pale. 'You have to talk to Mags. I don't know what else to say.'

I try to put it all out of my mind. Maybe Luke's right. It's ancient history. I should be more concerned with the here and now. The present. And the future. If Mam wants to keep relatives secret, that's her business. If Dad wants to be complicit, that's his. Lots of people have family they never see. It's not uncommon. OK, so this is a little different, pretending they never existed and all that. But there might be good reason for it. Perhaps they're not very nice. Maybe they did something horrible. I'd love to talk to Mam about them but I can't bring myself to ask. I don't want to cause her pain, or make her any more depressed, and I don't want to fall out with Dad. Whenever I call her, I imagine our words are like blades on ice, that our conversation skates a frozen lake that's always in danger of cracking. Tell me about your nephew, I want to say. About the sister I never knew you had. I know there's more to this story. What's the reason it's not being told?

I can barely contemplate a visit home. Work has become increasingly busy. Not just for me, for Luke too. We both find ourselves staying late at our desks in the evenings and I've a lot less time to be thinking about anything other than my cases. Even weekends are partly spent preparing legal submissions or drafting papers and pleadings. It's a good complaint, I know, but the extent of the workload almost makes me miss the email. I notice it in my inbox one afternoon, though I don't recognise the sender's name, one M. A. Zylinski, and the cheery title – 'Hi there!' – convinces me it's yet more spam from some far-flung destination, a hazard of having a profile on the Bar Council's online listing. It crosses my mind to trash it but, instead, I flag it for later attention along with all the other non-urgent messages. It's late, dark outside, before I finally get around to opening it.

> Dear Orla,
> I hope you don't mind me contacting you. My name is Maeve Zylinski and I'm living out here in Perth, Western Australia.

Australia? Makes a change, I think, from the usual origin of the begging letter/offers of millions in exchange for my bank details/notification of my huge lottery win.

> My maiden name is Mooney. I used to live in Ireland, down the road from you in Lissenmore.

OK, this is not what I thought it was.

> Last time I saw you, you were just a baby, so you wouldn't have any memory of me. I thought long and hard about getting in touch since my brother Donal

Skyped a couple of weeks back and mentioned he'd bumped into you in Castlefox. Not that he remembers you from all those years ago. He was very young when we all came out here. (He's only recently returned to Ireland. Poor thing's a bit homesick at the moment, missing the sunshine!) Anyhow, he was telling me about the photograph. The one you showed him. It clicked with me straight away when he described it. I'm the one who took it! Not that I ever saw it but I remember exactly the night it was taken. Donal said you understood when that was – not long before you were born – but that you didn't seem to know who the boy was and were asking about him. It was this that really prompted me to get in contact because that tells me something and, please, if I'm out of order or you don't want to reply, I won't be offended in any way. I looked you up – Googled your name and found you on the Law Library website. I forwarded your photo to Donal and he confirmed you were the same Orla Hyland he'd met (the world is such a small place now!). Again, I hope you don't mind that I'm contacting you. There are gaps to be filled here, and hearts to be helped. Broken hearts. Not in the lovey-dovey sense as such, but in the sense that all relationships stem from the need to connect on an emotional level, and emotion is a heartfelt thing. OK, I realise how that sounds, but what I'm really trying to say is that there's a story here, one I'm fairly certain you don't know. It's been out there all this time. It found me and now, I hope, it's going to find its way to you. I don't think it's any real coincidence that you bumped into Donal. I guess the past is always out there. Lying in wait.

I'd love to hear back from you. Writing this has made me feel hopeful. You'll understand what I mean if I get the chance to explain.

All the very best

Maeve

Once I've read the words on the screen, I go back to the start and read them again. And again. I take out my phone and scroll my pictures to find the shot of the photo. I sit there staring at it until the image blurs and swims in front of my watering eyes. *Hearts to be helped. Gaps to be filled. There's a story here.* My own heart pumps hard and fast as I zoom in on the boy's face, as I've done so many times before. A sharp pain rockets round my stomach, zips up my throat, bursts through the top of my head. Fear. I'm scared. Afraid of what I'll find out. Only the bad stuff gets buried: that's what I said to Luke. This is bad stuff. It has to be. Why else has it been kept hidden? Up to now it's been like a tug-o'-war. Me pulling hard against the might of the unknown. Now it's as though that unknown has given way, released its grip and let me tumble backwards in a heap. It's given up, exhausted, unable to continue. I'm closer now. She's thousands of miles away but contactable in seconds. What time is it in Perth now? I Google quickly: three thirty-five a.m. Should I leave it for a while? Should I think about it? If I reply now, chances are I won't hear back for hours anyway. But even as I contemplate, my fingers are beginning to type.

Dear Maeve,

It's difficult to know how to reply. First, thank you for getting in touch. As you can imagine, your email came as a bit of a shock. A bolt out of the blue. But, on the other hand, since what prompted you to write is something that's been on my mind almost constantly in the past weeks, the arrival of your email seems almost natural. I'm not sure what it is you can tell me, what gaps you can fill, so I'll give you a (fairly) brief outline of the scant details I already know.

I only became aware in January of the photograph I showed Donal. I was on a visit home and had told my parents I'm thinking of going to work in the States. Bit of a bombshell for them. My father and I got talking, mainly about my mother and how hard she'd take it if I do decide to go. She's suffered from depression for a long time but I've always felt there was something missing, something that caused the darkness within her. I got the impression that day that my father might be trying to explain what that something was. He got quite deep – very unlike him – and slipped the photo to me as I was leaving. I think he meant it to spark something off – a curiosity that would make me start fishing, start asking questions that would lead me to some sort of revelation about the past. If you know my father you'll understand how this might make sense. He wouldn't betray my mother by telling me something he'd sworn to keep secret. He'd just leave the way open for me to try to find out for myself. As soon as I saw the photo, I knew there had to be a story behind it. But I'd never seen the boy in it before, had no idea who he was.

I don't know if you remember Barry Kilbride? The local councillor as he is now. I figured he would've been around the same age as the boy and wondered if perhaps they'd been friendly. Quizzing my father at length had proved pretty much useless: he wouldn't tell me anything and made it clear I wasn't to bring the photo up with my mother. However, he did eventually reveal that the boy had stayed with them that summer so I decided to ask Barry if he knew who he was. I searched him out in Faranboy that weekend we stayed in Castlefox, and I worked my way round to producing the photo and asking if he recalled anything about the boy. He just clammed up. It was obvious he did remember but, for whatever reason, he wouldn't admit it.

When I got talking to Donal, I thought there was no harm in showing him the photo. I'm sure he must've thought me a bit strange but I was on a mission at that stage. It seems all I succeeded in doing was unearthing some traumatic memory he'd buried, something about the death of a dog.

In the village later on, I caught up with Katty Hackett (I'm sure you remember her, she used to run the post office) and I asked her if she knew the boy's identity. She recognised my mother and father – surprisingly, as she's often quite confused – and threw in a remark about 'her sister's boy'. When I told my father (I'd decided to come clean in relation to my detective work, just to see how far I could get with him), he broke a little and revealed to me something that came as quite a shock and, I'm guessing, something you already know. My mother had always told me she'd been the only girl in her family. Now, according to my father, it seems she has an older sister – Joan – with whom she'd fallen out years back (over what, he wouldn't say) and that the boy is her son. He was emphatic in stressing that he didn't want any more to be said about it. But digging for clues is part of my work and I was – and still am – sure there's more to this than the amount he told me. And if there is – perhaps this is what you can tell me?

This has become far longer than I intended and, now that I've read over it, more formal as well. But I felt it important to clarify the details I already know.

Looking forward to hearing from you.

With kind regards,

Orla

I inhale deeply and hit 'send'. Then I read what I've written and am washed through with a cold, clammy dread. I've been too revealing. *She's suffered from depression for a long time but I've always felt there was something missing, something that caused the darkness within her.* What was I thinking? In my haste to discover this 'story', I've disclosed far too much information to a complete stranger. I should've just sent a one-line reply. 'Dear Ms Zylinski, Thank you for your email. I'd be delighted to hear anything you have to say. Yours etc.' Should've been polite, professional, detached. Or maybe I've done the right thing in replying the way I have. I lean my head in my hands. Jesus, what does it matter now anyway? It's in her inbox. I can't call it back.

I won't say anything to Luke. In the last few weeks, there's been no discussion between us about the photo or anything surrounding it – a combination of being too busy and not wanting to keep going over old ground. If there's more to this whole story, I'll wait until I know what it is before disclosing it.

Over the next few days, I check and recheck my inbox so many times I almost drive myself mad. I'm convinced she's decided against pursuing things any further, that the language and tone I used put her off, made her rethink her decision to contact me. It helps that I'm busy. There are a couple of times during the work day when I think about emailing her again but my ongoing cases always intervene. At night, it's different. I have more time to think. I compose the opening lines of another email in my head on several occasions but the words never make it to the screen.

When her reply eventually pops into my inbox, I'm in court, forty minutes into a wait to have a case mentioned. I'm lost in it immediately, my eyes greedily eating up each word, my fingers shakily scrolling the screen of my phone.

Dear Orla,

Lovely to hear back from you and apologies for not being able to reply to you sooner. Over last weekend I had intended to, but life (i.e. kids) got in the way and I just didn't find the time. We've also been helping some friends out after the huge bushfires last month. Thankfully, we live a little way out from the worst-hit areas and our home wasn't damaged, but some people we know weren't so lucky. Anyway, aside from that, you've been on my mind. I was thrilled to get your reply and can see from what you wrote that it is as I thought – you don't know much about this whole thing but you've been scratching around. And you're right in assuming that there's more to it than the fact that your mother had a sister she never told you about. I can understand why she did that.

I've been wondering about the best way to approach this, and just earlier this evening I got a minute or two to talk to Paul, my other half. He's a practical kind of guy and used, in a way, to dealing with sensitive family issues (he's a school counsellor). He suggested I take it

> easy, tell you everything I know but kind of in a step-by-step way. So it might take a couple of mails to get it all out. I know you're probably wondering why we couldn't just Skype or call and I did consider it, but decided it would be awkward. It wouldn't work out right. Better to do it this way where you can read it at your leisure and

Shit. A colleague taps me on the shoulder. My case has been called. I direct my attention to the judge and prepare to speak. The courtroom is stuffy, airless. My ears buzz with the tense hum of expectation: whispering voices, shuffling papers, rustling robes. I falter, stuttering, in front of the judge. She peers down at me, eyebrows arched, her expression making it clear that patience is not her most obvious quality. I tell myself to get a grip, managing to do just that before she's forced to comment.

As the morning and then the afternoon wear on, the last sentence I'd read of the email sticks in my head: '... *read it at your leisure and* ...' Despite my own impatience, I make a decision to do just that. I need time to go over it without interruption. So I leave it till the evening when I'm back in the office.

Ciara's on her way out as I'm coming in. 'Staying late again? Busy-busy.' She belts herself into her black trench.

'Just a few things to catch up on.'

'Rather you than me. I've mountains to do but I can't be arsed. Going to dinner with Garret. Have to get ready.'

'I'll let you go, then. Wouldn't want to keep him waiting.' Or he might find another female who takes his fancy, I want to add. She turns her collar up and gives me a glacial stare, as though she can read my mind. It looks like she's about to say something, but then, for whatever reason, she changes her mind, sniffs and leaves. I open Maeve's email and take up where I'd left off:

> . . . better to do it this way where you can read it at your leisure and let it slowly soak in. I know you must be very busy, too – my brother Fintan's partner works in the legal end of things and he's constantly up to his eyes so I do understand. Time difference can be a pain as well, of course. All hail the wonders of email!
>
> So. Where to start? At the beginning, I guess. Back when I first met him. The boy with the white-blond curls. That summer was a memorable one, not just because of his arrival but because my father, Lord rest him, wasn't around. He'd disappeared after the previous Christmas. Never came back after going out to the shop one evening. My mother – she's gone too, Lord rest her – went to ground. (Though all was not as it seemed. More of this later.) I was fourteen, the eldest, with five younger brothers, and it was left to me pretty much to look after them. They were a handful, to say the least. It was Mammy who first told me that a boy was coming over from England to stay the summer with your parents. Mags's nephew, she said. Her sister Joan's only child. Mammy and Mags were good friends back then. The boy's name was Tim. Tim Swift. He was the same age as me and we hit it off straight away. He fancied me. I recognised that early on, and I did like him – a lot – but with Daddy gone, I didn't have much time or desire for anything other than minding the lads. And I suppose my head was turned a bit by Barry Kilbride, too. Boy about town he was, even back then. Always available

to be ferrying us around in his car, which, with Daddy gone, was something Mammy and I saw as a great thing altogether. I was too young to realise his motives. I thought he offered because he genuinely wanted to help.

Now, I got it into my head that something bad had happened to my father. I was a bit of a Daddy's girl and I couldn't accept that he would've just deserted us, upped and left without a trace. Tim was such a sweet boy – he wanted to help and I suppose me being suspicious rubbed off a bit on him and he started to believe it too. Anyhow, there was a disco on in Faranboy one Saturday night and I asked Tim along. That photograph you showed Donal, I took it with Tim's camera before we headed off in Barry's car. I felt bad afterwards because I spent the night dancing with Barry. But only because he was offering to take me over to Liverpool to look for Daddy (that's where Mammy said she had a feeling he was). So, being a bit put out, Tim walked across the fields back to your parents' house on his own. He told me the next day after mass that when he got back Father Coffey (parish priest at the time) was there, along with Mammy and your parents, of course. They all went quiet when he came in and he was told to go up to bed. Tim got it into his head that something bad had happened and he was sure – because Mammy was there – that it was bad news about Daddy. A few days later, Mags and Mammy went away for a couple of nights. To Dublin, they said. Your mother, of course, was pregnant with you at the time, and she said she had to go to hospital for some sort of a check-up, and Mammy was going to visit her auntie Gretta. Now, I knew something was up because Mammy took her good suit and I was sure that she'd found out from Father Coffey that Daddy was in some sort of trouble and she'd gone to wherever he was to sort it out. And, God love him, Tim was easily convinced and I had him believing it, too. But when they were gone, didn't poor Tim come down to us on the Friday after he'd been working with your father up in Castlefox for the week, all delighted with himself after earning a few bob, he was. Anyhow, we had a dog – Scamp – bit of a mad thing. Had to keep him tied up most of the time. The lads were tormenting him that day and didn't Tim feel sorry for him and untie him from the tree. Scamp rushed out onto the road and got hit by a truck. Killed stone dead. Of course, the lads were devastated. I was mad at Tim – even though it wasn't really his fault – and I sent him packing.

Barry came to the rescue, brought me out to some place to get a pup a week or so later, and I could see Tim was right sore when he saw us arriving back with it. You said in your email that you'd met up with Barry Kilbride and were sure he recognised Tim in the photo. He'd remember him all right – there's no way he'd forget. But I'm not surprised he pretended otherwise. He has his reasons. A lot of what I know now, I wasn't aware of back then, and sometimes my head's in a bit of a whirl with it all. So to make it clear (to myself as well as to you) I need to get it out the way I experienced it. You're probably wondering where I'm going with it all but you'll come to understand. There's a lot to reveal. It's a sad story, I have to tell you, but one I'm really hoping doesn't have to end that way.

I'm going to have to finish up for tonight, I'm afraid. Paul's over with some friends of ours, helping with repairs to their roof after the fires, and I'm going to have to get the kids to bed (we have three, who are, by the sound of it, pretty much beating the daylights out of each other downstairs). I'll pick a better time to write when I email again, hopefully in the next day or so. Bear with me until then.

All the best,

Maeve

Crap. *Bear with me until then?* If it's anything like the last time, God knows how long that might be.

Tim Swift.

So that's his name. Why did Mam lose touch with them all? What could've caused such a falling out? *It's a sad story … but one I'm really hoping doesn't have to end that way.* What was that supposed to mean? At this point, I'm left with far more questions than answers.

Tim walked home from Maeve's along a path paved with polished gold, studded with precious gems in vivid, scalding colours. He floated along just shy of the glittery ground, bursts of bright sunlight fanning out from the clouds above, hedgerows sprouting silver leaves that tinkled in the warm summer air.

Of course it wasn't really like that. It was the same grey stretch of road under a similar-coloured sky. But he was blind to his true surroundings. His mind made them far more beautiful than they were. His head was full of her. It was as if he knew nothing else. He hardly thought about what she'd told him – where Lar had been, the full extent of the deception – or even what she hadn't: *you have to talk to Mags . . . I know something I shouldn't.* None of that concerned him. Only later would he think of that. It was the touch of her hands. The nearness of her. Her faded blue T-shirt, her cut-off jeans. The satiny feel of her hair. Maeve. Even her name was soft and wistful, like the waft of a gauzy silk veil. *Maeve.*

And the kiss.

The kiss.

The sting of it reached down deep and bored right into his heart. He ached from the inside out. A pain so sharp he could barely breathe. And though it hurt, he wanted the agony. At that minute, he wanted it for ever.

But that was when he thought he knew why it was that she'd kissed him.

'There you are!' Mags greeted him when he got back to the house. 'About to send out a search party, so I was. Getting a bit chilly and you only up out of your sick bed. Don't want you heading back to square one now, do we?' She slipped her striped apron over her head. 'Going to start the dinner, so I am. Chicken and chips. What would you say to that?' She rolled up her sleeves. 'Well?' she asked, when Tim hadn't answered.

'I'm not really hungry.'

'Would you go away out of that! Not hungry. Sure you've eaten hardly a thing for days! And here's me jumping through hoops to make things you like.'

Tim gazed at her, swaying slightly on his feet.

'What's wrong with you at all?' she said. 'You look like . . . I don't know . . . like you're after being swung round on a rope. All dithery you are. Not over the worst of it, I'd say. Go on up and lie down. I'll call you when it's ready.'

He dragged himself up the stairs. In the bathroom, he peered at his face in the mirror again. He did look strange. Sort of dazed. Not quite fully awake. He inspected his just-been-kissed mouth. It looked completely normal, even though it felt swollen and after-the-dentist numb. In his room, he threw himself onto the bed and fell, immediately, into a thick, muddy sleep.

When he woke – or half woke – not long after, the gloomy light told him the sky had darkened further. He was hot, though the windows were open. He heard the warm wind strengthening, whistling through the trees, and watched how it made the curtains flit about the room, like spectres.

The kiss.

He kept reliving it. Playing it over in his mind. Again and again. The way she'd pulled him round. How her lips had pressed on his.

But, now that he thought about it, it hadn't been gentle. Not at all.

It had been . . . desperate. Vital. As if she'd had to do it there and then in case she never got another chance. Someone looking at them from afar would think they were like star-crossed lovers in a film, fearful it was their last ever meeting.

I know something I shouldn't. That was what she'd said, wasn't it?

Other thoughts came slanting through his brain, lighted daggers that shot in from the sides, slashing across the misty picture of her face.

You need to talk to Mags . . .

She'd been trying to tell him something. She'd cried on his shoulder, for God's sake.

Under his clothes, his skin was alive. Creeping, crawling, a cold rash of fear.

I don't know what else to say.

No. Stop. It's all in your head. Just accept the sweetness of the kiss, why can't you? She likes you!

But there'd been no sweetness. Nothing about it was right,

was the way it should've been. What did it all mean? He was afraid now. *Just ask Mags.* What did Mags know? Some secret? About what?

He was wide awake now. He put his feet to the floor. Standing up, the room spun a little, like he'd just had a rollercoaster ride. He felt as if his skull was about to burst, that the bone might split and crack and his brains would roll across the floor in flowery lumps, like Barry's cauliflower.

Mags and Tess. They'd known all along where Lar was. They'd both lied. Deceived. Pretended. Whatever you wanted to call it. He felt empty inside when he thought about it. Unsure. Saddened. But angry too. PJ couldn't have been ignorant of it. He must've known. He wouldn't have been happy about Mags being involved in the plan, being the go-between for Lar and Tess. PJ was straight up. Decent. Fair. It would be against his nature to be underhand. He'd want things out in the open. Mags was just helping Tess out, that's how she would've seen it. But to let those kids think their dad had run off and left them ... How must Maeve feel? How worried she'd been. And all that time ...

It wasn't right. It wasn't right at all.

He went to the back window and looked out over the fields. His heart lifted. Seeing the distant shimmer of the sea made him yearn for Mum and Dad and the journey home. Somehow, having miles of deep, dark water below him seemed more comforting, more solid, than having his feet planted firmly on the ground.

He leaned his head right out, the wind rippling his hair and thieving the breath from his throat. Then the van pulled up in the yard below and PJ unfolded himself from the seat. His stretchy limbs. His rusty halo of curls. He tilted his head and his tired eyes found Tim's. He nodded – just a barely noticeable movement of his head – before he disappeared inside.

Then Tim could hear Mags calling, her cheery voice announcing dinner.

His feet thumped out the rhythm of Maeve's words on the stairs.

I. Don't. Know. What. Else. To. Say.

Then say nothing. Stay quiet. I don't want to hear it.

Whatever it is, I don't want to know.

'You had a bit of a sleep, then?' Mags said, with a wink. 'Judging by the look of you.'

His hair. He reached up and patted it down. He sat at the table, where PJ was already ensconced, his face hidden behind the local paper.

'Put that down,' Mags said to him. 'I'm going to be serving now.'

PJ gave a loud sigh, folding the paper with exaggerated movements. He'd obviously had a tough day. His eyes had told Tim so when he'd seen him from the window. Mags put his food in front of him. 'Chicken and chips?' he said, frowning. 'Couldn't I get that down in Angelo's?'

'Go 'way out of that. Wouldn't be half as good and don't you know it.'

He shook his head. 'Chicken and chips. Would you believe it?' He looked at Tim. 'You've a lot to answer for, do you know that?'

He was only half joking. He said it without a hint of a smile.

'Don't be teasing the lad,' Mags said. 'If you're not happy you don't have to eat it.'

'Amn't I already eating it?' he said, forking a chip into his mouth. 'I was only saying.'

Mags flopped down in a chair, relief flooding across her face. She was tired. Only three weeks to go before the baby arrived. 'Well, you needn't be saying anything.' She drew her chin into her neck. 'It's nice to be cooking things Tim likes anyway.'

Tim sliced his chicken, though he didn't have any desire to eat it. 'Well, I won't be here very much longer,' he said. 'You can go back to cooking the things you're used to once I've gone.'

Mags wagged her knife at PJ. 'Now look what you're after doing.'

PJ chewed his food and stared at her until she had to look away.

Then there was silence. No sound except the scrape of metal across their plates. Tim knew what he'd said was a little cheeky. But he was annoyed. With Mags especially. And he wanted her to know it. Lying to Maeve. To the boys. To him. It made him feel small. He hadn't believed Mags was that type of person. The more he thought about it, the angrier he got. And what else was there? What else was she hiding? What was it that Maeve 'knew'?

'I know,' he blurted, after a few minutes. 'All about where Lar was. Maeve told me everything.'

PJ took a lengthy slug of his milk and eyed Tim over the top of the glass. Mags's face grew red. She searched for words. 'It's not . . . I mean . . . Don't . . .'

Tim faced her. 'Why did you have to lie?'

'Don't be silly. It . . . it wasn't a . . . a lie,' she said, with more than a little nervousness. 'I was doing it for Tess. For all of them. Can't you understand that?'

'But it was so unfair,' Tim cried. 'Maeve thought he might be dead!'

'Look, I . . . I know how it sounds. But, well, these are hard times, Tim. People are struggling. You'll understand more about it when you're older. I'm certain of that.'

PJ started getting fidgety. He shifted in his chair, wiped a big hand over his sweaty forehead and across the orange fuzz on his crown. Mags looked uneasy. She was breathing very deeply, up through her nose and out in long, loud streams from her mouth.

'You all right?' PJ asked, chewing.

'Fine. I'm fine. Just a bit uncomfortable. Nothing new there.' She gave him a weak smile. One he didn't return.

Tim played with his food. No matter what Mags said, he still thought what she'd done was wrong. She'd known all along where Lar was. How could what she had done have helped? OK, so they had a bit more money, but money wasn't everything.

Mags could see he wasn't eating. 'Come on, Tim. You need to build yourself up again.'

'I'm not hungry.'

'How about some peas?' She heaped a spoonful onto his plate from the dish in the middle of the table.

Tim noticed her hand was trembling. 'You're not supposed to lie,' he said.

'I told you. I did it for Tess. For all of them. Sometimes . . . sometimes we do things for other people because . . . we want to help. Please don't think badly of me. Let's just forget about it for the moment and eat our dinner.' She was trying to sound relaxed.

PJ laid down his knife and fork. 'Is that really how you see it?'

She turned to him. 'How . . . how do you mean?'

'That's how you convince yourself you did the right thing?'

'But you know it is. You know I only wanted to help. Tim'll come to understand.'

'And the other? Will he understand that?'

'Stop. We're talking about Lar here. That's all I'm trying to explain.'

PJ finished his food and pushed his plate away. He closed his eyes, rubbed the lids and shook his head. 'It's gone far enough.'

Mags swallowed hard, licked her lips, took a sip from her glass of water. 'What are you talking about?'

'You know right well what I'm talking about.'

'Look, I know you weren't happy about the whole thing. Him working and sending me his wages to give to Tess and she claiming off the state. And there's you trying to earn a decent, honest wage, working all the hours God gives and—'

'Mags.' PJ's voice was steady but stern. 'Stop it. That's enough. It's time now. We can't leave it any longer.'

Tim looked at their faces, his eyes flitting from one to the other.

Just ask Mags . . .

I know something I shouldn't . . .

'What is it?' he asked.

Mags pushed herself up from the table and began gathering the plates. Tim tried to look her in the eye but she kept her face down and didn't answer. He turned to PJ. 'Is this . . .' He gulped, had to start again. 'Is this something to do with . . . Well, I don't know what it's to do with but Maeve said I needed to talk to you. She said . . . she said she knew something. Something she shouldn't know.'

Mags stopped dead. Her shoulders slumped, her whole body deflated. She peered at PJ. 'Maeve? How would she . . . ?'

PJ shook his head. 'I've no idea.'

The wind gusted, slapped the back door against the wall. Mags jumped. PJ let out a half-stifled 'Jesus!' and got up to close it over.

'Is it something to do with Cornwall?' Tim went on. 'The postcard? Did you find the other one Mum sent? Can I see it? Are they coming over? Is that it?'

PJ stood up. He pushed his chair in under the table and he coughed, like someone clearing their throat before an important speech. 'Look, Tim,' he said, straight-backed and stiff, gripping the back of the chair. 'We didn't plan on things happening this way but—'

'No,' Mags said, her eyes panicky. 'Not yet. Let's—'

'We can't keep this up any longer, Mags. It's not fair on any of us. Least of all him.'

Mags clapped a hand over her mouth. 'Oh, God. Oh, God.' She leaned heavily on the table. PJ pulled out the chair he held. 'Sit down.' As she sat, exhaling loudly, Tim saw tears sliding down her face. 'Tim,' PJ said, his voice softer now, 'it wasn't that we weren't going to . . . We meant to but . . .' He trailed off, his head twitching, his hands resting on Mags's shoulders.

Tim looked at Mags. Her face was screwed up in pain, her arms wrapped round her middle. 'Mags? Mags? Are you all right? What's wrong? What is it? Is it . . . is it something to do with Mum and Dad?'

She reached a hand up to PJ. He took it, gripped it hard, his fingers entwining in hers. Her face was almost translucent now, the skin around her eyes silvery-grey.

Tim couldn't move. He looked between them. Two pairs of eyes staring at him.

They had something bad to tell him.

He knew that now.

A kind of stillness fell around him. He felt himself sinking, his body relaxing, readying itself. Preparing for what was coming next.

Mags reached out. 'Tim. Oh, God, Tim. I'm so sorry. I'm *so* ...' Then she could say no more. Her face crumpled and she rocked herself gently while she cried.

PJ spoke. 'We ... we didn't know how to tell you. Mags wanted ... We both wanted to give you a chance to get to know us, to ... to feel at home here first.'

Tim felt cold now. Freezing from the inside out.

'It was ... Well, you were only here a while and we would've told you earlier but Mags, she ... she wanted to wait.'

What was he trying to say? Tim's heart beat quick and heavy. It felt huge, swollen in his chest, squeezing the air from his lungs. He saw PJ turn, take the Bible from the dresser shelf. Mags was doubled over now, breathing fast, shallow breaths, her tears still falling, her hands still holding her stomach.

Silently, PJ opened the Bible and handed Tim a scrap of newspaper he took from between its pages. Tim took it and read the words. He let it fall before he could finish.

> SWIFT, 6 August (following an accident), Edward and Joan (née Rooney), Grimsmede, Cheshire. Sadly missed by son, Timothy. Funeral service will take place on ...

Tim stood up. He looked from PJ to Mags, trying to make sense of what they were telling him. He swayed. Stumbled. His legs gave way. PJ caught him before he fell and he sank into his uncle's body, breathing in the scent of him – cement and petrol and oil. Earth and paint and … life.

Life.

He could feel the thump of PJ's heart – mechanical and sonorous – but it gave him comfort for only the briefest moment. Then he railed hard against his grip but PJ held him tight. 'It's all right, Tim. Everything's going to be all right. Mags and me, we're going to look after you. We …'

His voice shrank. Faded in and out. The words Tim had read sped around in his head. Edward. Joan. Accident. Funeral.

Mum and Dad.

Dead.

No longer living.

And then he realised. The date: 6 August. Nearly three weeks ago. *Three weeks.* All that time. All that time it had been kept from him.

'It was an accident,' PJ was saying. 'The car … a truck … your mammy was … They hadn't a chance. Mags and me, we …'

Tim closed his eyes. He wanted darkness, craved the comfort of a dream. PJ let him fall gently onto the couch. He sank into its softness, brought his knees to his chest, curled himself tight. His whole body was charged, the root of every hair an electric pinprick.

Then the shivering began, his teeth chattering as the shock took hold. A soft weight fell on him – the warmth of PJ's jacket – and the soothing scent of the familiar. Of the world he'd come to know. The world they expected him to embrace.

He lay there, unseeing, unhearing, aware of nothing but the horrible, awful thoughts that pulsed inside his head – 6 August: the day of the disco. Father Coffey. He'd brought the news. They'd all stared when Tim came in that night and found them there. His parents were dead. And no one told him. Mass the next day, the family outing to the beach, trying to make things normal. PJ taking him to work, keeping him occupied. Days passing.

And no one told him.

They hadn't even allowed him to say goodbye.

He reared up and launched himself at PJ. His uncle reeled, feet scrabbling on the lino as he tried to stay upright. Again and again Tim struck out, punching hard, harder, wanting to inflict pain, to make PJ feel what he was feeling.

'Tim. Please,' Mags cried, pushing herself up from her chair, then falling back into it with a loud moan.

PJ stood mute, statue-still, accepting the blows, knowing it would last only so long. And when it was over, Tim slumped to the floor, his strength depleted, his eyes filling with acid tears. He made no objection when PJ helped him to his feet. 'Don't make it any harder for yourself, Tim,' he said. 'We're here to help.'

Tim stared into his face. 'How could you *do* that?' He turned to Mags. *'How?'*

'We thought . . . We didn't . . . We . . .' The rest of her words were lost in her tears.

'What am I supposed to do?' Tim cried. 'What's going to happen?'

'You're going to live here,' PJ said. 'With us. That's what's going to happen.'

Tim could see them. In his head. Mum and Dad. Asleep in their bed that night before he left. He remembered how they'd looked like they were dead. And now . . .

How could it be happening? Was it just a dream? Nothing made sense. Nothing at all.

'It's what's been arranged, Tim,' PJ said. 'It's what your . . . It's what Joan wanted. There was an arrangement. There's always been an arrangement. Mags was who they wanted to look after you if . . . if the worst ever happened.'

Tim couldn't understand what he was saying. What did all this even mean? 'Tim. You're still a child,' he heard PJ say. 'We're best placed to look after you.' PJ held out his hands. 'Look, let's not talk about it now. You need time. We all need time.' He moved closer.

Tim side-stepped him and made for the door. Time? They'd already had enough. How could Mags have kept it from him? How? In what way did she think that was best? He caught his breath and swallowed hard. He knew now why Maeve had been so upset, why she'd kissed him. 'Maeve knew, didn't she?' he heard himself asking. 'She knew before I did that my parents were dead.' It was as though it was someone else's voice. It didn't sound like his own.

'She must've . . . she must've heard Tess and Lar talking,' Mags whispered, wiping her eyes with a tissue she pulled from her sleeve. 'I'm sorry, Tim. I'm *so* sorry. I—' and she gave way again to her sobbing.

'Look, Tim,' PJ said, trying to sound reasonable. 'Whatever was done was done for your own good. Mags thinks the world of you. You should know that by now. She'd never do anything to hurt you. She . . . she . . . Well, she thinks the world of you, that's all I can say. She went over, Tim. She wasn't in the hospital that time. She was at the funeral. She saw them away, so she did. And Tess went with her, to mind her, like, and . . . '

His voice trailed off into nothing. Though Tim could hear him, his words became a muffled jumble that melted into an indistinct hum. 'Let him go,' he heard Mags say, as he walked towards the stairs. It was clear from the strangled way she said it that she was in pain. 'He needs time.'

Orphan.

The word ballooned in Tim's head, swelled at the back of his throat, as though the sound and shape of it might suffocate him. He found himself in his room and he sank down on the bed. The same bed. The same room. Same house. Same road. Same everything. Except it wasn't. How could it be? Everything was different. Every single thing. Nothing would ever be the same again.

Would he really never see Mum and Dad again? Ever? Would the last memory always be those moments in Holyhead? Dad handing him the money. Mum trying not to cry. He couldn't bear it. He wanted them. Wanted to be with them. Wherever they were.

He rolled onto his side. His nail scissors were in the bedside locker drawer. Mum had reminded him to put them into his toilet bag the night before he'd left. *Don't forget to keep your nails trimmed,* she'd said. Wiping his eyes with the edge of the sheet, he studied the blue-white undersides of his wrists. It would be painful at first but after that it would be only a matter of time. If he climbed in under the bedcovers, it would look to anyone, at a quick glance, as though he was fast asleep. He took the scissors from the drawer, lay back down and pulled the blankets up over his head.

I still haven't said anything to Luke about the emails. There's not enough to tell yet. No point in giving him half the story. Maeve seems to have her reasons for drip-feeding the details so I've little choice but to accept that and wait for the next instalment. I'm trying to stay focused, not to allow him to see my mind is elsewhere. But he knows me well. He can sense my distraction. It's lunchtime. We're grabbing a quick bite in the little Italian place round the corner from my office, sitting in our favourite spot in the sunny bay window. He talks about work. Bits and pieces. How he feels about the decisions in some of his recent cases. The upcoming retirement of a particular judge. The frequency of sending out invoices versus the infrequency of getting paid. I'm trying my best to keep engaged. He finishes the last of his minestrone. 'You're not really listening, are you?'

'No, no, I am, I'm . . .'

'You still obsessing about Curly Boy?' It's the first time he's mentioned it in weeks. He smiles. 'It's OK. I won't bite your head off.'

'No, I . . . Well, yeah, a little.'

'Thought so. Look, I'm sure you'll find out everything in time. It's only natural you're curious. But . . .' he takes my hand '. . . don't let it get under your skin.'

I shake my head and do my best to sound sincere. 'I won't. Don't worry.'

'Oh. Almost forgot. Don't suppose Ciara filled you in on the latest?'

I look at him blankly. 'Latest?'

'Dumped. By his lordship.'

'Seriously? When?'

'Last weekend. Big bust-up apparently.'

'Jesus. That didn't last long.'

'Longer than the previous one, by all accounts.' He signals to the waiter for the bill.

'She kept that to herself.'

'Well, she wouldn't want to admit her own failings. That's one reason people keep secrets, isn't it? Because they don't want to lose face.'

We finish up and walk back to our respective offices. All afternoon, I keep thinking about what he said. Is that Mam's reason? Is it guilt? Shame? Is she afraid I'll think less of her? What's going to happen when I finally find out what she's been hiding?

Tim Swift. At home that evening I Google his name. There are plenty of them. Doing all sorts of things in all sorts of places. I scan the page of images but none of those pictured bears any resemblance to the boy with the white-blond curls. Though who knows what he looks like now? Or if there'd be any reason for his picture to be online. Or if he's even still alive.

It's a sad story ... I don't really want to contemplate what that might mean. I'd replied to Maeve's last email. Just a concise 'Thank you so much and I can't wait to hear more', hoping she'd sense my impatience. That was two days ago and still there's been nothing further. Surely she won't leave me hanging much longer.

I wake in the middle of the night and lie there for what seems like hours. I'm alone. Luke didn't stay. A friend's thirtieth – drinks in his local. I didn't feel like going along. Eventually, I pick up my phone: 5:23 a.m. Not much point trying to sleep now – I'm usually up in little more than an hour. I tap the envelope icon on the lighted screen and wait for new emails to download. Finally. There it is. I switch on the lamp.

Dear Orla,

Been super busy here with everything the last few days so am only getting time to sit down and write this now. The kids are at school and I'm on a day off work, so here goes.

I told you about me being sure something had happened to my father, and Tim being all suspicious too? Well, Daddy turned up alive and well towards the end of August. He'd been working over in London and Mammy knew all about it. Came up with the plan after Daddy had been out of work for months. She'd been claiming benefits, pretending she'd been deserted, and Daddy had been sending money back through your mother (so as not to alert Katty Hackett's suspicions). Daddy missed us all so he came back and I was, naturally, mad at Mammy for lying to me. But I got over that quick enough, mainly because of what I found out about Tim. I wasn't meant to know anything but I heard Mammy and Daddy talking. Tim and I had been right to think something bad had happened. We just couldn't have known what it was all about.

I remember him coming down to our house that day. I hadn't seen him since we got the new pup, and he'd been sick in bed for a few days after that. He'd heard Daddy was back and he wanted to see how I was. I hated that I knew something so bad, something I shouldn't have known before him, and I kept telling him to go back to Mags and talk to her. Of course, he hadn't a clue what I was going on about. I remember walking out with him to the road and I kissed him before he left. I think I knew I'd never see him again after that. And I was right.

The truth was that his mother and father were dead. They'd been killed in a car accident a while after Tim arrived. Your parents had kept it from him all that time. I don't know when they'd been planning on telling him but it must have been absolutely devastating when he found out and realised it had happened weeks before. I hate to be the one to tell you this, Orla. I know you said you'd only just found out about the existence of your mother's sister but I think I'm right in assuming you didn't know that she and her husband had passed away? I only feel right telling you this because of what I found out later. There's a lot more to this story and

Jesus. My phone. Ringing. The noise of it like a drill in my ears. It can't be my alarm. Surely it's still too early for that? I reach to pick it up and see that it's a call. 'Dad'.

Mam's in hospital. Chest pains. I don't waste any time asking for details. All I want to do is go to her.

I'm dressed, in the car and on the road in under ten minutes. I drive across the river and up past Merrion Square. It's not bright yet and the city's Georgian streets are ghostly quiet, yet to come alive with morning traffic. I'm through Donnybrook and onto the Stillorgan Road in minutes. Now it's straight all the way. But it's far from an easy journey. I don't think I've ever felt so confused. So scared. So sad. That poor boy. His parents gone. Mam's sister, her brother-in-law. Dead. How could Mam and Dad have kept it from him? Why? Why all the lies and secrets? All the pretence. The withholding. All these years. And how serious are things now? How bad is Mam? The uncertainty. It's unbearable. Not knowing if Mam will be all right. Not knowing what else Maeve has to say.

I put my foot down. I'm driving way past the speed limit. I don't care about the danger.

A sad story, but one I'm really hoping doesn't have to end that way . . .

Tim couldn't do it. He tried. Dragged the scissors blade across his left wrist and drew a tiny bulb of blood. But that was as far as he got. He fell back, skin freezing, muscles locked, every bone seeming fused together. Exhaustion waved through him and he drifted somewhere outside himself, where he saw his own wretched tangle of limbs in a heap on top of the bed. In a haze of half-sleep he wondered what time it was, if Mags was up, if breakfast was ready. And then his chest was crushed with a boulder of despair when he remembered once again what had happened.

In and out he slipped. Remembering. Forgetting. Remembering again. Every word, every smile, every tear from the past few weeks. What was real? Really real? What was a lie? How could anything he'd done since it happened be true? How could any of it count? Thinking Mum and Dad were at home, doing the things they always did ... but they weren't. They weren't doing anything at all. And he hadn't been who he thought he was. All that time he'd been a boy whose parents were dead and he hadn't even known. Mum wasn't at the shops that day he rang. Or chatting to old Mrs Ball.

She was dead.

Dad was dead too.

Hot tears rolled from Tim's eyes. How could he be sure this was happening? Were they really not alive? How could he accept that they'd closed the door one day and never gone back?

Where was he supposed to call home?

He'd known something wasn't right with the postcard. *Greetings from Cornwall.* Those were Mags's words and it was her writing. Not Mum's. She'd had to think of some way to stop him leaving. He pictured her scrabbling about in drawers, looking for some old postcard to use, some old stamp, while he was being shoved to the ground by Barry Kilbride. She'd let him walk all the way to the phone box even though she'd known there was no point. No wonder she'd been watching out for him. She'd been terrified he'd arrive back before she'd managed to finish her little deception. 'Look what came for you . . .'

Love Mum and Dad.

How could she have done it? *How?* And he'd apologised to *her* for lying . . . And the second postcard. It had never existed.

It had been Mags's idea to keep the awful truth from Tim. That was obvious now. PJ wasn't happy about it. They'd been cool with each other since the night of the disco. All those things Tim had overheard them arguing about. Mags insisting it wasn't the right time. But when had she planned on telling him? And Father Coffey. Handing Tim those stupid beads and suggesting he say some prayers. He'd wanted Mags to tell. What had stopped her? Was she so afraid of dealing with it?

So afraid of letting him go? Something she'd said not long after he'd arrived. When she and PJ had been talking about the Mooneys. He remembered it now. *This is the perfect time. And I don't want it destroyed. I just wanted this summer for ... Well, you know what I wanted it for.* Whatever it was, Mum and Dad dying hadn't been part of it. She hadn't wanted her 'perfect time' shattered. Her perfect time before her perfect baby arrived. Was that it? *God knows how I'm going to feel come the middle of September.* Well, I'm sorry, Mags, he thought. Sorry this has all been so inconvenient for you.

Slowly, he swung his feet to the floor and stood up. His head thumped. He went to the open window, let the wind blast cold and fresh over his face. It could've picked him up, tossed him about in the sky, he felt so light and empty.

It was someone else's hands he saw hurriedly packing his rucksack. With someone else's clothes. He couldn't possibly be the person he had been. Mags and PJ couldn't hold him. Couldn't tell him what to do. He wasn't staying. Not now. Not after all this.

Oh, God. He could hear her. On the stairs. Steps slow and full of effort. Breaths heavy, rasping. He threw his rucksack into the wardrobe, leaped back into bed.

'Tim? Tim?' She opened the door. 'You awake?'

Pulse pumping in his ears. Heartbeats doubling, tripling. He rolled onto his side. Closed his eyes. Pulled the covers to his chin.

He felt her move across the room, heard the click of the windows as she closed them. Then, a moment without sound or movement as she – he could sense – stood over him, watching. Leaning in, a feathery kiss on his forehead, hands gently smoothing his hair.

A lump swelled and stung in his throat. His eyes burned. It was the hardest thing, not to reach up and throw his arms around her neck.

'Out for the count,' she whispered to PJ as she left. Then, from behind the door, Tim heard her say, 'No, I'm fine. Pain's not so bad now. Was just the shock of it all.'

He tried his best to stem the tears. If he let them flow, he was accepting it, allowing himself to admit the horror. He pictured their faces. Mum and Dad. Really focused on them as he concentrated on his breathing: inhaling deeply in sharp, measured sniffs; exhaling, deliberately, every drop of air from his lungs. In. Out. In. Out. Without meaning to, he fell asleep.

And the sea dream came again.

This time, he was sinking. Slowly, soundlessly. For ever. On and on.

Down, down, further, deeper.

To where it was deepest, blackest black. To where there was nothing else.

And it was black when he woke. The night was thick and dark, the wind swishing through the trees. He slipped out of bed and switched on the lamp, searching about in its hazy, weak-bulb gleam. He found his rucksack, pulled out the clothes he'd already stuffed into it and, this time, methodically rolled them into sausage shapes. Just like Mum had. Under the bed, he found the pair of leather brogues he'd sworn he'd never wear and slipped his feet into them, lacing them up tight, knotting them hard enough to hurt. Standing up, his legs shook, ice-cold, shivery waves rushing up and down his bones. He left his camera – it was no use now it was smashed.

He picked up the finished roll of film, ready to push it into his rucksack, but rage got the better of him and he flung it across the room. Why would he need reminding of this place and time? His eyes filled again when he found his drawing pad. In seconds, he'd ripped out every page and torn each one to shreds.

He tiptoed along the landing. Mags and PJ weren't asleep. He could hear murmurs coming from their room.

By the silver-blue light of a half-circle moon, he quietly eased open each kitchen cupboard in turn, cramming biscuits, a half-eaten bar of chocolate and a block of jelly into his rucksack. From the fridge he took some slices of ham, then filled a plastic beaker with water. A triangular hunk of brown bread sat on the counter but he couldn't bring himself to take it. He couldn't bear the thought that Mags's hands had kneaded the dough.

He was ready.

For what, he had no idea.

As he buckled the strap of his rucksack he heard a cry. It came from upstairs.

He couldn't describe the sound. Animal? Human?

And then again. Wild. Frantic. Then shouting. Someone calling. Calling his name. Tim. Tim! *Tiiiiiim!*

PJ leaped into the kitchen. He ran to Tim, grabbing his shoulders, shaking him hard. 'The baby!' he yelled. 'Help me, Tim! 'Tis coming. I swear to God. 'Tis coming!'

Tim couldn't move. He stared at his uncle, at his wide, frightened eyes. It was too early. Even through his own grief, he understood that. It shouldn't be happening. Not yet.

Another cry came from above.

PJ dragged him towards the stairs. 'Stay with Mags, you

hear me? I have to go and phone for help.' He pushed Tim upwards, following. 'Please. Stay with her. Help her.'

Mags lay on her side on the bed, legs bent at the knee, arms wrapped around her stomach. Her forehead and cheeks shone with sweat and her eyes were squeezed shut. 'The hospital,' she moaned. 'I need to get to the—' And then she roared again. That fierce, animal sound.

Tim didn't want to look at her but he couldn't turn away. He was scared. Terrified. Sometimes things went wrong when babies were being born. He knew that much.

PJ stroked Mags's hair. 'I don't know if we'd make it that far, love.' He tried to make himself sound calm. 'And I don't want it happening on the side of the road. I'll drive down to the phone box and call for the doctor. He'll be here quicker than an ambulance. Tim's going to stay with you. I—'

'Tim?' She went to reach out but pulled her hand back to her stomach and winced. 'Come here,' she managed to whisper. Tim didn't move. 'We want you to . . . stay.' She took a huge breath and shook her head, grimacing through another wave of pain. 'We want—'

PJ laid a hand on her arm. 'Mags, Mags. Shush now.'

'But—'

'Stop, Mags. Leave things be. We'll sort it all out later.' He bent to kiss her head. 'I'm going now. I'll be back before you know it. I—'

She grabbed hold of his shirt. 'Don't . . . leave me.' She held on to him, trying to pull herself up, but she flopped back down on the bed, the effort proving too much. 'Please, PJ. Don't go!' She was frantic now. 'I don't want to be here on my own! I'm scared. Please!' Tim could hardly believe this was Mags.

Everything was falling apart.

And then he felt it again – the crushing weight on his chest, squeezing his breaths to shallow rasps. *Mum*, he called out in his head. *What am I supposed to do?*

PJ sat down on the bed and took Mags's hand. 'We need to get the doctor. What if I ask Tim to go? Would that be all right, do you think?' He turned to Tim. 'Could you do it? Could you run down and phone? I know it's late but you might meet a car on the way and get a lift.'

'Lar,' Mags said, in a hoarse whisper. 'Couldn't he take him?'

'Sure he'd be there and back by the time Lar Mooney'd waken. Even if he was strolling.' PJ took a biro from the bedside table, scribbled a number on the back of Tim's hand. 'It's Dr Harris you'll be calling.' He pressed some coins into Tim's palm. 'Put these in your pocket.' He gripped Tim's shoulders. 'I'm sorry to be sending you off out like this. It's the last thing I'd be wanting to do after . . . well . . . after . . .' He squeezed hard, then released his grip. 'We'll see you back here, right?' Tim stared blankly. 'Right?' PJ repeated. Tim nodded slowly, and, as he turned to back out the door, Mags's arm shot out. Her eyes were desperate. She was crying now. 'I'm . . . sorry . . . Tim. I'm . . . so . . . sorry.' She tried to pull him closer. 'I . . . need to—'

'No.' PJ stretched over and lifted her fingers. 'Not now.' His voice was firm. Then it softened. 'I told you. Time for all that later on,' he said, settling her arm back by her side.

Tim's legs took him downstairs, brought him towards the back door, past the kitchen table where his rucksack still sat. He pushed his arm through the strap and lifted it, cradling it close to his chest as he went outside. At the gate, he let it slip to the ground, knowing the weight of it would only slow him down.

The warm wind curled about his face and the moon smirked down from the blue-black sky. His heart pulsed at the back of his throat. The night was thick and silent. Not a sound except the *slap slap slap* of his feet on the road. His legs pumped hard and soon he was running, as fast as his slippery leather soles would allow. He knew he'd be at Mooneys' soon. He could hardly bear the thought of having to pass. With every step, his body grew heavier until the cottage came into view, his knees buckled, and he had to stop. He felt sick now. Maeve had known before him. Her kiss had come out of pity. Nothing more. He'd thought he'd want the taste of her lips on his for ever. Now he wanted only to forget. He leaned down, panting, his hands on his knees as he tried to catch his breath. Then, out from the silence, came a low, rumbling growl. A car. Straightening up, he waved his arms above his head and watched as the headlights came closer. He was half blind when it came to a stop in the middle of the road. Leaning down to the open window, he blurted breathlessly, 'Please I . . . need a lift to the . . . phone box.'

'Do you now? At four o'clock in the morning?'

Tim knew the voice well enough by now, even before his eyes adjusted. Barry stared up at him through the open window, tonguing a piece of gum from one side of his mouth to the other. He'd been drinking. Tim could smell it on his breath.

'It's important. Mags . . . she's . . . she's having the . . . baby.'

Barry laughed. 'Ah now, come on,' he said, his words slurred. 'Even I know it's not supposed to be here for weeks.'

Tim's heart was a burning ball. He took a deep breath. 'I have to call the doctor.'

'Sure hasn't PJ his own transport?' Barry smacked the gum

round his mouth. 'Why would you need to be out hitching a lift?'

'Mags won't let him leave her.'

'Sorry. It's out of my way,' he sneered. 'Sure won't the run do you good?'

'It'll only be a few minutes in the car. Please. She's in pain. It's an emergency.'

'Better get your arse down to the crossroads, then. You wouldn't want them to be blaming you if anything bad happened.' He laughed, putting the car in gear.

Tim didn't think about it. He pulled open the door, grabbed Barry's arm and threw him out onto the ground. He'd never punched anyone before. Had never had the guts even to try. But things were different now. He wasn't who he used to be. Before the drunken Barry had a chance to consider getting to his feet, Tim shot a fist at his face and caught him full force on the nose. He fell flat on his back, his head hitting the road with a thump.

Tim stepped over him and settled himself into the driver's seat.

The engine was still running. Last year on holidays, Dad had allowed him behind the wheel on the quiet country lane that led to their rented cottage. If someone had asked him, he wouldn't have been able to explain how to drive but, somehow, the basics he knew came back to him. As the car lurched forward, he looked in the rear-view mirror and saw the dark shape that was Barry, still lying stretched out on the ground. At the sight of him, he pressed his foot harder on the accelerator.

The engine hummed in his bones. His head was clearer now. He picked up speed and the car began to veer all over the road. He managed to straighten up as he drove through the sleeping village and, as he came closer to the crossroads, he pushed his foot on the brake.

Dr Harris answered the phone surprisingly quickly. 'No need to panic, young man,' he said, after Tim had managed to explain. 'There's probably plenty of time yet. You go on back now. Tell your aunt and uncle I'll be there as quick as I can.' He sounded calm and kind, and Tim wanted him to say that everything would be all right. That there'd been some kind of mistake. Don't worry, he wished he'd say. Mum and Dad are fine. Just fine. Looking forward to you going home. Can't wait to see you. He hung on to those imagined words as he dialled his home number.

Please answer, Mum. Please.

He listened until it rang out. They're still asleep, he told himself. Try again.

He waited. And waited. Nothing.

He climbed back into the car and willed with all his might that this night was a dream. Please be a dream. *Please.* He wrenched the steering wheel round and the car began to turn. Surely it's time to wake up now. Just get me out of this. I've had enough.

Round and round. Further and further. Foot down hard. Too hard.

Spinning. Fast. Faster.

Then everything went black.

Dawn is breaking when I reach the hospital.

'My mother. Margaret Hyland,' I say to the bright-eyed nurse I meet just inside the glass doors. 'I'm not sure which ward. I—'

A reassuring hand is placed on my arm. 'Oh, yes,' she says cheerily, as if I've asked for directions to a funfair. 'There's someone with her at the moment. Your dad, is it? I'll bring you down.'

I follow her along a strip-lit corridor, the grisly hospital smell growing stronger with every step. She turns briskly into a small, airless ward, indicating the corner bed, tangerine curtains pulled almost all the way round. Dad gets to his feet when he sees me, smoothing down the front of his jumper. His face is grey and drawn, his eyes sunken. He seems thinner than before.

'How is she?' I ask. 'Will she be OK? Do they know anything yet?'

'Just spoke to a doctor, so I did. They think now 'twas some kind of panic attack.'

'Not her heart, then? Are they sure?'

He nods. I breathe out in relief. I want the detail now. 'What time did you get here? Was she admitted during the night?'

He gives me a sheepish look. 'Aye. Night before last.'

I almost want to lash out at him. 'She's been here all that time and you never called me? Jesus, Dad. Why did you leave it so long?'

'Didn't want to be disturbing you.'

'*Disturbing* me? This is my *mother* you're talking about.'

'Would you stop. Keep your voice down. I rang you, didn't I?' He tells me to take his chair and stomps off, arms swinging, to find another for himself. Mam's asleep, hooked up to several monitors. She stirs a little when I sit down, opens her eyes, shuts them again. She looks tiny in the bed, shrunken, enveloped in an oversized papery robe. Wires worm from the suction pads dotting her chest. A plastic ID band circles her wrist.

Dad returns. I light on him. 'What were you thinking, not telling me till now? It could've been serious.'

'I told you. I didn't want you to be worrying. Your mother wouldn't have wanted it either.'

'More of your secrets. Is that it? Yet another thing Orla doesn't need to know.'

'That's not it, I—'

'Then what is it? What is it, Dad?' I dig my nails into my palms. I can feel the threat of tears.

'Look,' he says, 'don't be getting yourself into a state. All that other stuff, that, that . . . picture and all. It's time we—'

'You don't have to concern yourself with that any more, Dad.' I'm sounding bitter but I don't care. 'Sooner rather than later it's all going to come out in the open.'

'Ah, lookit, you don't have to be so—'

It's Mam who cuts him off now. Her voice is hoarse, barely audible. Her eyes are still closed. 'What's going on? Why are you sniping at each other?'

I touch her arm. 'Mam. You're awake. How are you feeling?'

'Like I'm ready to get out of this place.'

I smile. 'That's good to hear. But we'll let the doctors decide when that'll be.'

'Sounded like they were thinking of this afternoon,' Dad says. 'Just have to wait for the top man to come round to see you.'

'I'll come home with you. I'll stay the night,' I say.

'There's no need,' Dad says. 'We can manage.'

'I'm coming. Decision made.'

Mam nods off again and we sit in relative silence. Soon the unforgiving overhead lights are switched on and, from somewhere distant, I can hear the rattle and clink of cutlery and teacups that signify the arrival of breakfast. A light-footed nurse flits about, checking end-of-bed charts and gently rousing each patient.

'You go and get yourself something to eat,' Mam tells me, when she's sitting up.

I sense she wants to talk to Dad so I do as she says, even though I'd prefer to stay beside her. Dad folds his arms tight across his chest, as though to protect himself from some kind of onslaught. He declines my offer to bring him back a cup of tea.

In the over-bright hospital café, I buy a coffee and something brown that resembles a croissant, sit down opposite a group of chattering nurses and take out my phone. My head thumps. I call Luke and explain everything. I have to put him off joining me. 'I'm fine,' I insist. 'And Mam's going to be OK.' I rub my eyes. Thankfully, I'm not in court; I've no need to hurry back. I take a bite of the suspicious-looking pastry. Whatever it is, it's long past its best. I lay my phone on the small, square table. I feel guilty reopening Maeve's email. Is this the time or the place? But then again ... The panic attack Mam had, maybe all the years of secrecy brought it on.

> ... and I only feel right telling you because of what I've just discovered. There's a lot more to this story and, if I'm honest, I'm not sure if I'm the right person to tell it. I could try but, really and truly, I think it would be so much better coming from the person who told it to me. Have a look at what I've copied and pasted here:
>
> Maeve,
> Thanks so much for this. It means such a huge amount. Can't tell you how happy I am that you're in contact with Orla. Please ask her if it's OK for you to give me her address so I can email. Really hope she's agreeable.
> Best,
> Tim
>
> I made contact with Tim again recently. I happened to come across a piece online about some photography prize he'd judged. When I saw his name, I wondered. So I looked him up and managed to get in touch. It's been nice, reminiscing about that summer, but sad, too, as you can imagine. When Donal mentioned he'd bumped into you and that you were curious about the photo, asking who the 'boy' was, I thought I'd let Tim know. It seemed strange to me that you didn't know who

he was and I thought maybe he'd like to get in contact with you. It was then that Tim told me the story and said he'd actually been thinking about trying to reconnect but wasn't sure how he should go about it. I said I'd look you up first, fill you in on some details, sort of ease you into it, as it were. The plan was that I'd put you two in touch, so I'm hoping very much that this is OK with you?

Hope to hear from you soon.

Maeve

My coffee grows cold and the noisy nurses return to their stations. I read and re-read, over and over, scrolling up and down through the lines as though I need to know it by heart. Part of me says, *Hurry up, just do it, say yes.* Another part says, *Take your time. What's the rush? Your mother's still in hospital, for God's sake.* I look through the café windows to the corridor. The place is filled with people making life-and-death decisions every day. Filled also, I'm sure, with those who wish they'd done things differently, who regret leaving things until it's too late. A bearded orderly pushes a skeletal old woman in a wheelchair, her face more bone than skin, her fingers like bleached twigs in her caved lap. She turns her head as they pass and we lock eyes for the briefest moment. I have to look away. She isn't old at all. Just ill. Probably dying.

I swallow hard, tap out a reply, tell Maeve simply 'Yes.'

The consultant, when he arrives at Mam's bedside, is reassuringly direct. They're satisfied with all the relevant test results and, although she'll have to return in a few weeks for some follow-up checks, they're happy to discharge her.

I ask him a few questions, which he answers in detail, his steady grey eyes firmly focused on mine as he speaks. When he leaves, I notice Mam and Dad are now holding hands, heads bowed, whispering to each other.

I have to force Mam to lie on the couch when we get home. She won't hear of going up to bed. She tries to make out she's fine but it's clear from her face that she's tired. She falls asleep in minutes.

Dad says he's not hungry. He's edgy, fractious. Definitely not his usual self. But, still, he settles himself in at the table and tucks into the omelette I've made him. 'You'll have to be off early, I suppose?' he asks, shuffling his feet under the table.

I'm in court next day but have already asked a colleague to stand in for me. 'I sorted something out. You'll have to put up with me. For tonight and tomorrow anyway.'

'But won't you need some of your stuff?' He takes a gulp from his glass of milk. 'Clothes and the like?'

'I have a few things in the car. I'll be grand.'

'All right so. If that's what you want.'

I can't stand the tension. I have to break it. 'Dad, I'm sorry I went on at you earlier.' His head moves, almost imperceptibly. A jerk rather than a nod. 'But you really should've called me when Mam was first admitted. All this secrecy, this not telling. It has to stop. Things have gone too far.' He says nothing, just stares at his plate. 'It's all going to come out soon, Dad,' I say, after a long silence. 'That's what you wanted, wasn't it?'

He looks up at me, eyebrows raised. 'And where are you getting that from?'

'Come on, Dad. The photo. It was no accident. You wanted me to see it, didn't you? You wanted this . . . this . . . whatever it is. It was all part of the plan.'

He leans forward, elbows on the table, rests his head in his hands for a moment. Then, slowly, he looks up at me, his eyes locked on mine. 'Your mother heard us rowing in the hospital. You know that, don't you? She's not happy that it's all come to this. And being in there, taking that turn, it's shaken her. I'm not sure she'll be looking at things the same way from now on. It's never been fair on you, Orla. Your mother and I, we both know that.'

If he was going to say any more, he doesn't get a chance. Mam stirs and calls out, sounding weak, disoriented. We go to her. He helps her to her feet. She's heading to bed now, she says, and wants Dad to stay with her.

Before they go upstairs, Dad reaches back and touches my arm. A short, tight squeeze that tells me he understands.

Later that night I lie in the metal bed in the spare room, staring at the ceiling. I'm close, so close. But to what, I don't know. Dad's words, his gesture, they mean a lot. Even after all this time. I can tell he wants an end to it and, from the way he was talking, Mam does too.

Tim is alive. And he wants to contact me. I've memorised his words. *It means such a huge amount ... Can't tell you how happy I am ... Really hope she's agreeable.* But what is it that he wants to say? What is this 'story' he wants to tell? I reach out for my phone and check my email. Nothing. I shift in the bed, trying to get comfortable despite the springs poking through the old mattress. I'm worried about Mam. And scared. Scared of what I might find out. What proof do I have that things will be better when I do? They might be a hundred times worse.

I dream I'm standing on a cliff, watching a boat sailing over the sea. There's something distinctive about its arrival, something I don't have words to describe. I watch it for what seems like the longest time and still it comes no closer to the shore. I inch nearer to the edge and then I'm falling. Floating. Swimming out to meet it. I plough through the waves, tasting salt water on my lips. And when I wake, my face is wet and sticky with tears.

I check my email. It's there.

Dear Orla,

I can't thank you enough for allowing Maeve to give me your address. It means a lot to me that you're willing to have me contact you, and I'm hoping that when you find out why you'll understand exactly how much. I really want to meet you, and I'm planning to come over to Ireland in the next couple of weeks – sooner rather than later. I have so much to talk about, so many things I want to say. To you, to Mags and to PJ. I've thought so long and hard about how to approach this, how I should begin, and I've come to the conclusion, crazy as it might seem, to say nothing. That is, of course we'll talk but, for the moment, I think it better that you uncover the truth about me for yourself. Maeve has filled you in on some of the story – about what happened that summer and your mother keeping my parents' deaths from me. But there's more. And this is the most important part.

I've attached a series of scanned letters here – please read them in order: 1, 2, 3. I know you'll figure it out – these words will paint a picture far more tellingly than I could ever hope to.

Yours, as they say, in anticipation,

Tim

Barry's car was a write-off. Tim was lucky to have come out of it with nothing more than a throbbing shoulder. He'd lost control somehow. Got confused with the pedals. He was tired. Exhausted. In shock. He'd hit a telegraph pole. He was pretty sure of that much. When he came to, the car was inside a hedge on the far side of a field, twigs and brambles protruding through the open window and the taste of petrol and damp grass in his mouth. The shattered windscreen slowly came into focus, tiny diamonds of glass threatening to burst all over the dash, and the fur-covered passenger seat, mangled and contorted, like a tormented beast. He heaved open the door, pushing back the undergrowth, and fell out into the field.

The sky was beginning to lighten. A faint yellow-pink tinge bleeding through the dark blue. He made his way towards the road. Birds sang all around. A new day. A brand new dawn. For one delicious moment, he was filled with joy. He inhaled the fresh morning air and closed his eyes in thanks. He was one lucky boy. It could've been so much worse. He could've been killed. Mum and Dad. They mustn't find out. No matter that he was OK, they'd be mad as hell. He'd be in deep trouble. They'd be ... He stopped. His throat was jagged and dry, his stomach was churning and his legs began to shake. A warning flashed behind his eyes.

Don't look back. Don't look back.

You know what you're going to see.

And he gagged himself empty onto the earth when his head turned and he imagined he could see them there. Half in, half out of the wrecked car. The only way he'd picture them for the longest time.

Staggering out of the field, he hunched down in the ditch and wrapped his arms around his knees. He could taste everything bad he'd ever eaten. He spat onto the road and wiped his mouth across his sleeve.

He remembered now.

Mags. The baby. The doctor. Barry's car. The happiness he felt about wrecking it was one grain of sand on a lonely beach. And the rest of it all – that was the deepest ocean of the fiercest waves. Washing away every bad thing that had ever happened. Every sad thought and feeling. Every horrible dream. They were nothing now. Not compared to this. He put his head on his arms. There was no way to fathom it. Someone somewhere could understand the most complicated mathematical problem, the most difficult scientific theory. But no one, anywhere, could explain this. This was a puzzle that couldn't make sense. That could never, ever make any sense at all.

He lifted his head when he heard a sound. He squinted. Away in the distance, beyond the crossroads, a tractor crawled towards him, emerging out of the early-morning mist like a rumbling, slow-moving dinosaur. Wishy Crowe. Even from a few hundred yards, Tim could tell it was him. No one else in Lissenmore drove like Wishy. Weaving over and back from one side of the road to the other, regardless of who or what might be behind him, though at this time of day he had the road to himself. Tim thought about running back into the field, hiding until the tractor passed. If it was anyone else, he probably would have. But Wishy lived in a world of his own making. A kind soul who did as he was told and took things as he found them. He loved telling you his own business but years of being put down by his brothers had taught him not to ask anyone about theirs. Tim stood up. He wouldn't have to worry about explaining himself.

Wishy brought the tractor to a stop, blinking at Tim through the broken lenses of his glasses. 'It's looking like you're in need of a lift. Hop up there now. I'll take you down the road a bit.' Tim pulled himself into the cab, tucking his body into the little bit of space there was. 'Off to Faranboy I am,' Wishy shouted above the splutter of the engine. 'Giving a dig-out to a fella up there wanting a field cleared. Mossy says I'm to be back by dinnertime so I'm heading up early.' As Tim had figured, Wishy didn't ask what he was up to. He might've noticed the tyre tracks gouged into the grass verge. Or, from his vantage point, might've been able to see the rear end of Barry's car poking out of the hedge into the field. But if he had, he said not a word about it. He kept his eyes on the road, his slight body bouncing up and down as the tractor made its way through the village. 'Would you look at that,' he said, and whistled through the crack in his front tooth. Tim raised himself up a bit then slunk further down when he spied Barry, sitting with his head in his hands, still in the same spot where he'd left him. Wishy didn't stop. Just gave Barry a quick salute as he passed. 'Worse for wear, I'd say. That boyo had better watch hisself.' Tim remembered the way Barry had treated Wishy the day he'd been up at Crowe's farm. Wishy probably wouldn't have offered him a lift even if he'd had room.

'There y'are now,' Wishy said, slowing the tractor down outside the house. 'This is where you'll be wanting me to let you off. That right?'

Tim straightened up a little and looked into the yard. A strange black car. The doctor. 'My mum and dad are dead.' His heart jumped when he said it. The words had put a shape on it, made it something that was almost understandable. He grappled with the dark, swelling spectre of it, but it floated up through the air and disappeared.

Wishy coughed, embarrassed. 'You head on in now.' He shifted in his seat, took his glasses off and wiped a hand over his face. He peered through the mud-smeared windscreen. 'More rain on the way.'

Tim slid from the cab. He stood by the gate until the gravelly sound of the tractor faded and the gentle twitter of birdsong took over, light and sweet in the morning breeze. He closed his eyes and listened. The day had dawned like any other. The birds didn't know any different. It was all still the same. Nothing had changed. Had it?

He was tired. He needed to lie down. To sleep. Maybe he could pretend. Maybe he could push everything that had happened into a deep, dark hole where he'd never have to see it again. Mags and PJ – why did they do it? How could they have thought—

And there it was.

A thin, reedy cry. The new life. Drawing a line that he couldn't cross. The sound of a beginning he couldn't be part of.

He leaned against the gatepost and slumped down to the ground. Something broke his fall. His rucksack. He stared at it. He knew now. Knew what he had to do.

He felt as though he was being chased as he ran. Across the yard, through the brambles, out into the fields. On and on, not stopping to catch his breath till he was in the grain field and the house and everything in it had melted away. Stalks rippled in the breeze. Skirting the field's perimeter, trees bent and swished, their dark, leafy branches scribbling against the sky. Still he kept going, kept running, chest heaving, throat thick with pain. Distance. That was what he needed. As much as he could get.

He saw the cliffs up ahead but turned before he reached them, slipping and sliding over the dew-soaked grass all the way down to the road. He walked along the desolate coast for miles, picked his way over the stones and rocks, stopping once or twice to pull food from his rucksack. The wind in his hair, the heat on his face, the ground under his feet – everything was heightened. Stronger, warmer, harder than it could really have been. His heart soared at the sight of a seagull – its wings blinding white against the bluest sky – then sank to the depths of under-earth black as he watched it hover over the waves. Nothing was as it had been. Nothing at all. Everything was upside-down. What was sharp was soft. What was bright was dull. He was free and yet he was caught. Light, but heavy as stone.

He was Tim Swift. But not the way he remembered.

Back on the road, he took a lift from a kind-faced delivery

driver on an early-morning run. He was friendly, talkative, but Tim dodged his questions by pretending to nod off. His stream of chatter filled Tim's head and, after a few minutes, he'd fallen asleep for real. When he woke, the first thing his eyes focused on was a sign with a picture of a ferryboat under the words 'Dún Laoghaire'. He didn't think about it, just asked him to stop, said they'd reached the place he was going to.

He still had his money. He bought a ticket, boarded the boat when it arrived. He sat stock still in his seat, didn't move one inch, looked neither left nor right, just stared out at the sea for the entire length of the journey. When they docked in Holyhead and he followed the throng, his stomach did a somersault and he threw up all over the gangway.

He took a crowded train to Chester, a quiet bus to Grimsmede. Maybe it was all a mistake. He had to make sure, had to see for himself if it really was true. He hid behind a wall, waited for the coast to clear, rushed across the street, smashed the kitchen window of his house and crawled to the hall, collapsing in a heap against the front door.

The light faded.

It grew dark.

The rooms swelled around him, the walls moving, sliding, the furniture coming alive, the carpets billowing over the floors like waves.

He was sure he could hear them.

Through the strained, electric silence of the night. Rising. Falling. Murmurs seeping through the ceiling. Bricks cemented with their voices. Wood ingrained with their words. And then the sound crept along his skin, burrowed into his bones, infiltrated the blood that flowed in his veins. It swam upstream, filling every opening, stopping every gap, until it reached the dead end of his brain and stayed there, roaring, until it was more than he could bear and he smashed his head repeatedly on the cold, hard floor.

He passed out. Came to. Passed out again. When he opened his eyes, a thin, greyish light was licking edges, marking corners, making sense of the shapes around him. The noise in his head had shrunk to a vague shush, there but not there, still maddening but comforting all the same. A deliciously present pain. And mingled with it – milk-bottle clink, front-door thud, jingle-jangle, cling-clang, bye-bye – whooshing, bubbling in his ears.

The day grew into itself and still he lay there. He shivered, sweated, shivered again, wrapped his arms around his knees, pulled them tighter to his chest. He tried to figure out time, how long it had been, how much had gone by. Already everything seemed so far away, more deep-rooted in his memory than things that had happened long before. Some part of his thinking told him otherwise, that less than one full day had passed. But he didn't believe it. How could it be possible for so much to happen in such a tiny stretch of time?

The feel of paper in his hands. Smooth and crisp. He must have crawled or rolled a few feet to the bottom of the stairs. A stack of letters lay on the first step. He could see it in there, the blue envelope among the brown and white. They'd never seen it, never heard what he'd had to say. Carefully, he opened it and, in the afternoon silence of the house, sent the words up into space to find them.

'"Dear Mum,"' he whispered, '"I'm having a great time. I went strawberry picking. I brought some back and Mags made jam. Mags showed me some pictures of my grandparents and my uncles. Maybe you can tell me about them when I get home. I've made friends with a family called the Mooneys. They live . . .'"

And then his eyes watered and his voice cracked and the paper fell to the floor.

Someone had to have sorted the letters, laid them neatly on the stairs. It wasn't long until that someone arrived. He found Tim asleep, the envelope under his face, Mum and Dad's name and address imprinted backwards on his cheek. When Mags and PJ had realised Tim was gone, they'd made contact with Uncle John. John had already begun to sort things out; he'd been in the house several times since the accident. This time, he came to see if his hunch about where Tim might be was correct, and when he saw Tim curled on the hall floor, he held him in his arms and rocked him while he cried.

John had thought it strange that Tim wasn't at the funeral. But Mags had told him Tim didn't want to go, that he was too upset, and John had accepted her explanation. Earlier that day, down a crackling line in the hospital corridor, she'd held her newborn baby daughter close and told John the truth. He didn't blame her. He understood. Perhaps he might have done the same.

Mum and Dad had left the house in trust to John, to transfer to Tim when he was twenty-one. He moved in and, with a kindness that surpassed any Tim could have imagined, cared for him until he was old enough to look after himself. In time, Tim went back to school and, with John's support, he made it through to the end. John was patient, accepting, understanding. It was he who encouraged Tim's interest in photography, to the extent that it became his full-time career.

There had indeed been an 'arrangement' in Mum and Dad's will that Mags should look after Tim. But Tim's wishes were taken into consideration. He wanted to stay in Grimsmede, close to his friends, his school – everything he was familiar with – under the care of Gentle John. Mags kept in touch with John, writing often and, once the phone was finally installed, calling every month or so. Tim never felt able to speak to her. She was sorry for not telling him about Mum and Dad – he knew that from John. And that was enough. He held no grudge against her but it was easier for him just to get on with things, not to think any more than he had to about what had gone before. Mags persisted. Sometimes Tim sat at the top of the stairs and listened in. He'd hear John saying, 'Not a good idea,' or 'Not at this point in time,' or 'I will, Margaret, but I can't promise anything.' After a couple of years, Mags's calls were less frequent. And then came a time when they didn't come at all.

Tim couldn't have known the effect it all had on her. That, in many ways, it was far more difficult for Mags than it was for him. That summer he'd spent in Lissenmore and the things she'd kept from him – that was only part of it.

There was so much more he didn't know.

On his eighteenth birthday, John sat him down and handed him a file of papers. 'You're an adult now, Tim. I hope you're ready for this. What you do with it is your own decision.'

He was hardly able to take it in.

What he read explained so much. And not just about those few weeks that summer, about what had happened before. Mags's overlong and overtight embraces now made sense. Her sudden exits, her bouts of tears. And his dream ... he understood it now. Now there was meaning to it all. And yet he'd never felt so utterly confused.

For a long time afterwards he refused to confront it. It might have been the truth of his past but did he have to drag it into his future? He lived on, fooling himself into believing that the life he was living was the only one that mattered. That what others had done with theirs – Mags, Mum, Dad – was of no concern. Whatever mistakes, decisions, difficult choices they'd had to make had been theirs alone to come to terms with. They were nothing to do with him.

He told no one.

He shut it into a box and buried it deep, tried not to think about it and, mostly, he was able to put it out of his head. Refusing to deal with it was the only way he could cope. Though sometimes, late at night, he'd find his mind straying and the box lid easing open, its contents almost escaping until he slammed it shut and forced himself to think about something else. He knew he had to learn to admit it. People were hurting.

But it wasn't the right time.

He went to college, made new friends, got on with things. There were girlfriends, but none he could imagine spending his life with. That was what he needed if he was ever to admit this truth. To admit it would be to accept it. He couldn't do that in isolation, without the help of a partner who would be with him for ever. He couldn't bear the thought of telling someone who was there and then gone.

Then, just as he was beginning to make a name for himself as a commercial photographer, John became ill. Diagnosed with lymphoma. His gentle uncle dealt with death as he had dealt with life – stoically, patiently, without drama. It was a slow journey, if it was compared to Mum and Dad's. Three years. During that time he managed a few short trips with Tim to places he'd always wanted to see – Rome, Vienna, Bruges. 'We'll leave Istanbul for the moment,' he joked from his hospital bed not long before the end. When he was gone, Tim's tears were shed not just for his own loss but also for John's. He'd lived his life without a partner to share it. The enormity of that fact shocked Tim more than his uncle's death. John hadn't been old – still in his early fifties. There had been someone special once. Marjory. A secretary in one of the schools John had visited in his job as a stationery salesman. Wafer thin, with long, dark blonde hair in a plait down her back, she'd worn white ankle socks and sensible laced-up shoes. It had lasted – on and off – for three or four years. The problem was, she and John were too alike. Both thoughtful, both kind. Tim had found it painful to watch them together, each terrified of offending the other. Tim always suspected that he was part of the reason John couldn't commit. He felt guilty about that. He often pictured himself grabbing his uncle by the shoulders and telling him that it was OK, he didn't mind if he married Marjory and she came to live with them. But he never did.

They'd have had to use Mum and Dad's room. He wasn't sure if he'd ever have been able to cope with that.

Arranging John's funeral. That was when it had hit him the hardest. Not the grief – it went without saying that he was devastated – but the loneliness. That would've been the time to do it. To reach out and connect again. He thought about it, spent many nights imagining how it might change his life. But he couldn't do it.

Not until he met Beth. No one before her had come close.

He was well into his thirties by then, more aware than ever of how little time we really have. When finally he shared the story with her, the shift came, as he'd always known it would. He lifted the lid. It was out there now, not just part of him but part of her too. He was no longer in sole control. Beth encouraged him to think about it.

To think about going back. Confronting the truth. He'd done just that for several years. The year of his fortieth, he thought he might find the courage. But he continued to put obstacles in his way, excuses, reasons why not. Then Beth became pregnant. After years of waiting. I can't do it now, he told himself, there are more important things. But when he felt the soft, warm weight of the tiny boy in his arms, he realised there was no way to separate what was now and what had come before. They were one and the same. It was all important. Every bit of it was the most important thing. And he understood. More than ever. How impossible it must have been for her. For Mags.

Then Maeve got in touch.

The night he read her words, the dream came again. Dragged up from the deep, the sea dream from that summer. He'd known for a long time what it meant. He felt it even more strongly now, pulled in and out of it by the hungry cries of his own small boy. Beth listened to him calling out in his sleep. She begged him when he woke, 'Please, Tim. For everyone's sake.' So he told Maeve everything. The full truth. Words pinging to and fro across thousands of miles. She understood. And she helped, giving Orla the background detail, paving the way for Tim to get in touch.

Late one night, he sat up in bed, staring at his laptop, the bright screen the only light in the darkened room. He typed, deleted, typed again, over and over, the soft silence soon succumbing to Toby's strangled little mewls. Beth rose, slipping over to the cradle like a shadow, her bare feet making no sound on the wooden floor. 'Remember,' she whispered, climbing back in beside him, Toby snuffling at her breast. 'It's not just your history now. It's ours.'

But what was he supposed to say? After so much time thinking, composing reams of sentences in his head, nothing he thought of sounded right. His mind kept wandering back. To that night. The last night. The sound of her first cry the sharpest knife through his ribs.

And then it came to him.

Her mother's words would tell it far better than any of his own.

He pressed his lips to his baby's cheek and left the warmth of the bed. Downstairs, he opened the drawer where he kept the papers John had given him and, hands trembling, scanned three of Mags's letters to Joan, the ones from all those years ago, from the time when she was only a girl. When he sent them through to Orla, he closed his eyes and prayed to a God he wasn't sure he believed in that she – and Mags – would welcome him home.

Pale dawn light washes through the curtains, showing up the room's patterns in all their terrible glory. I jump up, wash, hurriedly throw on my clothes, slip downstairs. I fill a glass with water, gulping it down as I look out over the fields. Frosted grass sparkles under the hazy, low-hanging sun and the trees spread their bare black branches against the bluest sky. I can't be here, in the house, when I read them ... *scanned letters* ... *I know you'll figure it out* ... What if this 'truth' is too difficult? If it's something bad? Whatever it is, I know I need to be on my own.

I scribble a note on the back of an envelope, prop it against the kettle.

Back soon. Need some sea air. Just gone for a drive to Faranboy.

Several times on the way I have to tell myself to slow down, reduce speed, take it easy. I turn a corner too fast, veering onto the opposite side of the road before I can straighten up. Taking the left to the town, I see the sea glittering in the distance, the broad stripe of grey-blue that fades to mist as it stretches towards the line of the horizon. I park along the seafront and walk back to the cliff path, zipping my coat up to my chin against the harsh sea breeze.

I climb quickly, slipping once or twice, but regaining my balance easily. Once at the top, I sit down on one of the new wooden benches, their placement, according to the local paper, arranged by Councillor Barry Kilbride. A weekday morning, there's no one around. Nothing but me, the sky above, the sea below. The only sound the cries of seagulls flapping about the cliff edge.

I don't hesitate.

I open number one, holding my phone close as I read.

It's handwritten. On lined paper. Neat. Copperplate. Clearly executed with focus, by someone young. Someone aiming to please.

21 February 1969

Dear Joan,

I'll be getting the boat over from Dún Laoghaire on Saturday, 29 March. Mammy says I have to be there in plenty of time. It's lonely here on my own now the lads are gone. Even though I hate them all. I sent a letter to Christy O'Hara. He's staying in the same house as them, Mammy said. I told him he's a bastard for what he did. I don't want to ever see him again. He can stay in Canada for the rest of his life for all I care. I knew he'd be gone in a shot as soon as he found out.

Daddy's back talking to me now. He says he's a good mind to slap the arse off me or worse for what's after happening and he's never been so ashamed in all his life. And haven't you only yourself to blame, says he, and you riding crossbar on his bike all the way to Baltinglass? As if that made ME the sinner. And the lads were no better. Even Francie said it was my own fault for leading Christy on.

Mammy says isn't it only the mercy of God that you went over to England and that He hadn't blessed you with one of your own? She'd be sending me off to the nuns in Tuam or Roscrea if you and Edward hadn't offered the adoption. So I suppose I have a lot to be grateful for. I've been trying to eat properly like you said and I'm not throwing up as much any more. The only thing I'm happy about is that it's winter. No one down the town thinks it's strange that I'm wearing my duffel coat all the time.

From Mags

17 March 1969

Dear Joan,

Only two weeks to go before I come over. I have my case mostly packed. Francie sent us a Saint Patrick's Day card. I didn't think you'd be able to get them in Canada. Mary Donnelly wanted me to go to the parade in Faranboy with her today but I told her I had to stay home and help make the dinner. The road is awful bumpy. I don't think he'd have liked it. I can feel him kicking away all the time now. The money came. There's more than I need for the boat and the train so I'll give you the change when I get there. I'll wait for you at Chester station like you said.

So I'll see you soon. I hope you and Edward are well.

From Mags

10 April 1969

Dear Joan,

How is he? I miss him so much already. I'm sorry I made a fuss at the station. It was just that, after what happened on the way over, I didn't know if I was going to be able to get on the boat again. It was awful. I cried the whole way home. I really needed the toilet but I couldn't go in. I was too scared to look at where it happened. I hope he'll be all right. I really didn't want to leave him but I know you're going to look after him well. I was wondering what normally happens to babies born out in the middle of the sea. Will he be Irish or English or something between the two? Timothy is a nice name. I hope I can come over soon. I can't wait to see him again.

From Mags

Oh, my God.

1969? I count back in my head to 1953, the year Mam was born. Sixteen. She was *sixteen*. Only a child. Taken advantage of and made to shoulder all the blame.

I know now why I used to find her in the spare room, staring out to sea. She was looking out to where he'd been born. Between here and there. And those summer days on the strand, the way she'd gaze out over the waves. What must it have been like? To go through that all on her own?

Christ almighty.

That's why she couldn't tell him about his parents. Only a mother would want to spare her child the pain.

Oh, Mam. I bring up the photo on my phone. No wonder she looks so happy. Her arm around the child she'd had to give away, her hand placed on the one yet to be born.

It's probably the happiest she's ever been.

I sit thinking about it all. Going back over the years.

Everything makes sense now. Horrible, awful sense.

I pick my way down the path on unsteady legs, wiping the tears from my eyes. Driving back, the road seems different. But, then, everything is different now.

I walk through the back door and into the kitchen. Mam is up, standing by the sink. She turns when she hears me, hands clasped tight together, face drawn and pale.

My mother.

Is she the same woman I've always thought her to be? Am I?

I'm not her only child. I have a brother.

I've always known something was missing. Always.

'Orla.' She takes a step, falters a little. 'I've been waiting for you.' She sounds brittle, shaky. 'No, I'm fine,' she says, when I move towards her, knowing my instinct is to reach out and take her arm. 'I want you to sit down. There's something I have to tell you. Being in the hospital, taking that turn, it made me realise it's time. I don't want to keep it from you any longer.'

It's as if every cell in my body has been flooded with light and warmth. My eyes brim. 'You don't have to say anything, Mam. I already know.'

We both sit down at the table. I smile at her. The broadest, happiest smile. The joy I feel comes not only from the fact that she finally wants to tell me, but from knowing that she doesn't need to find the words.

She looks at me, puzzled. 'No, love. You don't understand. What I mean is . . .'

I stretch across and take her hand. 'It's OK. I know all

about him. We found each other. Tim and I. We found each other, Mam.'

'But how . . . That's not . . . What are you talking about? Is he . . . Are you being serious?'

'Yes, Mam.' I widen my eyes. 'I'm serious.'

I tell her everything. The emails from Maeve. Mam's letters to Joan. She keeps her eyes downcast as she listens, shaking her head, incredulous at what I know.

'I'm so sorry,' she whispers when I finish. 'So sorry you had to find out the way you did.' Her eyes find mine now. 'I just couldn't . . . I never had the . . .'

'It's all right,' I tell her. 'I understand. I understand everything now.'

'Things were different back then, Orla. The shame of it. Made to feel it was all my fault, I was. Then expected to just carry on as if nothing had happened. But at least I knew where he was. There's many whose children were taken and they hadn't a clue what happened them. Not a clue. All those years he was growing up I longed to see him, for them to come over. But Joan, she . . . she was only doing what she thought was best, I suppose.'

'But she let him come that summer. What changed her mind?

'You did.'

'Me? I don't understand.'

'Once she heard I had another little one to think about, she seemed to relax about the whole thing. I think, up till then, she worried that if I got Tim on my own I might let it slip. That all my focus would be on him and I wouldn't be able to help myself. But I'd never have done that. I know times are different now, and it's not that long ago really, but people weren't as understanding back then. He might've been looked down on. And I'd never have wanted him to feel bad about himself.' She wiped away a tear that had begun to trickle down her cheek. 'The truth is the thought crossed my mind. Not to tell him who I was, but to keep him there. I was so happy to have him over. I had my son with me for the first time since he was born and I had you on the way. I didn't want that time to end. And then when Joan and Edward were ... the accident ... well, I felt so guilty. As if somehow I'd willed it to happen so that Tim could stay with us for ever. And I was grieving too. All over the place, I was. Thought I was doing the right thing by keeping it from him. I know I should've told him but I didn't want him hurt. I was used to keeping secrets, see. I'd never told a soul about him before then. Only my family knew.'

'What about Dad? When did you tell him?'

'Not till you were on the way.' She sees the look on my face. 'I know, I know. Only a month or so before Tim came over. 'Twas hard on him. A lesser man might've walked.'

'He did this for you,' I tell her. 'He didn't want to be disloyal but, at the same time, he knew it was time for it to come out.'

She smiles. 'He's not without his faults, mind you, but I couldn't have wished for a better man.'

'Where is he? Where's Dad?'

'Waiting upstairs. I asked him to. I wanted it to be just you and me.'

I rise from my chair and I go to her. I don't want to ask her about the worst of it. Getting pregnant when she was barely more than a child herself. Being blamed for it by her family. The father doing a runner. Giving birth on her own. On a boat in the middle of the sea. I don't want to contemplate it.

She stands up and almost falls into my arms. 'Oh, Orla,' she cries into my shoulder. 'I was never here for you the way I should've been. All that time. All those dark days.'

Her thin frame is shaking now. 'Don't cry,' I tell her, though I'm weeping too. 'You'll see him soon. Your son. You're going to see him soon.' We stand there for the longest time, entwined, our embrace tighter, stronger than it's ever been before. And when finally we relax our hold, we look into each other's faces and we smile. And I'm certain that our happiness for what we hope is ahead of us is far greater than our sadness at what has passed.

When Dad appears, Mam breaks down again and he insists she needs a rest. I bring her up to bed. She's asleep in the time it takes me to draw the curtains.

Back downstairs, I sit with Dad and go over it all again with him. He can't believe how much I've managed to find out in such a short space of time. But he's grateful I already knew. He's glad Mam was spared having to recount every detail. As we talk, my mind is still trying to comprehend, to navigate its way through the maze of revelations.

'What must it have been like, Dad? Having to go through it all on her own? And on the boat?'

'I've often wondered.' He scratches his beard. 'Didn't tell a soul what was happening. Went into a toilet cubicle and well . . . I can't even imagine what 'twas like for her. Stayed there till the boat docked, kept him under her coat all the way to Chester.'

A young girl. A child. Giving birth on her own. In secret. My mother. His wife.

'March the twenty-ninth,' I say, after a few moments.

'That's the day he was born. That's tomorrow.'

'Don't think I don't know. Same thing every year. Used to get a bit better round this time, so she did. After her winter episodes. Always hoping he'd get in contact. He lived with an uncle. Your mother used to speak to him on the phone. Nice man, she said. But Tim never wanted to talk. Even after the uncle told him the truth about everything. I think every year your mother always hoped he'd want to get in touch. "He's twenty-one now," she'd say. "He's bound to want to." Or then 'twas "He's twenty-five, this might be the year." On and on it went. But it never happened.'

'Well, it's happening now, Dad. He's coming over.'

'Not going to be easy. For all her wishing and hoping. She still feels bad about what she did. Not just that she gave him away, but that she didn't tell him about the accident when he was here.'

'Maeve said the night you told him ... she said that was the night I was born.'

''Twas and all. Never told you you were early, did we? Weren't expected till well into September. Sent Tim out to phone for help, so we did. Middle of the night. Your mother wouldn't let me out of her sight. So scared, she was. Brought it all back to her. What had happened the first time. Never saw the lad again after that night. Ran off and got the boat home, so he did. But sure you couldn't blame him. Apart from everything else, there was that stuff with the Kilbride fella.'

'Barry?'

'Aye. Only found out about it after. Bit of a scrap between the two of them by all accounts. Kilbride wouldn't give him a lift to the phone box at the crossroads. He admitted that much at least. Said he thought Tim was only cod-acting. Took

Kilbride's car and drove it down, so he did. Crashed it into the field. But he managed to ring for the doctor. You arrived only a couple of minutes after he got here. Not a sign of a breath from you for a full minute. Wouldn't have had a notion what to do on my own.'

'But . . . was I not born in hospital? I thought—'

'Wouldn't have made it there in time. Got you both there soon after.' He swallows hard. ''Twas touch and go for a few hours. Whatever way you want to look at it, you mightn't be here if 'twasn't for Tim.'

I can't put into words how that makes me feel.

'There's no doubt you were the best thing that happened us,' Dad continues. 'But for your mother . . . the two things got mixed up in her brain. Him leaving, you arriving. She had one but she'd lost another and . . . she'd so much she wanted to remember about that night. And so much she wanted to forget.'

'I've always felt something was missing, Dad. Things could've been so different if only I'd known.'

'Well . . . I knew and it didn't make it any easier. But I suppose you're right. If she'd been able to have some sort of contact with him . . . Spoiled him awful when he was with us. Wouldn't let him lift a finger. A different woman, she was, back then. A different woman.' His eyes glisten. 'Everything changed after that. You're right. A part of her was missing.'

'But it's not any more. He wants to meet us. And I want to meet him. I want to meet my brother.'

'Never really looked at it that way. I suppose he is your brother, right enough.'

'He sounds nice. Friendly. I wonder what he looks like now. If he's married. If he has kids.'

'Well, if he's that eager to come over, you'll be able to ask him all those questions yourself.'

I take a detour on the way back to Dublin that evening, turn off the main road and head for Dún Laoghaire. I park the car and walk the path along the seafront, the wind doing its best to blow me onto the road. The day is at an end and the pier is almost deserted, just a few anoraked dog-walkers, a couple of joggers, a girl in a red Puffa jacket pushing a buggy. A huge ferry leaves the terminal as I walk the length of the pier, easing its way out of the harbour, slowly making its way back out to sea. When I reach the end and can go no further, I stand in the falling darkness, watching, until it disappears.

Tim is heading back. After he sent the scanned letters to Orla, he freaked out a little. He didn't hear from her for twenty-four hours. He started to regret the way he'd gone about it, wished he'd just explained it straight. Maybe she hadn't grasped it, hadn't figured it all out. Perhaps she didn't want to know him. It was too much, too soon. Then her reply came. Full of heart and understanding. She got it. She got it all. And, just to show him exactly how much, she wished him a happy birthday.

At first, he decided to go alone. He thought that was for the best. But when Orla heard he had Beth and Toby in his life, she persuaded him to bring them too. But he asked if she'd keep their arrival a surprise. He wants to see his mother's face when she learns she has a grandson.

He's bringing his best camera. To record his return. As he packs it into his case, he's reminded of the last time. His Kodak stuffed into the rucksack. All the snaps he took. And Barry Kilbride stamping it to bits. Over the years, he was often sorry that he'd left his roll of film behind. But, then, if Mags hadn't had it developed after he left, he might not be preparing himself for this visit now. It might have taken a lot longer. Knowing that Orla was wondering who he was, trying to find out about him – that made all the difference. He knows he's going to get along with his sister. Already he can feel they've formed a bond.

They're taking the ferry over. It was Beth's idea. And, when Tim thought about it, it seemed the natural thing to do. They take the train to Holyhead, a long journey from their London home but, as it speeds through the countryside, he's glad he has the time to think.

Once on the boat, he finds seats beside a window, the glass grimy and spotted with spray. He takes Toby from Beth, holds him to his chest, feels his little head nestling against his neck. Pulling out of the dock, they soon gather speed. The hills recede, the waters widen and the deep hum of the engine fills Tim's head. But as they plough on, it fades, until the only sound he can hear are the sobs that crouch, pulsing, in his throat.

He cries for the lives of his mothers. For the short years one lived, for the long years one lost. For the times that never could be. He cries for their desires and denials. For the past that's now buried, for the future that's yet to be found. For the men who quietly watched them, accepting, patient; for the silence of their thoughts. He cries, too, for the keeping of secrets. The not telling. The hiding away. They both shared the burden, each sister. Both sure they did the right thing.

Embarrassed by his tears, he closes his eyes. And there it is, the deepest, blackest black. The deep of the dream, as they pass over the place where he began.

* * *

Orla is waiting at the ferry terminal. Tim knows her without needing to be told. Her father's daughter, no denying. They shake hands, then embrace. Beth gives her Toby to hold and Orla smiles through her tears.

The journey seems so much shorter. Their words fill every second of the space. So many things along the way look different. So many look the same. And then they're driving through the village. New shop fronts. Hanging baskets, window boxes. Further along, the pebble-dashed cottage is no more. Replaced by a pink-painted bungalow. Gone is the big cedar, gone the yard. In their place, a neat lawn, a trampoline in the middle, a row of tidy saplings bordering the road.

The fir trees are still there – taller, thicker. The gate is new. Orla slows as they turn, tyres crunching over gravel where, back then, there had been just bare earth.

There's PJ, hand extended in a wave, the years showing plainly across his face. He smiles, walks over, firmly shakes Tim's hand. Then he kisses Beth, beams at their little boy. His words are kind, welcoming. He makes a joke about how much Tim has grown.

And there she is. Mags. Waiting at the door. Like the first time. Orla takes Tim's hand. They stand for just a moment, then they go to her.

They close themselves together. Tight. Tighter. Squeezing out the space that parts them. Leaving nothing in between.

ACKNOWLEDGEMENTS

My thanks to:

My agent, Lucy Luck, for her sound and sensible advice, her wisdom and support; my editor, Ciara Considine, for her thoughtfully considered suggestions, her commitment and belief; the team at Hachette and everyone involved in bringing *The Boy Between* into the world.

Claire Coughlan and Jamie O'Connell for their friendship and encouragement.

Justin Merrigan of *sealink-holyhead.net* for kindly clarifying certain aspects of the Dún Laoghaire-Holyhead ferry in times past; Brian McMahon of *brandnewretro.ie* for generously sharing memories of telephone boxes in the 1980s.

The Arts Council of Ireland for their assistance while I was writing *The Boy Between*.

Last, but not least, my wonderful family, especially my children, and Derek, for his support and understanding and also for providing me with an insight into the workings of the Law Library.

Reading is so much more than the act of moving from page to page. It's the exploration of new worlds; the pursuit of adventure; the forging of friendships; the breaking of hearts; and the chance to begin to live through a new story each time the first sentence is devoured.

We at Hachette Ireland are very passionate about what we read, and what we publish. And we'd love to hear what you think about our books.

If you'd like to let us know, or to find out more about us and our titles, please visit www.hachette.ie or our Facebook page www.facebook.com/hachetteireland,
or follow us on
Twitter @HachetteIre